JACQUELINE WILSON'S SUPERSTARS

www.kidsatrandomhouse.co.uk

Jacqueline Wilson
Superstars

The Suitcase Kid

and

The Lottie Project

Illustrated by Nick Sharratt

CORGI YEARLING BOOKS

JACQUELINE WILSON SUPERSTARS
A CORGI YEARLING BOOK : 0 440 86455 0

PRINTING HISTORY
This collection first published in Corgi Yearling 2000

7 9 10 8

Copyright © 2000 by Jacqueline Wilson

THE SUITCASE KID
Doubleday edition published 1992
Corgi Yearling edition published 1993

Copyright © 1992 by Jacqueline Wilson
Illustrations copyright © 1992 by Nick Sharratt

THE LOTTIE PROJECT
Doubleday edition published 1997
Corgi Yearling edition published 1998

Copyright © 1997 by Jacqueline Wilson
Illustrations copyright © 1997 by Nick Sharratt

Set in Century Schoolbook

Corgi Yearling Books are published by Random House Children's Books,
61–63 Uxbridge Road, London W5 5SA,
a division of The Random House Group Ltd,
in Australia by Random House Australia (Pty) Ltd,
20 Alfred Street, Milsons Point, Sydney, NSW 2061, Australia,
and in New Zealand by Random House New Zealand Ltd,
18 Poland Road, Glenfield, Auckland 10, New Zealand
and in South Africa by Random House (Pty) Ltd,
Endulini, 5a Jubilee Road, Parktown 2193, South Africa.

Made and printed in Great Britain by
Cox & Wyman Ltd, Reading, Berkshire.

The Suitcase Kid

Jacqueline Wilson

Illustrated by Nick Sharratt

CORGI YEARLING BOOKS

In memory of Hilda Ellen Smeed

When my parents split up they didn't know what to do with me. My mum wanted me to go and live with her. My dad wanted me to go and live with him. I didn't want to go and live at my mum's new place or my dad's new place. I wanted to stay living in our *old* place, Mulberry Cottage, the three of us together. Four, counting my pet Sylvanian family spotted rabbit Radish.

There were all these arguments about who would get custody of me. I thought they were talking about custard at first. I hate custard because you can never tell when there's going to be a lump and it sticks in your throat and makes you shudder.

My mum got mad and my dad got mad and I got mad too. I felt *I* was being split up. Half of me wanted to side with Mum. Half of me wanted to side with Dad. It was much easier for Radish. She just sided with me. She lives in my pocket so there's never been any hassle over who gets custody of her.

We had to go for family counselling. It seemed a bit daft because my mum and dad didn't want to be a family any more. This lady chatted to me. She was trying to be ever so casual but I knew she was trying to suss things out. She had some little dolls in her office, a mummy doll and a daddy doll and a whole set of children dolls in different sizes. She wanted me to play with them. I poked the mummy doll and the daddy doll in the stomachs and said I didn't like playing with silly old dolls.

But this lady saw me fiddling about in my pocket and she got a glimpse of Radish. I like to hold her tight when I'm feeling funny.

'Oh, what a dear little toy. Do let me have a look,' she said, in that silly voice grown-ups always use when they're trying to get you to like them.

'She's not a toy, she's a mascot,' I said. I didn't want to show her Radish at all. She's mine and she's private. But I had to let this lady paw her about and undo her frock and turn her upside down in a very rude sort of way.

'What's Bunny's name?' she asked.

You'd have thought I was two years old, not ten. I just shrugged and shook my head.

'That's Radish,' said Mum. 'Andrea's had her for years and years. She's a very important member of our family.'

'Actually, I bought Radish for Andrea. As a silly Saturday present. I like to give her a little treat every now and then,' said Dad.

'You did not give Andrea Radish! *I* bought her one Christmas to go in Andrea's stocking,' said Mum.

'Look, I can vividly remember buying that rabbit in the corner shop—'

'They don't even sell Sylvanian families at the corner shop. I bought it from the toy shop in town and—'

I snatched Radish back and put my hand gently over her ears. She can't stand to hear them arguing.

'Never mind,' said the lady, trying to shut them up. She was still smiling at Radish.

'Hello, Radish,' she said, peering right into her little furry face.

I scowled at her. OK, Radish is real for me, but I can't stick it when grown-ups act like she's real too.

'I expect you're feeling a bit sad and worried about where you're going to live, little Radish,' said the lady.

Radish kept her lips buttoned.

'We know what Mummy wants and we know what Daddy wants, but what do you want, Radish?' said the lady.

Radish wouldn't say a word.

'I think she's a bit shy,' said the lady. 'Maybe it's hard to say anything in front of Mummy and Daddy.'

So she asked Mum and Dad to step outside the room for a few minutes. They didn't really want to. They both kept looking at me. You know what it's like at school when you're the team leader and everyone wants to be picked first to go in your team. Pick me, said Mum.

Pick me, said Dad. I stared down at Radish until they'd gone outside.

'Poor Radish. This is a bit tough on her, isn't it,' said the lady.

Radish and I stayed silent. The lady was quiet for a bit too. And Mum and Dad outside. I wondered if they were listening. But then they started up another argument. They whispered at first, but then got really cross and let rip.

'Oh dear,' said the lady. 'Well, Radish. Here's Mummy. And here's Daddy.' She propped these horrible dolls up at either end of her desk. Then she got some toy bricks and built a little house for the mummy doll and a little house for the daddy doll. She reached out and took Radish, putting her in the middle. Then she looked at me. 'Where does Radish want to live, Andrea? Does she want to live in House A?' She pointed to the mummy doll's house. 'Or does she want to live in House B?' She pointed to the daddy doll's house.

'She wants to live in House C. Mulberry Cottage, where we've always lived. With Mum and Dad and me,' I said.

'I know she does. But she can't. Not any more. It wouldn't work out. Just listen to Mum and Dad,' she said. They were shouting now.

'They can't be happy living together. You can see that for yourself, can't you, Andrea? But they both love you very much and they want you to be happy. So which house do you think you and Radish would be happiest in? House A?' She pointed to the mummy doll's house again. 'Or House B?' Daddy doll's turn.

I looked at House A. I looked at House B. I looked at Radish. I made her walk one way. I made her walk the other. I made her trek backwards and forwards across the desk.

'She still wants to live in House C. But if she can't do that – and I still think she could – then she wants to live in House A *and* House B.'

'Ah,' said the lady. 'You mean she wants to live in House A one week and House B the next week?'

So that's how it was decided. Radish lives with me, in my pocket, as she's always done. She's the luckiest one. And I get to live in my mum's house one week and my dad's house the next. It's as easy as A B C. I don't think.

is for Andy

My name is Andrea West but I mostly get called Andy. My sly little stepsister Katie calls me Andy Pandy. Everyone just thinks she's being cute. Katie specializes in cute. We are exactly the same age – in actual fact she's five days older than me – and yet she barely comes up to my waist. I happen to be big. Katie is extremely small. People don't twig she's ten. They think she's only about seven or eight, and she plays up to this for all she's worth. She blinks her blue beady eyes and wrinkles her small pink nose and puts on this squeaky little sugar-mouse voice. People go all drooly and practically nibble her ears. Katie is not a sugar mouse. Katie is a King-Size Rat.

She's very spoilt. She's got her very own television set and video in her bedroom. When it's my week to sleep at my mum's place I have to share with Katie. She always insists that she gets to choose what's on television, and she always gets first pick of the videos. She's got heaps. She's got some pretty impressive creepy gory horror films that her dad knows nothing about. She hides them inside her Care Bears cases. She's also got the usual Walt Disney stuff. And then she's got this WATCH WITH MOTHER video. Have you seen it? It's a bit dopey really, with little kids programmes that my mum and dad used to watch on telly donkey's years ago. Including a little clown puppet called Andy Pandy. We watched it together, and that's when Katie started calling me Andy Pandy.

I couldn't stick it and I told her to shut up and she wouldn't. So I had to make her. My mum saw us thumping each other and she was furious. She didn't say a word to Katie. She just picked on me.

'How dare you hit Katie! I can't believe you could be so mean. You're twice poor Katie's size. I simply won't have this hateful bullying. You make me desperately ashamed of you. Katie's gone out of her way to welcome you into her home and then you behave like this!'

I wanted to hit my mum then as well as Katie.

'It's not fair. You don't know what she's like,' I wailed, only I just sounded like a tell-tale-tit.

I stalked off and shut myself in the bathroom, Radish clutched tight in my hand. We stayed in the bathroom for ages and even when we came out we didn't speak to anyone all the rest of the day. Mum tried to make it up with me when we went to bed, but I still wasn't saying anything, not with Katie grinning away in the dark.

It wasn't until days afterwards that Mum and I were on our own for once. Uncle Bill was working late. Only he's not my uncle. He's my horrible stepfather and I simply can't stick him. I can't understand what my mum sees in him. I take a good look and all I can see is this great hairy baboon. He's got all this thick black hair like a baboon. He's got a squashed-up ugly face like a baboon. I've never caught a glimpse but I bet his bum's bright red like a baboon's too.

Paula was round at her friend's house. Graham was shut up in his bedroom playing computer games. And Katie was out at her ballet class.

'So it's just you and me, pal,' said Mum. 'What shall we do, eh?'

I shrugged and made out I was busy watching the telly. I was still feeling a bit miffed. But Mum came and sat beside me on the sofa and put her arm around me. I made myself go stiff at first but Mum went on cuddling and soon I sort of collapsed against her. I ended up on her lap. My mum's quite little and I'm big and I probably squashed her but she didn't seem to mind.

'Cheer up,' said Mum, fiddling about with my hair, doing it in little tiny plaits.

I'm growing my hair but it's taking forever. It hasn't even got near my shoulders yet. Katie has got long hair right down her back and it's a glossy bright black.

'It's a very unusual combination,' she told me smugly. 'Blue eyes and black hair. I take after my mother.'

Her voice always goes all sad and holy when she talks about her mother. It's as if she died only last week and so you've got to be sorry for her. In actual fact Katie's mother died when she was little and so she probably can't remember her properly. Maybe she wouldn't even know her mum had blue eyes and black hair without the colour photo in the silver frame on the window-sill.

My eyes are muddy brown. So is my hair. It's a bit depressing.

'I don't feel like cheering up,' I said grumpily, though I didn't budge off Mum's lap.

'What was all the hoo-ha with Katie the other day?' said Mum.

'She called me names.'

'What?'

'Andy Pandy.'

Mum burst out laughing. 'That's not too dreadful!'

'Yes it is,' I said, and I shifted sideways, back on to the sofa.

'Andy Pandy. That's just a friendly nickname.'

'It's after that television programme.'

'Yes, I know. Well, Andy Pandy's OK. He's the hero. I suppose he's a bit wet. Anyway, *you're* not wet. Why don't you call Katie Looby

Lou and tease her a bit? But don't fight with her, I won't have that.'

'You don't understand.'

'Oh, mums never understand,' said my mum, ruffling my hair. 'Let's watch *Neighbours*, eh?'

She turned the television up. I didn't bother explaining about Andy Pandy. He plays all these daft little games with Teddy and Looby Lou and then the lady with the silly voice says something.

'Time to go home.'

And Andy has to get in his basket while she sings the Time to Go Home song. Katie calls me Andy Pandy and she sings Time to Go Home in this sweet little voice but it's as if she's spitting at me. Because she knows I haven't got a home any more.

is for Bathroom

We're all crammed in together when I'm at Albert Road. That's my un-Uncle Bill's house. I'm never going to call him Uncle. I don't even call him just plain Bill. Though he *is* plain. I don't call him anything at all. I don't even speak to him if I can help it.

I can't stand the way Mum talks to him. She snuggles up to him and hangs on his every word and roars with laughter at his stupid jokes. She doesn't even get cross if he goes out drinking with his mates after work. That's really stupid, because she used to nag my dad like mad if he came home late. Though that was probably when he was seeing that dopey Carrie . . .

My un-Uncle Bill is a painter and decorator though you'd never think it if you saw his house. (That's how he and my mum met. When he came to paint our hall and stairs at Mulberry Cottage, because it was too high for Mum to reach. Bill the Baboon had a special set of planks. I'd like to make him walk his rotten plank. Right to the edge and over.) His own house in Albert Road is dead scruffy, nowhere *near* as nice as Mulberry Cottage, so I can't see why my mum makes out she likes it here. She's starting to do the decorating herself, changing it all around. Making it her place.

There's nowhere that's *my* place though. The others are always barging about the kitchen and the living-room. My mum shares a bedroom with old Billy Baboon, so I'm certainly never going in there.

He's got three children: Paula, Graham and little ratbag Katie. I don't like any of them, but I suppose Paula's the best. She's fourteen and she doesn't think much of my mum and they keep having rows. I encourage this like mad, because then my mum might get fed up and want to leave. And then all I've got to do is get my dad to leave Carrie and we could all be a family again. We might even be able to buy back Mulberry Cottage and start all over again, living happily ever after.

Paula has her own bedroom and she's got pop posters all round the room and she plays her stereo system so loud that the whole house shakes. She's got special earphones but she deliberately doesn't use them. *We're* the ones that need earphones.

It's funny, Paula's so noisy, yet Graham is the most silent boy you could ever imagine. He's twelve, yet I'm much taller than him. If we had a fight I know I'd win, easy-peasy. But he's not the fighting sort. He's pale and twitchy with glasses and he just likes to shut himself up in his box-room and plug into his computer. I think he'll turn into a robot one day. He moves in this jerky sort of way, and the rare times he does speak his voice is flat like a machine.

Katie's got the biggest bedroom so she has to share it with me. It's not *my* fault. I don't want to share with her. I can't stick it. I can't ever dress up or practise pulling silly faces or play a good game with Radish because Katie's always there. I can't even get lost in a good book because Katie turns her television right up or sings some silly song right in my ear to distract me.

So do you know where I go when I need a bit of peace and quiet? I lock myself in the bathroom.

There aren't any really good places to sit. The toilet gets a bit hard after a while. The edge of the bath is too cold. I wouldn't dream of sitting *in* the bath. I always just wash in the basin. The baboon has a bath every day and he leaves dark wisps of hair all over the place, and little crumbs of plaster and flakes of paint.

I collected some of his foul scummy hairs in a matchbox, together with a nail clipping and a shred of one of his dirty tissues. Then I concocted an evil spell and threw the box out of the window. I waited hopefully all the next day for the news that he'd fallen off his ladder. But he didn't. Magic doesn't work. I should know that by now. I wished enough times that Mum and Dad and I could be together again in Mulberry Cottage and it hasn't happened yet.

Even when I'm locked in the bathroom I can't always concentrate on my book. I used to read heaps and heaps and I got through every single story in the Book Box at school, and I went to the library too and I had my own collection of paperbacks, nearly fifty of them, some of them really big hard nearly grown-up books. But now my own books are shoved in a cardboard box somewhere and I can't get at them, and all the books from school and the library suddenly seem boring. I can't get into the stories. I just keep thinking about Mum and Dad and Mulberry Cottage.

So now I choose really babyish books to read, stuff I read years ago, when I was six or seven or eight. I can remember reading the stories the first time round and sometimes I can kid myself I'm little again, and everything's all right.

Sometimes it doesn't work, even in the bathroom by myself. So then I generally play a game with Radish.

She loves the bathroom. It's her favourite best ever place. Don't forget she's only four centimetres tall. The basin and the bath are her very own Leisure Pool. I generally fix up a Superslide by knotting Paula's tights together and hanging them from the door hook to the bath tap. Radish hasn't got a very slippery bottom so I soap her a lot to make her slide satisfactorily. This means Paula's tights get a bit soapy too but that can't be helped.

Radish certainly doesn't fancy a swim in the baboon's hairy lair but she likes a quick dip in the basin, and she's getting very good at dives off the window-sill down into the water. Sometimes she turns somersaults as she goes.

When she starts to get a bit shivery I dry her in the towel, and then she warms up using the sponge as her own Bouncy Castle. When she's tired of this she generally begs me to make her a snowman. I know this will get us into trouble but I don't care. I take the baboon's shaving foam and we make all the snowdrifts and then we start sculpting them into snow people. Last time I got a bit carried away. I made a snow girl and a snow rabbit and then I made a snow cottage. All right, it looked more like a big blob than a cottage, but the snow girl and the snow rabbit liked it a lot. I tried to do a tree too but the shaving foam went *phut* and I realized I'd used it all up. Nearly a whole can.

The baboon beat his chest and bellowed in the morning, but Radish and I didn't care.

is for Cottage

We didn't always live in Mulberry Cottage. We used to live in this pokey flat in the middle of London when I was very little. It was noisy and there was lots of rubbish everywhere and we kept getting burgled. Mum and Dad used to talk about moving to a pretty little cottage in the country but it was always just like a fairy story.

Then one day we went for a run out in the

car and it was very hot and I got bored and started whining and they got cross with me so I howled and wouldn't shut up and Dad stopped at a little corner shop to bribe me into silence. I stopped yelling and started happily slurping my way through an icecream. Mum and Dad had an ice too, and we all went for a little walk in the sunshine. And that was when we saw it. The cottage at the end of the road. A white cottage with a grey slate roof and a black chimney and a bright butter-yellow front door. There were yellow roses and honeysuckle growing up a lattice round the door and the leaded windows, and lots of other flowers growing in the big garden. In the middle of the garden was an old twisted tree with big branches bent almost to the ground. Mum and Dad were so taken by the cottage that they'd stopped keeping an eye on me. I toddled through the gate and made for the tree because it was studded all over with soft dark fruit. I picked a berry and popped it in my mouth. It tasted sweet and sharp and sensational. My very first mulberry.

There was a For Sale notice on the fence. It seemed like we were meant to buy Mulberry Cottage. It wasn't quite in the country. It turned out to have a lot of dry rot and woodworm and for the first year there was dust everywhere and we couldn't use half the rooms. But it didn't matter. We'd found our fairy-tale cottage.

I found it. After all, I was the one who started yelling so they had to stop the car. It was my cottage. I was the one who called it Mulberry Cottage right from the start.

Mum made mulberry pies the first year we were there. And then she made mulberry jam. It didn't set properly but I didn't care. It was fun pouring your jam on your bread. I didn't mind a bit when it ran down my wrist and into my sleeve. I liked licking it off.

When Mum went back to work she stopped doing that sort of cooking. Dad had a go at a pie once, but his pastry was all burnt and crunchy. It didn't really matter though, because the mulberries softened it up. He didn't have another go so I just used to eat my mulberries raw.

Have you ever had a mulberry? They're better than raspberries or strawberries, I'm telling you. You have one mulberry and you want another and another and another. They stain quite a bit no matter how careful you are. You end up looking like Dracula with mulberry juice dripping bloodily down your chin, but who cares? You also often end up stuck in the loo with a tummy upset but honestly, it's worth it.

My mouth is watering. I want a mulberry so much. I can't stand to think that there's someone else living in Mulberry Cottage now, picking my mulberries off my tree. There's someone else in my bedroom with the funny uneven wooden floorboards. I kept trying to prise them up hoping that someone in the past would have hidden treasure underneath. And I was sure there was a secret passage because the walls were so old and thick. I know I'd have found the treasure and the passage if I could only have gone on living there.

is for Dad

Dad came to collect me on Friday evening. I got so excited and fidgety before he came that I couldn't even sit still to watch *Neighbours*. I couldn't wait for him to get here — and yet when he tooted his car horn I suddenly clutched Mum and didn't want to go after all. It's always like that.

Dad doesn't come to the front door any more. Dad and Mum still row a lot if they're together for long. And once Dad and the baboon nearly had a fight. They both had their fists in the air and circled round each other. Mum yelled but they didn't take any notice of her. I kept tugging at Dad but he just brushed my hand away. It was Katie who stopped them fighting.

'Oh please stop, Daddy, you're scaring me,' she squeaked, blinking the famous blue eyes.

I can't stick Katie.

There's one really good thing. My dad can't stand her either.

'I had another fight with Katie,' I told Dad when we were driving over to his place.

'And who won?'

'*I* did.'

Dad chuckled. 'Good for you, Andy. She's a spoilt little brat if ever I saw one.'

'Uncle Bill said I was spoilt the other day,' I said.

I'd made a fuss because I didn't get the cream off the top of the milk for my cornflakes three days running. He said we all had to take turns. I said I never had to take turns in my old house with my mum and my dad. Uncle Bill said it was about time I learnt to share. I said a whole lot of other stuff and I ended up getting severely told off. But I didn't care, because Paula let me have the top of the milk when it was her turn, because she says she's slimming.

'What a cheek that man's got! I don't know what your mother sees in him,' said Dad.

'Yes, he's horrible,' I agreed happily.

'Is he horrible to you, Andy?' Dad asked, reaching out and giving my chin a little tickle.

'Well. Sort of.'

'You tell me straight away if he tells you off again or does anything else horrid, OK? Get on the phone right away. It's madness your having to live with them half the time. You'd be much happier with me, wouldn't you?'

'Mmm,' I said, and I reached for Radish in my pocket.

'I miss you so much when you're at your mum's place,' said Dad.

'I miss you too,' I said.

When I'm with Mum, I miss Dad. When I'm with Dad, I miss Mum. Sometimes I can hardly believe that we all used to live at Mulberry Cottage together.

'Come here, sweetheart,' said Dad, slowing down so he could give me a hug.

I cuddled up against his chest and he kept kissing the top of my head. I felt as if I was a juicy stretch of grass and he was a hungry sheep.

'My little girl,' said Dad.

I love it when he calls me that. Even though I'm not little, I'm big.

He looked at his watch and gave me a squeeze.

'We're quite early you know. Shall we go and have an icecream soda together, just you and me?' He winked. 'No need to tell Carrie.'

Carrie is his new wife. She disapproves of anything that tastes really good, like icecream and fizzy drinks and hamburgers and chips and chocolate. She serves up the most horrible brown muck for our meals. She gives her children Zen and Crystal carrot sticks to eat instead of sweets. (They cheat though. They're always swiping Smarties from the other kids in their Infants class).

Icecream sodas are my all-time favourites. I can never decide whether I like strawberry or chocolate best. My Dad knows I always dither between the two.

'How about two icecream sodas today? One strawberry, one chocolate?' he suggested.

'Wow!' But I hesitated. Seeing he was in such a good mood . . . 'Dad?' I said, trying to sound all sweet and wheedly like Katie. 'Hey Dad, as we've got lots of time could we maybe do something else instead?'

'Instead of icecream sodas? Gosh! OK pet, what do you want to do? Anything for my little girl.'

I took a deep breath.

'Could we take a little drive and go and see Mulberry Cottage?'

Dad's arm went stiff. His face lost its smile.

'Oh Andy. Don't start.'

'Oh Dad, please. I'm not starting anything. I just want to see Mulberry Cottage again, that's all.'

'Why? There's no point. We're not ever going to be living in Mulberry Cottage again. There's another family living there now.'

'I know. I just want to see it, that's all. Because I like it. And the mulberries should be out soon and we could maybe pick some and we could get Mum to make one of her pies and—'

'Don't be silly, Andrea,' said Dad, and he started up the car and we drove off.

I didn't get to go to Mulberry Cottage. I didn't get a strawberry or a chocolate icecream soda. It wasn't fair. It never is.

is for Ethel

For most of my life I was an only child. I didn't mind a bit. And then all of a sudden I get lumbered. I have five and a half stepbrothers and sisters.

There's Paula and Graham and horrible little Katie who are my un-Uncle Bill's children. Then there are Zen and Crystal, Carrie's five-year-old twins. Yes, Zen and Crystal. Did you ever hear such dopey names? Mum fell about when she heard.

And then there's the half. Carrie is going to have another baby.

I didn't suss things out for a bit. Carrie is very thin but she often wears long droopy smocky things so I didn't really notice her tummy. But then one Friday night when I was unpacking all my things I started up an argument with Zen. Crystal isn't too bad. She's got long fair hair and a little white face and she sucks her thumb a lot. Zen bites his nails. He's going to chew his fingers right down to the knuckle soon. He's got long fair hair and a little white face too. When I first saw them I thought they were twin girls. But though Zen looks a wet little wimp he's as tough as old boots. He *wears* old boots, sort of miniature Doc Martens, and he doesn't half kick with them too. There's a big poster about the Peace Movement in Carrie's kitchen but no-one gets any peace at all when Zen's around.

He's got his old Teenage Mutant Hero Turtles poster on his side of their bunk-beds. Crystal's got one of a ballet dancer and she's started lessons herself and keeps twirling about in her pink satin ballet slippers. Carrie tried sending her to junior karate instead but Crystal hated it. Carrie tried to get Zen to go to ballet with Crystal but he just mucked about and was silly and the teacher complained. No wonder.

Anyway, I have to sleep in Zen and Crystal's bedroom every other week and it's a right bore. They've got their bunk-beds but otherwise it's not like a bedroom at all. Carrie lets them get all their toys out at once and they never have to put anything away. They have a tent in there too, and a weird Wendy House made out of the clothes-horse, and heaps of cardboard boxes that are supposed to be trains and shops and caves. You have to wade through all this junk to get across the room to the big cupboard. It's falling to bits and half the drawers don't fit properly, but Carrie's painted it with dragons and mermaids and unicorns and all sorts of other fairy-tale stuff so it looks quite pretty if you like that sort of thing.

I think I'd have maybe loved a cupboard like that when I was Crystal's age. I wouldn't mind one now. If I could have it back in my own bedroom at Mulberry Cottage.

Mum says it sounds as if I have to sleep in

a rubbish tip and she gets particularly narked that I don't have a proper bed. Carrie's made this weird cotton sleeping-bag that she says is like a Japanese futon. She embroidered little Japanese ladies and butterflies and birds all over the front and I thought it was specially for me and I couldn't help liking it a lot. But then I found out that Zen and Crystal's creepy little friends come to stay sometimes and they sleep in the Japanese bag too, so I went right off it.

I made a great fuss about my back hurting and my neck hurting and my everything else hurting after a night trussed up in the bag.

'Don't be such a whinge, Andy,' Dad said sharply.

'Whingy-pingy,' said Zen, trampling on my feet in his boots.

'You can share my bunk-bed with me if you like, Andy,' said Crystal.

'No thanks. You wet the bed,' I said.

'Only sometimes,' said Crystal, blushing.

I felt a bit mean then. I wasn't really cross with Crystal. I was cross at Carrie because if my dad hadn't gone off with her then I'm sure we'd all be living happily ever after in Mulberry Cottage.

I say heaps of mean things to Carrie but

she's never mean back. She always acts like she's pleased to see me but I'm sure she's not. She doesn't want me around half the time. She wants my dad to herself. I bet that's why she made the Japanese bed-bag. She can fold it up and stow it away in the cupboard. I bet she'd like to fold me up and stuff me out of sight too.

Anyway *again*, I was busy trying to clear a little bit of space for *my* stuff so I had to chuck some silly junky toys out of the way and Crystal didn't mind when her Barbie went whirling across the room and landed with her legs in the air and she just laughed when her My Little Ponies went flying through the air like Pegasus, but Zen started yelling that I was mucking up all his Transformers and he started kicking me really hard. So I hooked my leg through his and tripped him and he gave a roar of rage and punched me right in the stomach.

'Stop it, Zen!' Crystal shouted. 'You mustn't hit people in the stomach. Carrie said.'

'She said I mustn't hit *her* in the stomach, because she's going to have the new baby,' said Zen. 'I can still hit anyone else.'

'Oh no you can't,' I said, and I pushed him over and sat on him. 'What's all this about a new baby?' I said, breathing hard.

'It's Carrie and Simon's new baby,' said Crystal.

She was sucking her thumb so it came out very indistinctly. I made her repeat it again, while I tried to catch hold of Zen's kicking legs.

'Stop that, Zen, you silly little squirt,' I said, and I pulled his hair which he hates.

He started yelling and Carrie and Dad came running and there was a bit of a fuss because I was the one on top of Zen, and I suppose I am twice his size.

'But he did kick Andy quite a bit,' Crystal said fairly.

Maybe it's not so bad having Crystal for a step-sister. But I know one thing. I can't stick the thought of *another* one. One that will be my dad's little girl too.

'You're having a baby,' I said fiercely to Carrie.

'That's right. Isn't it lovely?' said Carrie, smiling nervously.

'Why do you want more children when you've got Zen and Crystal?' I said.

'I want Simon's child too,' said Carrie.

That made me feel a bit sick. Dad was a bit red in the face too.

'We were going to tell you this weekend, honestly,' he said.

'It's all right. I'm not really interested. I don't like babies,' I said.

'Oh come on. I think you'd like a baby sister,' said Dad.

'No thanks. Anyway, you don't know it's going to be a girl. It could be a boy. A boy like Zen,' I said.

My dad doesn't go a bundle on Zen either. I'm glad. I don't see why Zen and Crystal get to have my dad all the time just because they haven't got one of their own. (Carrie said their dad couldn't face commitment. He probably took one look at Zen and scarpered.)

'*Twin* Zens,' I added triumphantly.

But Carrie shook her head.

'No. I had a scan. In case it was twins again. And it's just one baby. A little girl.'

'Oh.' I couldn't think of anything else to say.

There was this great long silence. Carrie looked at me. Then she looked at Dad. He didn't do anything. So Carrie came and put her arm round me.

'What shall we call your little sister, Andy?' she said.

Dad brightened up. 'Yes, Andy. How about you choosing a name for her?'

Carrie looked a bit worried, but she nodded.

'OK,' I said. 'I'll choose her name.'

They're going to have to let me choose it now. They practically promised. And I'm going to pick the worst name ever.

I used to have this Great-Great-Auntie Ethel who smelt of wee-wee and shouted at everyone. She took one look at me and said 'Who's that great gawky child with enormous feet? Let's hope she's got brains because she's certainly no beauty.'

I've got brains all right. My little step-sister-to-be is going to be called *Ethel*.

is for Friends

Aileen was always my best friend right from the time we were in the first year at Infant school. Her mum and my mum were friends too and Aileen's mum would drive us all home after school. Sometimes we'd go back to Aileen's and her mum would make hot chocolate with marshmallows and Aileen and I would play with her Barbie dolls. Sometimes Aileen and

her mum would come back to Mulberry Cottage
with us and we'd have fruit juice – once we had
mulberry juice – and Aileen and I would play
Sylvanian families.

Then we got old enough to do things without
our mums and so we'd go to the park and
play on the swings and we'd go down to the
corner shop to buy crisps and Coke and we'd
creep through a hole in the fence on this bit of
wasteland and play games in the bushes.

We had such a great time. But now it's all
different. When we left Mulberry Cottage, I
couldn't go on playing with Aileen after school
every day. My mum's new house with the
baboon is miles and miles away. My dad's
flat with Carrie is even further away in the
opposite direction. Mum did let me have Aileen
round to tea one time, but Katie kept hanging
round us and we didn't have anywhere private
to play so we just ended up listening to Paula's
records. We couldn't be secret and special the
way we used to be.

I still see Aileen every day at school but
it's not the same. Aileen's mum gives a lift
home to Fiona now. Aileen and Fiona play together after school. We go round in this sort of

threesome at playtime. Aileen keeps insisting she's still my friend but when we have to join up with a partner in class now she always goes with Fiona.

is for Garden

I come home from school by myself now. There isn't anyone to give me a lift. I have to walk down Seymore Road and round Larkspur Lane and up Victoria Street into the town. I go to the bus station and then, when I'm staying with Mum, I get a 29 as far as *The Cricketers* pub and then I have a ten-minute walk. I have to get two buses when I'm at my dad's, a 62 and a 144 and then I have a fifteen-minute walk even after the two bus rides. I'm exhausted when I get back, I'm telling you.

I'd go crazy if I didn't have Radish to talk to on the way. Once or twice just at first I got lost and forgot the way and got that horrible hot swirly feeling in my stomach. I had to clutch Radish tight to stop myself crying. Then I calmed down and asked a safe-looking lady with children to show me the way to the bus station.

Then another time my purse must have fallen out of my coat pocket because when I was queuing up for the bus I went to get my money out ready and my purse had gone. I thought for a moment I'd lost Radish too but then I found her clinging to the pocket lining. She made me feel a bit better but I still didn't know what to do.

I could simply have told the bus driver I'd lost my purse but I was scared he'd get cross. He was one of those big fat men with a frowny face.

But I didn't have to ask him in the end because an old lady had been watching me frantically searching my pockets.

'What's up, dear? Lost your bus fare? Here, don't you fret, I'll pay your fare today.'

I was very grateful and asked Mum for extra bus fare the next day to pay her back. Mum got ever so fussed when she found out what had happened.

'Poor old Andy. You must have been so worried. Oh dear, I do hate it that you have to come home by yourself now.'

Mum can't come and meet me because she works nine to five in a chemist's shop now to help pay the bills. I wish she'd chosen a more exciting shop, like a cake shop or a toy shop or a pet shop. You can't get very excited when she brings home half-price loo rolls and stale cough sweets.

'*I've* been coming home from school by myself since I was six years old, Auntie Carol,' said Katie smugly.

'That doesn't count. Your stupid old school is just down the road. A baby of six months could crawl it,' I said.

'I wish you'd swop to Katie's school, Andy,' said Mum. 'It would be so much more sensible.'

'But if I went to Katie's school then it would take me hours and hours to get there when I'm staying at Dad's,' I said.

'Well. All this to-ing and fro-ing is getting ridiculous anyway,' said Mum. 'You're getting worn out, Andy. I'm thinking about you, darling. It would be so much better if you settled down in one place for a while and went to the local school.'

'That's what Dad says. He wants me to settle down with him. And go to Zen and Crystal's school,' I said.

I'm not going to go to any other old school. I like *my* school. Even though it isn't really the same any more. Aileen isn't the same. The teachers aren't even the same. They made a bit of a fuss of me at first when Mum and Dad split up but now they often get cross with me. I forget to do things or I lose my books or I don't listen in lessons.

'If you'd only try to *concentrate*, Andrea,' they say.

I am concentrating, but it's not often on lessons nowadays.

There's only one good thing about all these boring journeys to and from school. I've discovered another mulberry tree. It's in a garden in Larkspur Lane so I get to see it whether I'm living at my mum's or living at my dad's. It's not as nice as our mulberry tree at Mulberry Cottage of course. It's very old and knarled and bent over, but it still grows lots of mulberries.

I watched them ripening from red to purple to bright black and brimming with juice. No-one seemed to be picking them. The grass grew lavishly and the flowers were in tangled clumps and the creepers were crawling all over everywhere. Perhaps no-one was living there any more.

I peered over the high fence every day, trying to see the house, though it was hidden by another tree. I never heard a radio or saw a deckchair out in the garden. I started to lean right over the gate, peering in. Sometimes I got Radish out so she could peer too.

The garden would be fairyland for Radish. She could trek through the grass playing Jungle Explorers, swinging on the creepers like a tiny Tarzan. And she could eat mulberries . . .

My mouth watered as I looked at those great big berries. One day I could stand it no longer. I got my leg up over the gate, I jumped down into the garden, I ran through the long grass, I reached the mulberry tree, I snatched a handful of berries and then rushed back. I scratched my hand on the tree and banged my shin badly climbing back over the gate but I had the mulberries safe in my hand. I crammed them into my mouth and the juice spurted over my tongue and I closed my eyes because it was just just just like being back at Mulberry Cottage.

I still stop at the mulberry garden every day. And mostly I slip inside.

is for Haiku

I wish I was
in Mulberry Cottage
with Mum and Dad
and Radish.

That's a Haiku. We did Haikus in English. When the teacher said that we were going to learn about Haikus we all got excited because we thought it was going to be like Kung Fu.

But Haikus are little Japanese poems. She read us some and there was one about a garden in the moonlight with a willow and wild berries. I started listening properly. I decided I liked Haikus a lot.

> In my dreams
> I am as small as my rabbit
> and I am safe
> at home.

That's another Haiku.

> I live with Mum
> I live with Dad
> I live with Radish
> Can't we join up?

And another.

I

is for Ill

I always seem to be getting ill nowadays. I get
these headaches or sometimes they're tummy-
aches or other times it's an ache all over and
I'm either much too hot or so cold I'm shivering.
It's always worse on Fridays. That's change-
over day.

A few Fridays ago I had a bit of a sniffle on
Friday morning. I burrowed right under the
bedclothes till I got boiling hot and sweaty and

then I called Mum, sounding all sad and sore and pathetic.

Mum felt my forehead and gave me a worried cuddle. I knew Katie would tease me later about being a baby but I didn't care. Mum always makes far more fuss of me on Fridays. I clung to her and said I felt really lousy.

'I think you've got flu,' said Mum. 'Oh dear. Well, you certainly can't do that awful journey to school, not in this state. You'd better stay in bed.'

'All by myself?' I said, hunching up as small as I could.

Mum hesitated. 'Maybe I'd better stay off work.'

'Oh Mum, would you?' I said.

'They won't like it. But it can't be helped. You're really not at all well, pet. You'd better stay in bed all weekend.'

'What, at Dad's?'

'No, you'll have to stay put here. You're not up to travelling,' said Mum firmly.

I started to feel really sick then. I wanted to stay with Mum and have her making a big fuss of me – but I still wanted to go to Dad's too.

But I made the most of that Friday all the same. Katie flounced off, forbidding me in a whisper to touch any of her videos or records – 'Or I'll get you later.'

I can beat her in a straight fight but she's got all sorts of devious hateful ways of hurting me. She hides my stuff. She scribbles inside my schoolbooks. Once I found poor Radish floating miserably down the loo and I just know Katie threw her there. She had to spend the night in a bowl of disinfectant and she didn't lose the smell for days and days, so that whenever I cuddled her close my eyes stung.

But I didn't need to play Katie's records or videos or touch any of her boring junk. Mum came and sat on the edge of my bed and she read the paper and I read one of my old baby books and then when I started to act a bit droopy Mum read some more books aloud to me. She fixed me a lovely lunch, tomato soup and a soft white roll and then she made me a special bowl of green jelly. She even let me pretend it was lettuce-flavoured so that Radish could wade through this wonderland and get her paws all sticky.

We all had a nap after lunch and when I woke up Mum lent me her white lace hankie and I played Brides with Radish. I said I was starting to feel a lot better and suggested I could get up, but Mum wouldn't hear of it. And then the others came home from school and the baboon came back from his work and then about seven o'clock I heard the car toot outside. It was Dad come to pick me up.

I tried jumping out of bed then but Mum hauled me straight back. She went to speak to Dad. Only they didn't do much speaking. They were shouting in less than a minute. Then Dad stormed right into the house and up the stairs to see me. Un-Uncle Bill said he had no right to come barging in and Dad said he had every right if his daughter was ill. Dad gave me a great big hug but then he held me at arm's length and looked at me.

'You seem fine to me. Maybe you've got a cold, but everyone's got the sniffles just now. Come on, Andy, get dressed and we'll get cracking,' said Dad.

I started to do as I was told, but Mum started shouting that it would be madness taking me out into the cold air when I had flu and that I was to get back into bed this instant.

I stood in my pyjamas shivering in the middle of Katie's bedroom, not knowing what to do. Mum won that battle in the end. Dad stormed out and I was so scared he was blaming me that

I started crying. Mum bundled me back to bed, insisting that it was wicked for Dad to get me in such a state.

I had to stay in bed most of that weekend and it stopped being a treat and started to get really boring. I didn't have Mum to myself because all the others were around. And then on Sunday Katie insisted she'd caught my 'flu' and she stayed in bed too. She didn't want my mum nursing her. She just wanted her dad.

So the baboon sat her on his lap and called her his poor little princess and other sickening stuff. He nipped out to the off-licence at lunchtime and bought her a huge box of chocolates. Katie wouldn't eat any of Mum's chicken and roast potatoes and peas but she hogged almost that whole box of chocolates to herself.

I hated seeing her all cuddled up with the baboon. It made me miss my dad even more. I couldn't wait till the next Friday so I could see him again. But then he was all huffy with me for ages, acting like it was my fault I'd stayed on at Mum's.

'You can't kid me, Andy. You were play-acting,' he said crossly, and when I tried to get on his lap he tipped me off and said I was behaving like a big baby.

He was a bit nicer on Saturday and by Sunday he was OK and he played Snap with me and one evening that week he came home early from work and took me out and bought me an icecream soda . . . but it still wasn't such a good visit as usual.

Maybe I'd better not get ill again for a while.

J

is for Jelly

I was ill the very next time I went to Dad's. Not just a little sniffle. I felt a bit shivery and strange on Thursday, but then I generally do at Carrie's house. She has the basement flat and it's always got this sour damp smell even though she burns joss sticks all day long. She's got storage heaters. I don't know what they store but it's certainly not heat. I wear a thick cardi even in the summer and by the

Autumn I wear two of everything, even two pairs of knickers.

Carrie doesn't seem to feel the cold herself and floats around in her filmy smocks without a shiver. Zen and Crystal are the same. They wander around stark naked after a bath or play for hours in their pyjamas while I hop about in the Japanese bag absolutely perished.

I told Dad I felt funny but he didn't take much notice. Carrie tried to put her arm round me to give me a hug.

'It's Friday tomorrow, isn't it. Poor old Andy.'

I wriggled away from her. I don't like her holding me at the best of times. I especially can't stand it now, when she's got this big tummy full of the baby sticking out in front. Zen and Crystal put their hands on her tummy and giggle when they feel the baby moving. It gives me the creeps.

I kept dreaming about the new baby that night. Carrie's tummy swelled and swelled until she got as big as a whale and couldn't even waddle around any more. And then the baby was born and it was huge too, even taller than me, with a great big lolling head and beady blue eyes that glared balefully at me. It bawled whenever I got near it so Dad said I'd better keep out of the way. It went on yelling even when I was in the bathroom so Dad said I had to go right out in the freezing cold garden.

I started yelling too then, and Dad got really cross and said I wasn't setting my little sister Andrea a good example.

'What do you mean, Andrea? *I'm* Andrea. The new baby can't be called Andrea too. I've got to give her a name, you said I could. She's Ethel. I'm calling her Ethel.'

The baby roared and Dad pushed me right out into the road.

'Don't be so silly. You're not Andrea. My baby's my little girl and she's called Andrea,' Dad shouted from the house, struggling with the giant baby.

'*I'm* your little girl! I'm Andy!' I screamed as I dodged in and out of the traffic.

Then a car hit me hard in the chest and I opened my eyes and there was Zen sitting on top of me.

'Wake up, Andy!' he said, jiggling up and down.

'You were shouting, Andy,' Crystal said, bending over me, her long hair tickling my face. 'Were you having a bad dream?'

'Mm. Get off me, Zen,' I said. My voice came

out in a queer croak. It hurt a lot. I wasn't shivery any more. I was boiling hot.

'Get *off* her, Zen,' said Crystal, pushing him. 'I don't think you're very well, Andy.'

'I don't think I am either,' I said, and I started to cry.

'I'll get Mum,' said Crystal.

'No, get my dad,' I croaked.

They both came. Carrie sat cross-legged beside me, her tummy huge under her nightie. She sighed sympathetically.

'Poor little fruitcake, Friday always makes you feel bad, doesn't it,' she said. 'Would you like me to show you the relaxation exercise I do at my childbirth class? It really helps stop you feeling tense.'

'She's not feeling tense, she really is ill,' said Dad, his hand on my forehead. 'She's got a fever, feel, Carrie.'

I squirmed away from Carrie's cool fingers and clutched at Dad.

'My throat hurts. And my head. And my neck and my arms and my legs. Everywhere hurts. Oh Dad, will you stay off work and look after me?' I begged.

'My poor old tuppenny. Yes, you've got a

nasty sore throat. All right, no school. But Carrie will look after you.'

'I want you, Dad.'

'Now you're being silly,' said Dad, but he didn't sound cross. He ruffled my hair and hugged me close. And to my amazement he phoned his office after breakfast and told them he was taking a day's leave.

'I can't help it if it's not convenient,' he said. 'My little girl needs me.'

I was really glad I had a sore throat then, even though it hurt so much. Dad tucked me up in his and Carrie's bed, making a special nest for me, and then we played paper games all morning, noughts and crosses and Hangman and Battleships. We haven't been able to play paper games properly for ages because Zen and Crystal are always around and they're too little to play and just scribble and waste the paper.

Carrie made this bean casserole thing for lunch but the only sort of beans I like are baked beans out of a tin so I wouldn't eat any.

'My throat's too sore,' I said, making it croak a little more.

'Oh dear,' said Carrie, looking sad. 'Isn't

there anything I can get you, Andy? What would you really fancy?'

'Jelly.'

'Jelly. Right. I'll make you a lovely fruit jelly for tea,' said Carrie.

She went out and bought some oranges specially, and spent ages in the kitchen.

'I've never made a jelly before but I *think* it's going to turn out all right,' she said.

'It's easy peasy to make jelly, you just pour on boiling water and stir,' I said.

'Oh, that's jelly out of a packet,' said Carrie, looking shocked. 'I'd never give you junk food, Andy. You need natural fresh food with lots of nourishment.'

Carrie's jelly didn't look very nourishing when she brought me a plate at teatime. It was supposed to be orange jelly but it wasn't orange-coloured. It was a weird sickly brown. It wasn't jelly either. It didn't stick. It sort of slid about the plate. Radish was quivering in my hand, ready for another glorious jelly glut, but when she saw it for herself she jumped back into my pyjama pocket, her ears drooping.

'Come on, Andy, eat up your nice jelly,' said Dad. 'Isn't Carrie kind to make it for you specially?'

'I'm not really hungry now.'

'Don't be silly, Andy. You've got to eat something.'

'I feel sick.'

'Now don't start.'

But I did feel sick, and it wasn't just to do with the jelly. Mum was due to come and collect me and I knew there was going to be trouble.

I lay waiting. I heard my un-Uncle Bill's van draw up outside. I heard Mum's footsteps and the tap on the steps down to the basement flat. I heard the door-knocker. And then I heard the quarrel.

'What do you *mean*, Andrea's in bed? My God, I simply can't believe this! I didn't think even you could stoop so low! Just because Andrea was genuinely ill the other weekend . . . Oh, of course she's not ill this time! You're just being deliberately obstructive, trying to get your own back in as nasty and spiteful a way as possible . . . It's just typical! Come on, hand Andrea over this minute.'

'The child is very ill. She has a sore throat, and a fever—'

'Well, I'm not surprised, stuck in this damp old flat. It's disgraceful, no place for young children—'

'Well, if you hadn't bled me dry over the divorce we could afford a better place—'

'Oh don't give me that rubbish. And you don't even make sure Andy has a proper bed. She's told me about having to sleep on the floor. I can't believe it, you're too mean to buy a proper bed for your own little girl – and yet *her* kids have got bunk-beds, I know. Well, if Andy really *is* ill then I insist she comes home with me where I can nurse her properly. Andrea? Andrea, where are you, darling? It's Mummy. I've come to take you home with me.'

I heard her blundering about the flat for quite a while before she got the right room.

'You poor little lamb!' she said, rushing to me. 'Why have they stuck you in here? Ugh, in their bed. Come on, let's put your coat on over your pyjamas. You're coming home with me this instant.'

I jumped out of bed obediently and stepped straight into the plate of jelly. I stood shivering, up to my ankles in brown slime.

'Oh my God! *What's that?*' Mum screeched.

'It's jelly. Carrie made it for me.'

'Jelly!' snorted Mum. 'That stupid hippy's been feeding you that muck and calling it *jelly*?'

'Will you quit calling Carrie names?' Dad roared.

'I'll call her anything I like, the dirty slut! She's not looking after my daughter again, do you hear me? I'll send the social services round. You're daft enough to take on her hippy twins and she looks as if she's about to have your baby any minute, but I'm telling you one thing – she's not looking after *my* daughter, not any more.'

is for Katie

Mum took me home with her and said I wasn't
ever going to go back to Dad's. Dad phoned
up and came round and sent furious letters.
I stayed in bed with my sore throat and tried
to forget about them both. I played lots of
Under-the-Bedcovers games with Radish. She
had a sore throat too and we knew the only
possible cure would be a sip of magical mulberry juice so we searched high and low across

the dark and barren land (you try crawling around under your bedcovers) but our throats remained sorely parched.

'What are you doing under there, you daft berk?'

It was Katie, back from school.

'How's the poor lickle invalid then?' she said nastily. 'When are you going to shove off back to your boring old dad, eh? I'm getting sick of you cluttering up my bedroom. Your mum's not *serious*, is she? You're not going to be here always?'

I emerged red-faced from under the covers.

'I don't know,' I mumbled.

Katie slotted a video into place and pressed the button. A horribly familiar little puppet wobbled into view.

'Oh ha ha, very funny,' I said.

Katie played the fast forward so Andy Pandy and Teddy jerked about like crazies and then stopped the tape the moment she spotted the basket.

'Time to get into your basket, Andy,' Katie said, in the lady's silly high-pitched tone. 'Did you get that, Andy Pandy? Fold up your great huge horrible arms and legs and stuff your fat head into your basket, right? I'll post you off to your dad. Only once the new baby's born they won't have room for you there either so you'll just have to stay stuffed up in your basket for ever, OK, because nobody wants you.'

I clutched Radish tightly. I knew Katie was just winding me up deliberately. But it was working. I *felt* wound up. Tied up so tight I could hardly breathe.

'They do so want me,' I croaked. 'My mum wants me. My dad wants me. That's what all the fuss is about now. They both want me so much.'

'Oh no they don't,' said Katie. 'They only go on about you because they want to get at each other. If they really truly wanted you then they'd have stayed in that boring old cottage you keep going on about. But your dad left and your mum left. Your dad wants his new lady. Your mum wants my dad. They want them, not you.'

'Shut *up!*' I said, and I reached out of bed and tried to hit her.

It was just a flabby punch, it couldn't have hurt her at all, but she immediately started squealing and Mum came running.

'Whatever's the matter now?' Mum shouted above the racket, taking hold of Katie.

'Andy's poked my eye out and it *hurts*!' Katie roared.

'Andrea! I thought I'd put a stop to this nonsense! I won't have you bullying poor little Katie. Come here, Katie, let's see. Of course your eye's all right. Although, oh dear, yes, it is a bit red. Andrea, how *could* you?'

'I didn't touch her silly old eye,' I protested truthfully. But then I looked at my fist. Radish's ears were sticking out of it. It looked as if Radish had done the poking for me.

I tried to explain but Mum wouldn't listen. She was very very cross. Then the baboon came home and I eavesdropped anxiously and she told him. And Katie started crying all over again just so that he would make a fuss of her. Then he came into the bedroom to see me and I got really scared.

I decided to poke his eye too if he shouted or smacked me. He had no right to tell me off. He wasn't my dad. I suddenly badly wanted my own dad and burst into tears.

'Yes, well, I'm glad to see you're feeling sorry, Andrea,' he said. 'Dear oh dear, you little girls! And I thought it would be smashing for you both, being the same age and that. But listen to me, Andrea. I know you've had a hard time

71

and you're not very well just now but that still isn't really any excuse. You must stop hitting Katie or you'll really hurt her. She's only small and she's not used to such rough and tumble. Her poor old eye is very sore. It could have been really nasty, you know. I don't want my baby to end up getting badly hurt. She's been a good little girl sharing her bedroom and all her precious bits and bobs with you. So I'd like you to try to be a bit grateful, Andrea. I know you're a nice little girl underneath even though you've got a bit of a quick temper. You've inherited that from your dad, obviously. But you've got to learn to control yourself, dear.'

I had the greatest difficulty controlling myself right that minute. I wanted to scream and kick and hit and rage because it wasn't fair. Katie always hurts me far more than I can hurt her. And I don't want to share her horrid bedroom. I want my *own* bedroom, back in Mulberry Cottage. My own place with my own things where I can be with my own rabbit.

is for Lake

The garden in Larkspur Lane has got a lake! Well, not a *proper* lake. It's really a round brick goldfish pond – but it's a magnificent lake for Radish.

We go there nearly every day after school, even though the mulberries are finished now. We've started to explore the garden properly. Once we thought we saw a face at the window and we had to run like mad. We didn't go back for several days, walking quickly past the gate without even looking in, but we missed the garden badly.

Radish jumped over the gate by herself so I had to go after her. I wanted to stay close to the mulberry tree, but Radish found a crazy-paving path and followed it round a corner behind a hedge and there were three mossy steps down into another garden. The lawn was long and lush there too, right up past Radish's ears, and if I crouched down at her level I couldn't see the lake until we were right on top of it.

I don't think I've ever seen Radish so excited. She loves her dips and diving sessions in the bathroom at Mum's place (there's no proper lock on the door at Dad's and there's a gap under the bath where the spiders live so Radish doesn't like playing there) but the lake was pure paradise by comparison.

She wanted to wade right in straight away, but I kept her paddling cautiously at the edge in case it got too deep. We both got a shock when an orange whale suddenly rose up out of the water and nibbled Radish's paws. I snatched Radish out of the way. We've done the story of Jonah and the Whale at school and

I didn't fancy the idea of gutting a goldfish to retrieve my Radish. But she didn't seem too bothered by the fish. I looked very carefully at their mouths. They just opened and shut as if they were blowing harmless kisses. They didn't seem to have *teeth*. Still, maybe they could suck at Radish and then swallow her down whole.

I decided Radish had better go boating. I found various big leaves but as soon as I stood her on board the leaves started sinking. I tried collecting twigs but I needed something to stick them all together. I snaffled some Sellotape from the kitchen drawer at Mum's place and stuck the twigs together the next day and made quite a good little raft but Radish didn't seem too happy on it. It tipped about too much. I was scared she'd sail right into the middle of the lake and then slide in under the water, out of her depth.

She needed a proper boat, not a raft.

I sidled up to Graham after tea the next day.

'Hey Graham,' I said, smiling at him.

He blinked a bit behind his glasses. We've barely spoken to each other ever since my mum's lived at his place. He generally makes himself scarce in his room with his computer.

He's clever and gets a lot of extra homework. The baboon calls him the Boy Wonder. I don't like the way he says it. He doesn't seem to think that much of Graham. He's dotty about Katie and he cares a lot about Paula too though he's always nagging at her for wearing too much make-up and staying out late. But he often makes these snide remarks about Graham. Graham doesn't say anything back. Graham hardly ever says anything very much.

'Graham, you haven't got a toy boat, have you? I mean, I know you're too old for toys now, but did you use to have one?'

Graham shook his head. 'I made myself one with a second-hand Meccano set once.'

'Did you? Did it float OK?'

'No, it's metal, so it wouldn't float.'

'Well then it was a pretty stupid boat, wasn't it?' I said, disappointed. 'What does float, Graham? I've tried wood, but it's not right.'

'Cork.'

'Cork. What's that? Oh, I know, like in the top of a bottle. But it wouldn't be big enough. What else floats?'

'Rubber.'

I shook my head, thinking about the eraser in my pencil case.

'Still too small. Come on, Graham, what else?'

'Plastic.'

I thought hard. I went back to the living-room. I borrowed one of the baboon's tapes, making sure no-one was looking. I tried floating the plastic case in the bath. It did OK, but as soon as I tried to launch Radish on it they both sunk. It needed to be bigger. A video case. Aha.

The next day after school Radish sailed the good ship *Video* from one side of the lake to the other. She had the sail up and stood on the sun deck, her black eyes bright with bliss.

is for My Mate Graham

Mum still said I couldn't go back to Dad's. Dad got on to his solicitor. We had to have another family counselling session. It was the same lady, the one with the mummy doll and the daddy doll and the bricks to make House A and House B.

'Hello Andrea. How's Radish?' she said.

I just shrugged, but I was impressed that she'd actually remembered Radish's name.

Mum and Dad ranted on and on. I didn't
say much at all. Neither did Radish. The lady
kept looking in my direction and asking me
what we thought. We shrugged so often our
shoulders ached.

It was quite good fun hearing Mum slagging
off Carrie and Zen and Crystal and it was quite
good fun hearing Dad slagging off the baboon
and Paula and Graham and Katie but it was
no fun at all hearing them slagging off each
other. I started to get my sore throat back, and
I felt sick and I had a pain in my tummy. I went
off to the toilet down the corridor to see if that
might help the pain. I crept back and listened
for a bit outside the door.

'How do you think Andrea's coping with all
this?' said the lady.

'It's awful for the poor little lamb,' said
Mum.

'Yes, it's really unsettling her,' said Dad.
'Though when she's been with me a few days
she calms down – and by the end of the week
she's almost her old happy self.'

'That's because she knows she can come back
to me soon.'

'That's absolute rubbish! The poor kid's been
missing me dreadfully, she says so herself.'

'Have there been any behaviour problems at all?' asked the lady.

I tensed a little.

'She's always fine with me.'

'We get on like a house on fire, always have done.'

'It's just that the school says she's rather withdrawn and isn't doing very well at her lessons.'

'What do you mean, withdrawn? She's always been very outgoing and she's got heaps of friends.'

'And she's extremely bright, nearly always top of the class.'

'Yes, of course, but she has had quite a lot to cope with recently.'

I nodded bitterly behind the door.

'Children in these circumstances often develop worrying little habits which show they're under stress. They get whiny and demanding. They bite their nails. They often wet the bed.'

'Cheek!' I whispered. 'I do *not* wet my rotten old beds.'

'Sometimes they start stealing, but it's not as serious as it sounds. It's simply a way of looking for affection, taking a few treats because they feel very hard done by.'

'Oh dear,' said Mum, her voice catching. 'You see the thing is, Andrea has started taking a few things recently.'

'*What????*' I whispered. 'I haven't! I'm not a thief! What are you *on* about, Mum?'

'Well, Andrea's never stolen anything when she's with me. So it just shows she wants her dad.'

'It's not really stealing. And she takes such silly things. Things she can't possibly want. It's not as if she helps herself to money or chocolates or anything like that,' said Mum, sounding nearly in tears. 'I haven't said anything to her, but I've been getting really worried. It started off with her taking my Sellotape. And then she took one of Bill's cassettes. I knew she doesn't like his music so I thought she was just trying to be annoying. But then she took Katie's video case. That's what's really puzzled us. She doesn't like that video, the *Watch with Mother* one, the Andy Pandy puppet gets on her nerves. But she didn't take the video, just the *case*. What in the world would she want the case for? It doesn't make sense.'

I stuck my tongue out at the door. It made perfect sense.

'Perhaps she just wanted to annoy Katie?' said the lady.

'Perhaps,' said Mum. 'She certainly doesn't get on with her. They're always fighting.'

'She fights a lot with Zen and Crystal too,' said Dad, 'but if only Andrea could be with us for longer then I'm sure she'd put down roots and we'd be like one big happy family, especially when the new baby's here.'

'She needs to be with me,' said Mum. 'She can't cope with the idea of a new stepsister, she's talked about it to me.'

'Yet she's already having to cope with five ready-made siblings,' said the lady. 'You can't expect Andrea to get on with them. She doesn't want to be with them, she doesn't want to be with your new partners – she simply wants to be with you two.'

I nod, clutching Radish.

'And of course that's not possible.'

It *is*.

'I wonder where Andrea's got to? I'd better go and look for her.'

I take my cue and go back into the room. They all three give me big false smiles. I don't smile back. I still don't say anything. They think they've sussed me out but they know nothing.

And they're wrong about my new brothers and sisters, as a matter of fact. I don't think much of Zen but Crystal's OK, she can be quite sweet sometimes. I detest and despise little sugar-mouse Katie but Paula's funny, though she gets narked with me when I use her drying tights as a slide for Radish. But the best one of all is Graham. We are now mates.

He kept out of the way as usual for a few days and then he suddenly waylaid me on the stairs.

'I've got something in my room for you,' he muttered.

It was a boat. He'd made me a real little Radish-sized boat out of pieces of wood carefully nailed together and then painted. There's a real sail made from an old hankie and a little red ribbon flag on top.

'This one floats,' said Graham. 'I've tried it out in the bath. And it'll take one passenger easily.'

'Oh Graham!' I gave him a big hug. He went very pink and his glasses misted over. 'It's a lovely boat. It must have taken you ages. Why did you do it for me?'

'Because I like the way you keep bashing Katie,' said Graham, grinning. 'I can't stick her either. She always used to get on to me and tease me and muck up my stuff. Now she leaves me alone because she's got you to plague.'

'Yeah, it's not fair. And I can't ever get away from her.' I considered, my head on one side. 'It's awful sharing a room with her. Tell you what, Graham, I could come in here with you sometimes, couldn't I?'

'Oh, this is too small for two people what with my computer and everything,' Graham stammered, blinking anxiously.

'It's OK. I've got my own secret place where I go actually.'

'The bathroom?'

'No, much much better than the bathroom. I go there after school. That's where I'll sail my boat. Thanks ever so much, Graham. Here, we're mates now, aren't we, you and me?'

'Yes OK, if you like,' said Graham.

I do like. And so does Radish. She liked the video vessel very much but she *adores* her real sailing boat. She'd sail the lake all day long if I let her.

is for Night

Katie keeps me awake half the night. She won't have the light out for a start. Well, she'll switch the main light off but she's got this little china lamp in the shape of a toadstool with all these dinky rabbits and squirrels perched on little china chairs inside (Radish squeezed through the little door and tried to make friends but they didn't want to know). The lamp glows all night long, and then Katie has her own torch and she nearly always has her television on too. She turns the sound down low but the picture goes on flickering.

The only way I can find a bit of proper dark is right under the bedclothes and then I nearly suffocate.

'Switch that stupid set *off*!'

'It's my telly. It's my bedroom. I can do what I want.'

'I'll tell my mum.'

'I'll tell my dad.'

'I want to go to sleep.'

'Well *I* want to stay awake.'

'Look, I'm turning it off, so tough titty,' I said, jumping out of bed and switching off the set.

'And *I'm* turning it on, so tough titties with knobs on,' said Katie, bouncing out of bed and switching it straight back on.

She likes it when we have these long arguments late at night. She likes to stay wide awake. Sometimes I have a bad dream and I wake up at two or three in the morning and if I look over at Katie's bed her eyes are nearly always open, big and blue and unblinking.

It's not that she can't go to sleep. She fights terribly hard not to. She almost never lies down comfortably. She sits up with all her pillows propped behind her. She eats biscuits and drinks a lot of water so she has to keep nipping along to the bathroom. She even wears an old angora jumper under her pyjamas. It's so tight and tickly it does a splendid job keeping her awake.

'You aren't half a baby, Katie. Ten years old and scared of the dark.'

'Oh, I'm scared am I?' said Katie, and she touched the volume control on the television. She was watching one of those awful *Nightmare* films and just the sound of the creepy music made me put my head back under the covers.

It was my mate Graham who helped me suss things out. He gets a bit fussed and fidgety if I barge into his bedroom but we sometimes have these little chats on the stairs now. He used to share a bedroom with Katie when they were both little so he knows what it's like.

'She didn't have a television then so she used to make me play all these games with her and then we'd have to take turns telling ghost stories and whenever I fell asleep she'd pinch me and once she hit me so hard with her torch I had a black eye in the morning *and* I got into trouble with Dad for it because he said I was a right little wimp if my kid sister could get the better of me in a scrap,' Graham said, sighing.

'Doesn't she get tired like other people?'

'Yes, of course she does. Haven't you seen the dark circles under her eyes? And she sometimes falls asleep at school.'

'So why won't she go to sleep at night like anyone else?'

'Because she's scared.'

'But she *makes* herself scared, watching all those horrid videos.'

'No, that's to keep her awake. She's scared of going to sleep.'

'Mm?' I stared at him. 'What's there to be scared of in going to sleep?'

Graham fidgeted quite a bit. He screwed up his face several times and took his glasses off and polished them.

'She's just scared, that's all.'

'But what *of*?'

Graham's eyes looked very strange and bare and pink without his glasses. They blinked a lot.

'When our mum died they told us she'd gone to sleep,' he said, swallowing. 'Paula and I knew she'd been ill and then we knew she was dead. But Katie was just this little squirt and she didn't know what dead meant. So they said it was just like going to sleep. They meant to be kind but she got very scared of going to sleep after that.'

'I *see*.'

'Andy?'

'What?'

'Don't tease her about it, eh? I mean, I know she's a right pain, she's my own sister and yet I can't stick her, but all the same, don't go on about it.'

'I won't.'

And I didn't. That night I didn't even moan when she kept bumbling about the bedroom hour after hour. I settled down and went to sleep myself. I woke up about midnight. I looked over. Katie was still awake, sitting bolt upright staring at the television screen.

'Katie.' I reached out and touched her. She was icy cold. 'Hey. Why don't you switch that off and come in my bed for a cuddle, eh?'

She paused. There was a little silence. Then she gave a sniff.

'What on earth makes you think I want to come in your bed, Andy Pandy? You're so big and fat I'd get squashed flat in five minutes.'

I *still* didn't tease her. But I didn't half want to.

is for Old People

I don't like Old People. They really get on my nerves.

Miss Maynard is old. She's my headmistress. I had to go and see her the other day. She started off being quite matey and she even offered me one of her special toffees but then she started in on me.

'It's just not good enough, Andrea. Your schoolwork's gone to pieces this year. You don't hand your homework in on time, or you don't even bother to do it. You don't have your P.E. kit for your lessons. You don't bring a proper sick note when you've been off school. What's going on, mmm?'

My teeth got jammed in this huge wodge of toffee so I could only manage to urgle-urgle in response. Anyway, how could I explain properly? I'm so busy flitting from my mum's place to Dad's and back again that I leave half my stuff behind. I hand Mum my P.E. stuff to go in the wash and then I forget to take it with me to Dad's. It's no use expecting Carrie to do it. She washes but she doesn't ever iron anything and I get teased when I'm at Dad's because my school blouses are all crumpled and once they went shocking pink because Carrie shoved my stuff in with Zen's scarlet sweater. Carrie didn't even say she was sorry. She said she thought the pink shirt looked lovely with my bottle-green uniform, much better than boring old white.

I don't always bring a sick note because I forget to ask Mum or Dad . . . and maybe just occasionally I'm not exactly sick, I'm just staying off school because I've got fed up with it.

No-one knows. I pretend to Mum or Dad that I'm going to school and I get on all the right buses but I don't always get off in the right place. I slope about the town instead. Sometimes I go to the garden in Larkspur Lane and Radish and I spend hours and hours there. She sails backwards and forwards across the lake and then she treks through the jungle or climbs the north face of Mount Mulberry . . .

'Andrea!' Miss Maynard put her thin wrinkly face close to mine. 'You've gone off into a day-dream! For goodness sake, girl, you must stop this silly habit. I know things have been difficult for you at home.'

'I haven't *got* a home any more. Mum and Dad—'

'Yes, I know. And I do sympathize. But I can't help thinking you're making a rather unnecessary fuss. You know as well as I do that lots and lots of parents divorce and move house. It's very upsetting, but it's not the end of the world. We've been making allowances for you long enough, Andrea. Now it's time you started pulling yourself together.'

She gave my shoulders a little shake as if she was really pulling me together. I felt that if she went on pulling I'd go twang like elastic.

Mr Roberts is old too. Really old, with white hair and whiskers, but he still serves in his sweet shop though he can't bend any more because he says his knees have gone. You can't see whether they really have gone or not because of his corduroy trousers. Bill the baboon doles out pocket money on Saturdays. I get it too when I'm around, and then we all go down the road to the local shops. Paula's always fussing about her figure so she doesn't go to Mr Roberts' sweet shop, she buys tapes and magazines from the newsagent's on the corner. Graham and Katie and I go to the sweet shop.

'Hello, my darlings,' Mr Roberts says as soon as he sees us. He's always twinkling and stroking his beard. You expect him to go Ho-ho-ho like Father Christmas.

Graham is very shy with most people but he gets quite chatty with Mr Roberts. But it's Katie who is the favourite. Naturally. She twirls about the shop like a sugar-plum fairy and Mr Roberts chuckles and claps and calls her his Little Precious and his Cute Little Sweetheart. He always lets her have a free go in his Lucky Bag, five pence a dip.

He offers me a free go too but I just stick my nose in the air and say no thanks. I have to buy my sweets and chocolate from him because there's nowhere else to get it, but I'm not going to make friends.

Mr Roberts and I are deadly enemies. The very first time I went into his shop with Graham and Katie he looked me up and down and then he whispered to Katie, 'Who's the Jolly Green Giant then?'

It was a loud whisper and I heard. Katie sniggered and snorted and even Graham smiled. He said later that Mr Roberts just called me that because I was wearing my green school raincoat. Rubbish. It was a studied insult because of my size.

The grannies and grandads are all old too. I can't stick any of them. I have my own Nan and Grandad but they live in Canada with my auntie so they're no use. They're Dad's mum and dad. Mum's mum and dad are dead so they're no use either. It's not fair, because Paula and Graham and Katie have got two full sets of grandparents and they're always coming to see them, and Zen and Crystal have a granny and grandpa too. *They* aren't too bad, because they took me to the zoo with them, and we all got icecream and an animal colouring book. Paula and Graham and Katie's lot are awful. The baboon's parents are squat and hairy like him, even the granny. I'd hate to kiss her because she has a moustache. But the worst ones of all are the other gran and grandad. They used to help look after Paula and Graham and Katie after their mum died. They still come and visit a lot. They don't think much of my mum. They keep going on about the past, and how devoted Bill was to his first wife, and Mum gets very pink in the face. They practically ignore her. And me. You will never believe this but when they come on a visit they always bring presents for Paula and Graham and Katie. Sometimes they're really big presents, new clothes or books or records. Sometimes it's just boxes of chocolates. But whatever it is, I don't get anything at all. Not a sausage.

Mum got pinker than ever, pinker than my spoiled school shirts, and eventually I heard her ask the gran and grandad if they could include me in the present-giving so that I wouldn't feel left out.

'But Paula and Graham and Katie are our grandchildren,' they said. 'Andrea's nothing to do with us.'

Well, good. Catch *me* wanting anything to do with *them*.

P

is for Photographs

Dad's got a camera. We're back to the old routine now. One week at Mum's. One week at Dad's. You know. As easy as A B C. Carrie was a bit huffy at first because she'd had a social worker round to check up on things.

'And she said everywhere is spotless,' said Carrie. 'You tell your mother that. We might be a bit untidy, but the flat is perfectly clean and she said that Zen and Crystal are delightful intelligent children who have obviously had a lot of loving care and stimulation.'

The delightful and intelligent twins were having a fierce pillowfight as she spoke, lovingly and carefully stimulating the pillows until they both burst simultaneously and scattered a snow of feathers.

Carrie just laughed. Even Dad didn't get cross. He got his camera and took lots of photos.

'You'll wear that camera out before the baby's even born,' said Carrie, still laughing. She turned to me. 'I bought your dad this second-hand camera so he can take lots of photos when the baby's being born. Won't that be lovely?'

I stared at her. I know how babies are born of course. I didn't think they were going to be the sort of photos you could put in a silver frame and prop on top of the television set.

Dad saw me looking doubtful.

'I want to take lots of photos of my number one daughter too,' he said. 'Come on, Andy, give us a smile.'

I gave him a smile. And then another. And then I put my hand on my hip and gave him a little wave. Then I pointed a toe. Then I pirouetted round the room, Dad going *snap snap snap*.

'That's the girl, Andy. Hey, that's great. You've really got the idea, haven't you?'

It was wonderful. I felt like a film star. Crystal came and joined in and she smiled and waved and pointed too, but she didn't do it as naturally as me. And Zen was hopeless, galumphing about and pulling hideous faces at the camera.

'No, Andy's the star model,' said Carrie. 'Here, let's dress her up like a real model, eh? Come and help me choose some clothes, Crystal. And we'll make her up and give her a posh hair-do. Would you like that, Andy?'

I liked it enormously. Carrie dressed me up in one of her long droopy fancy frocks and Crystal draped a shawl round my shoulders and stuck a ring on every finger. Carrie stroked dark shadow on my eyelids and purple lipstick round my mouth and then brushed my hair up into a crazy kind of bun. Crystal squirted me all over with scent even though it wouldn't show in a photograph.

Then we had a long, long, posing session, Dad snapping away until he eventually ran out of film. He developed the photographs himself, blundering round the bathroom in the pitch dark. I couldn't wait to see the finished photographs. I felt as if I'd been transformed into this new grown-up magical pretty person. I looked for her in the photographs – but I just saw myself, looking a bit funny in a long frock with stuff smeared all over my face.

'I don't like them. Tear them up, Dad. Ugh, I look awful,' I said hastily.

'No, they're very good. The lighting's a bit haywire and you're out of focus here and there, but on the whole they're great,' said Dad.

'*You* look great, Andy,' said Carrie. 'You know what? You'll have to be a fashion model when you grow up. You're nice and tall already. Fashion models have to be very tall.'

I didn't know that. I thought about the idea. Maybe the photographs weren't too bad after all.

Dad gave me some copies to show to Mum when it was her turn to have me.

'Oh for Heaven's sake!' said Mum. 'Look at the way they've got you up! You look awful, Andy. All that dreadful make-up. And you're wearing that Carrie's clothes. Why on earth couldn't your father take some proper photos of you in your own clothes, instead of all dolled up like a dog's dinner.'

'I was being a fashion model, Mum. Carrie

said I could be a model when I grow up, she did, Mum, honestly.'

'She would,' said Mum, shuddering.

'Fashion models aren't *fat*,' said Katie, poking me in the tummy.

'I can go on a diet when I grow up,' I said, but I was starting to wish I hadn't taken the photos with me.

But then Paula came and had a look.

'Don't you look grown-up, Andy? No-one would ever think you were only ten. You look almost as old as me.'

That pleased me quite a lot.

And then Graham had a quick shuffle through the photos too.

'Don't, Graham. I look such a twit,' I said, going hot.

'Yeah, you said it, Andy Pandy,' said Katie.

'I think you look pretty,' said Graham.

That pleased me even more.

is for Questions

'What's Miss Maynard on about in this letter, Andy? She's moaning about all your dental appointments, saying it would be better if you could go after school. But you haven't *had* any dental appointments, have you? You went for a check-up in the summer and you didn't even need any fillings. So what's going on, Andy? *Andy??*'

'How did you do in your English test, Andy? And how's the old arithmetic getting on? Why won't you let me see your schoolbooks nowadays? You are still top of the class, aren't you? Andy, what's the matter?'

'Come along, Andrea, answer the question. It's no use looking at Aileen, she's not going to tell you. You weren't paying attention, were you? It's simply not good enough. Do you want to end up a complete dunce, is that it?'

'Who's been mucking around with my tights? They're all wet and soapy. You've been messing about with your little rabbit again, haven't you?'

'How are things working out for you and Radish, Andrea? Do you mind going from House A to House B and back again?'

'Do you know what time it is, Andy Pandy? Time to go home. Only you haven't got a home any more, have you?'

is for Radish

I didn't dare stay off school for a bit because
Mum went to see Miss Maynard and they had
a Long Talk. I'm not ever going to be able to
make out I've got to go to the dentist now
even if I get a gum boil and half my fillings
fall out. I can't even get a cold or a cough or
a tummy upset. Miss Maynard showed Mum
my forged sick notes. And then Mum told Dad
so I won't even be able to swing things when

I'm at his place. I have to stay at boring old school even though the teachers just shout at me now and Aileen and Fiona whisper secrets and won't play with me properly and I keep coming bottom in all the tests.

I can't even go to the garden for long after school because Mum knows what time I should get back to her place and even though she's not there Katie always tells on me. It's even worse when I'm at Dad's. Carrie comes to meet me off the bus and she looks awful now with her great huge bump and I'm scared people will think she's a proper relative instead of just a stupid stepmother. I just have time to charge down Larkspur Lane, climb over the gate, give Radish one quick sail across the lake and back, maybe let her take a two minute trek in the grassy jungle, and then it's home again home again *jiggetty jig* only I haven't got a home any more and Radish seems to be getting a bit fed up with my pocket.

I wish I could make a real home for her. I tried making her a Japanese bag out of one of Dad's hankies and then I thought about making her a proper little Japanese house but Crystal kept trailing round after me asking what I was doing, and then when I got the big box of kitchen matches to construct a wooden house Carrie suddenly swooped and snatched them away.

'I'm sorry, Andy, but I can't let you play with matches.'

'I'm not going to *play* with them. I'm going to make something with them.'

'Yes, it's going to be a little house and she's made a tiny screen out of a cigarette packet and a baby tree out of a bit of twig and she's going to make Radish a special frock called a kimona,' Crystal burbled.

'Shut *up*, Crystal,' I hissed, because it would all get spoilt if everyone knew.

It was spoilt anyway. Carrie still wouldn't let me have the matches. I did try to think of making the house with something else but then Zen trod on the screen after I'd spent ages colouring in little tiny Japanese things all over it. Carrie helped me a bit. In fact she did the drawing part and she had the ideas and Zen kept pestering and eventually he just went *stamp*. Carrie said we could do another screen but I said no thanks. I didn't really want her poking her nose in anyway. I wanted it to be a secret for Radish and me with no-one else involved, not even Crystal.

I tried again when I was at Mum's. I snaffled an old shoe-box and I spent ages getting all the thread off some cotton reels but Katie was poisonous.

'Oh how sweet. Little Andy Pandy's playing house with her dinky toy rabbit. But I think it's rather a dodgy site. I have a feeling this is an earthquake area. What's that? Did you feel a tremor? Whoops!'

She reached out and Radish and her home went flying. So then I reached out and Katie went flying.

Mum was furious and wouldn't even listen why.

'I've told you and told you, Andy. You are *not* to hit Katie, no matter what. You *must* stop this disgraceful bullying, especially when Katie's so much smaller than you.'

And as if that wasn't enough, Katie deliberately pulled two buttons off her school blouse. Mum saw and tutted and went to her sewing-box – and then I got into another row because she said I'd mucked up all her thread.

I was in so much trouble that I decided I might just as well stay for ages in the Larkspur Lane garden and miss my bus. Miss two buses, even three. Katie could blab all she liked to Mum as I'd stopped caring.

'Do you hear that, Radish?' I said, as we climbed over the gate. 'We can stay here as long as you like.'

Radish wriggled excitedly in my hand. She could hardly wait till I got her boat unpacked from my satchel. She hopped on board and was soon sailing across the lake, expertly skimming her way through the shoals of orange whales. I let her sail under her own steam, squatting down on the muddy shore and watching her, but after a while it got a bit cold and damp so I found a long twiggy stick and started propelling her round the lake in uncharted territory. Together we discovered Step Creek and Lily Land and for a while we were caught up in the foetid swamps of Waterweed Bog but we escaped at last after Radish heroically hacked her way through with her bare paws and my scrabbling fingernails.

She was a bit tired of sailing after that and we'd both got very wet so we ran round and round the lake to get warm. We were hungry too and looked longingly at the mulberry tree but the berries were long since over. I searched the lining of my satchel and salvaged a few biscuit crumbs but they weren't much of a feast for Radish and they didn't help my hunger at all.

I don't have a watch but I knew it was teatime. I was really really late now. It was starting to get dark. Mum would be back from work and she'd be so cross. She'd tell the baboon and he'd have another go at me. And Katie would give a smug little smile and then whisper about it half the night. I wouldn't even be able to cry because she'd see.

I leant against the mulberry tree clutching Radish in my fist and had a bit of a cry there. But then as I moved about to stop my face getting scratched my hand holding Radish suddenly slipped under a branch and went into a little hole.

'Radish? Come back!'

But Radish was running about inside the dark little hole, getting excited. It was just like a secret cave. I tried to peer in but it was getting too dark to see properly. Radish insisted that she could see. She loved the little hole. Only it wasn't a hole to her. She wanted me to help her make it into a proper home. Not a proper permanent home, but a holiday home for her visits to the lake.

'OK, Radish. We'll make it really cosy for you. We could get some moss for a soft green carpet. And I could stick some shiny leaves together to make matching curtains. And we'll have to see about some sort of light because I can't see in the dark even if you can.'

And at that moment a light went on. Not inside the hole. Outside. In the big house behind me. It made me jump and my hand jerked and then suddenly Radish wasn't there.

'Radish? Radish, where are you? Come back! Come here!' I said, feeling frantically. And then I felt the drop at the back of the hole. I pushed my arm in as far as it would go. I scrabbled and stretched but it was no use. Radish had fallen out of my reach.

'Radish!' I screamed.

And then the door opened and there was a dark figure in the garden and I had to tear my arm out of the tree and run for it.

S is for Starlight

'Where on earth have you *been*?' Mum shouted.

I was too choked up to answer properly.

'I was just . . . playing,' I mumbled.

'Playing!' said Mum, and she smacked me hard across the face.

We both gasped. She's never hit me before. Then I burst into tears. And Mum did too.

'Oh Andy,' she said, and she was suddenly hugging me tight. 'I'm sorry. I was just so worried and I've been phoning everyone. I phoned Miss Maynard, and I had to phone your father and he blames me for going out to work and yet if he'd pay his share of the bills then I wouldn't have to and— Oh darling, never mind all that. All that matters is you're safe.'

'But Radish isn't,' I said, and I started really howling. I'd held it in while waiting for the first bus and then on the journey and then on the second bus and then on the walk back to Mum's place but now the full awfulness washed over me like a giant wave.

'I've lost Radish,' I sobbed, and I buried my head in Mum's shoulder so I could shut out all the other faces round me. Graham looked sympathetic and Paula patted my shoulder but Katie had her eyebrows raised in mock amazement and the baboon looked impatient.

'For goodness sake, is that why she's so late? Because she's lost her little toy?' he said, sighing.

'She's *not* a toy, she's a mascot,' I shouted.

'Hey hey! No need to take that tone. Look, your poor mum's been worried sick. You're two hours late home, young lady. It's just not good enough.'

'Yes, I know, Bill, but Radish is very special to Andy,' said Mum, still holding me close.

'All the same, it seems a bit daft to have the whole family going demented because she's lost a little rabbit that isn't even real.'

'She *is* real to me!'

'Come on now, Andy, calm down. You really are being a bit of a baby, you know,' said Mum. She said it quietly but the others could still hear. I pulled away from her. 'Andy? Now don't be like that. Look, maybe Radish isn't lost for ever. When did you last see her? Did she drop out of your pocket on the way home?'

'She fell down inside a tree,' I whispered, thinking of poor little Radish tumbling backwards down that dark hole.

'Which tree?' said Mum, but I couldn't tell her because I'd get into more trouble for going into someone else's garden. Oh how could I have run off like that and left my Radish down in the depths of the mulberry tree? And she wasn't the only thing I'd abandoned in my hurry to save my own skin.

'I've lost your lovely little boat too, Graham,' I said crying harder.

'Never mind. Look, I can easily make you another,' Graham said gruffly.

'But there can't ever be another Radish,' I said, sobbing.

'Of course there can,' said the baboon. 'I'll get you a new one in the morning. They sell them in the toy shop down the road. Katie had some of those Sylvanian family things when she was little.'

The 'little' stung, but I was so overwhelmed with misery and guilt I hardly cared.

'I don't want a new Sylvanian family. I want *Radish*.'

Radish hadn't died. She hadn't stopped being. She was still there, alone in the dark tree, probably hurt, certainly very lonely and scared. She'd be wondering where on earth I was, why I wasn't coming to rescue her . . .

'I've got to go back,' I said desperately. 'I can't reach her, but I could call down to her, try to comfort her—'

'Don't be so silly, darling,' said Mum. 'You're certainly not going out again. You're going to have some tea and a nice hot bath and then you're going straight to bed.'

There was no arguing with her. There *was* a lot of arguing going on, but that was between Mum and Dad, because Dad came round to see if I was safe and then started up all the old rows. My hand kept reaching out for Radish and then clenching in despair.

It was even worse when I went to bed. I couldn't remember ever going to sleep without Radish. She always tucked into my hand and I put my finger in between her dear little ears and rubbed her soft furry forehead until I went to sleep. So now of course I couldn't possibly sleep. I lay awake for hour after hour. Mum crept in to see me and gave me a special kiss and tucked me up while Katie made vomit noises from the next bed, but it didn't help. I heard Graham go to bed. Then Paula. Then Mum and the baboon. Soon the whole household was asleep except me. And Katie. She started.

'Down a tree, is she, Andy Pandy? In with all the bugs and spiders, eh? You get lots of creepy crawlies inside trees. And maybe some bird's fallen down the hole too and died and your little Radish is lying on its *corpse*. Yeah, all the maggots are going *wiggle wiggle wiggle* all over her and she won't even be able to cry for help because rabbits don't talk. She's just opening her little mouth and screaming silently, wondering why you don't come.'

'I *am* coming,' I said. I got out of bed and started pulling on my clothes.

'What are you doing, you dope?' Katie whispered.

'What do you *think* I'm doing? I'm going to comfort Radish,' I said, pulling on a jumper.

'But it's after midnight. You can't go *out*.'

'Just watch.'

'But your mum—'

'I don't care. She won't know. And if you tell her I'll . . . I'll tell you're such a scared baby you won't even lie down properly to go to sleep. And I know why and I'll tell everyone – if you tell on me. Understand?'

She understood all right. She still looked worried.

'Andy, you are just kidding, aren't you? You can't really go out in the middle of the night. Look, those things I said about Radish, I was just making them up to annoy you, they're not true.'

'They could be,' I said, and I put on my coat and wound a scarf round my neck.

'But it's so dark outside,' said Katie.

She was wrong about that. When I'd crept down the stairs and out the front door I looked up and saw there was a big round moon and hundreds of stars shining in the sky. I saw the Pole star shining brighter than all the others. I threw back my head, staring at it until my eyes watered, and I whispered the wishing song.

Starlight, star bright
First little star I see tonight
Wish that I may, wish that I might
Have the first wish that I wish tonight.

'I wish that I can find Radish and work out a way of reaching her so that I can have her back, please, please, *please*.'

is for Time To Go Home

There aren't any buses in the middle of the
night. Larkspur Lane is a long bus ride away.
I wasn't sure how long it would take me to
walk. I'd never been out that late at night
before. Certainly not by myself. The stars
and the street lights stopped it being too dark,
but it was still pretty scary. It was cold and
strange and all the streets seemed so empty,
and yet whenever a car went by or a man

walked past I shrank away from them.

I tried to think of poor little Radish stuck down the tree – but I couldn't stop thinking about poor little *me* too. I remembered all the things Mum and Dad had said about strangers and when a man slowed down when he saw me and said 'What's up, dear? Why are you out all on your own at this time?' I shot past and went flying off down the street. He called after me and then started running too.

I ran faster, heart thudding, feet pounding, dodging down an alley and round someone's garden and down another passage and out into another road and then another, running and running and running – and when at last I stopped, spread-eagled against a wall with a great tearing stitch in my side the man was nowhere to be seen.

He might have been a kind man trying to look after me. He might have been a monster ready to make off with me. There was no way of telling.

I didn't even know where I was any more. I stared round at the dark unfamiliar buildings in panic. I could try going back along the alley but the man might be waiting . . .

I started shaking and shivering. My cheeks

got a bit wet. My hand seemed horribly empty – but then I tucked my thumb inside my fist and tried to kid myself it was Radish and it helped just a little bit. I ran on down the road and when I turned the corner I was at the shops. I knew how to get back to Mum's place in less than five minutes. But I couldn't go back. Katie would be still lying awake, and how she'd sneer if I came creeping back so soon. And Radish was still down the tree, so lost and lonely and frightened. I thought of her tiny heart beating violently under her soft fur and my face screwed up in pain.

'I'm coming, Radish,' I whispered. I stared up at the stars. 'You've *got* to make my wish come true.'

So I set off walking. I walked and walked and walked. I walked until I was so tired I started to wonder if I was dreaming. Everything seemed so strange and silvery in the starlight and every so often my head would nod and I'd stumble and start. I kept expecting to blink my eyes and find myself tucked up in bed at Mum's, but it didn't happen. So I just walked some more, my head down, shoulders hunched, feet going *left right left right left right*.

I missed my way several times but then I'd

suddenly recognize a shop or a house and I'd
know I was back on course again. But then I
found myself in streets I was certain I'd never
seen before. I walked on and yet it was all new
and different and I realized I was lost again. I
tried going back but I kept getting to corners
and not knowing whether to take the left turn
or the right. So in the end I kept on walking
anyway, and after a while I stopped thinking
about finding the way. I just looked up at the
stars and whispered Radish's name and walked
on and on and on.

Then I suddenly recognized a house at the
end of a road, with gables and a curly iron gate
and a caravan parked in the front drive. It was
Aileen's house and she went on her holidays
in that caravan and we'd swung on that gate
together and she was probably asleep in her
bedroom under the gables right this minute.

'Aileen's house?' I whispered. Then I'd somehow missed Larkspur Lane altogether. I'd by-
passed the school. I was back in my own old
territory, the other side of the school. The part
of the town where I never went any more. If
this was Aileen's house then I knew what was
down the road and round the corner.

I stood still, shivering. No. I had to go to

Larkspur Lane and find Radish. I couldn't waste time going anywhere else. But I had to. My feet started walking and I couldn't stop them.

I went past Aileen's house. Past all the other houses in the road with their neat privet hedges and their pointed roofs making a zig-zag pattern against the starry sky. I got to the corner. I stood still again, holding my thumb. Then I started walking, very very slowly.

I could see it in the starlight. A cottage at the end of the road. I could only see in black and white but it was easy to paint in the colours. A white cottage with a grey slate roof and a black chimney and a bright butter-yellow front door. There were yellow roses and honeysuckle growing up a lattice round the door and the leaded windows, and lots of other flowers growing in the big garden. And in the middle of the garden was the old twisted tree with the big branches bent almost to the ground, and at the tip of each twig grew big bunches of black mulberries . . .

No, no mulberries. The berries had long ago withered on the tree. No roses, just tangled thorny branches. No sweet-smelling honeysuckle, just leathery stems trailing untidily. But it was still Mulberry Cottage. I was back. I was home.

is for Unconscious

'Andy? Andy darling, is that you?' Mum's at the door, smiling at me. 'Come in, sugar-lump, I've got tea all ready on the table.'

'Yes, come on, Andy, Mum's made a lovely mulberry pie and my mouth's watering,' Dad calls.

'Dad?' I step inside, shaking my head. 'Dad, what are you doing here?'

'He got off work early, didn't you, darling,' says Mum.

'But what are *we* doing here?' I say, dazed.

'We live here, silly,' says Mum, and she ruffles my hair. 'What's up, Andy? Don't you feel very well?'

'No, I feel . . . wonderful. I can't believe it. Was it all a dream then – all that about leaving Mulberry Cottage and you having Bill and Dad having Carrie and . . . ?'

'I think you're still half asleep, pet. Come on, let's have tea, we're all hungry.'

Mum takes my hand and leads me into the living-room. Dad's sitting at the table, smiling at me. There's a big bunch of our own pink roses in a pretty white vase, and there are little fairy cakes with pink icing and white rosettes and the newly-baked mulberry pie, dark wine-red juice bubbling up through a crack in the golden pastry and filling the whole room with the rich fruity smell.

Mum cuts me a huge slice and tops it with vanilla icecream. I bite into hot and cold, crunchy and smooth, sweet and sharp, and close my eyes with the bliss of it.

'Mmmmm,' I say, and Mum and Dad laugh.

'Doesn't Radish want some too?' says Mum.

'Radish?' I say, and there she is, safe and sound, tucked up in my pocket, half asleep too.

Mum lets me fetch a doll's-house saucer and a china thimble and Radish eats and drinks with us.

'But wait. This is the thimble I swopped with Aileen ages ago,' I say, puzzled.

'Well, you must have swopped it back again,' says Mum.

'And maybe you'll get swopping yet again because I've got a little surprise in my pocket for you and your Radish,' says Dad.

'A present!' I jump up and run to Dad.

'Oh darling, you do spoil her,' says Mum.

'I like spoiling both my best girls,' says Dad, and he gives me a present out of one pocket and Mum a present from the other.

Mine is a small square cardboard box and inside is a tiny Radish-size gilt table and chair, and sellotaped safely to the table top is a tiny pink china cup and saucer and plate, delicately edged with a wisp of gold paint. Mum's present is in another cardboard box and it's a proper size pink china teacup and saucer with cherubs flying all round the rim, and a little message in looping writing at the bottom of the cup. The message says 'I love you'. Dad says it too. Mum goes as pink as her cup and they give each other a long kiss. Radish and I grin at each other. We are all very pleased with our presents.

We eat up the pie and icecream and every one of the fairy cakes and then we all do the washing-up together, making it a game. Dad keeps flapping the tea towel and I put my fingers on my head to make horns and rush around pretending to be a little bull and Mum makes out we're getting on her nerves but she keeps laughing, and we're still all in a giggly mood when we go back into the living-room, as if it's a special day like Christmas.

We switch on the television and my very favourite film *The Wizard of Oz* is just starting and so Mum and Dad and Radish and I all cuddle up to watch it. I've got my red slippers on and Mum and Dad keep calling me Dorothy and I turn Radish into Toto and make her give little barks. We sing along to all the songs and at the end of the film when Dorothy clicks the heels of her ruby slippers and whispers 'There's no place like home' I suddenly start crying.

'What's up, darling?' says Mum.

'Don't be sad, little sausage,' says Dad.

'I'm not sad. I'm crying because I'm so happy,' I say, sniffling.

'You funny old thing,' says Mum, and she pulls me on to her lap for a cuddle.

When the film finishes I climb on to Dad's lap instead and he reads me a story, lots of stories, from all the story books I had when I was little.

'But they got lost somewhere, I'm sure they did,' I say.

'Well, we found them again, specially for you,' says Dad, giving me a kiss.

'You don't mind reading me such babyish stuff, Dad?'

'You're our baby, aren't you?' says Dad, giving me a tickle. 'Come on, little babykins, say *cootchy-coo* for your Dad-Dad.'

'Oh Dad, don't be so daft,' I say, shrieking with laughter.

'I don't know – tears one minute, a great big fit of the giggles the next. I think it must be bed-time,' says Mum.

'Oh no,' I say, but I don't argue too much because I don't want to spoil anything and it's easy to be good when I'm so happy. I get in the bath and Radish gets in with me and floats about as merry as a little duck. Then

we both get dry and powdered and into our
nighties and then Dad comes and carries me
into bed as if I really am a baby. He tucks me
up and he tucks Radish up too, and he kisses
both our noses which makes me giggle again.
Then Mum comes and she tickles us both under
the chin and we giggle some more. Then Mum
and Dad stand arm in arm at the foot of my
bed, chatting softly to each other while Radish
and I snuggle up. The bed's so soft and I feel so
safe with all my own things round me, my own
rabbit pictures on the wall, my own wardrobe,
my own toy cupboard, my own bookshelf, my
own Radish in my hand, my own Mum and Dad
right by my bed, together. I'm so happy I want
this moment to last forever but I'm so sleepy
too and I can't stop my eyes closing and I know
I'm going to sleep and I'm suddenly worried
because I know it can't last and that it's going
to be very different when I wake up and I try
to open my eyes wide but they're so heavy and
I have to rest them just for a second and then
they won't open again and I'm going to sleep
in spite of myself, I'm going to sleep . . .

is for Vagrant

I woke up and it was dark and I was so cold and I felt for Radish but I couldn't find her and then I remembered and I couldn't bear it and I huddled under an old sack at the bottom of the garden and tried to get back into the dream . . .

And then I woke up again and it was light and I heard someone out in the garden, over by the bird-table.

'Come on, little sparrows, nice toast crumbs for breakfast. Come and have a little peck. And I've got some nuts for you too and— Oh my goodness! Harry, come quick! There's some little old vagrant sleeping under the mulberry tree!'

A vagrant. For a moment I thought she meant a real vagrant sleeping somewhere beside me. And then I realized. She meant me.

Vagrants sleep rough. They don't have their own bed. They don't have a proper home. Nobody wants them. They keep shifting around and getting moved on and everyone acts like they're a general nuisance.

I'm a vagrant.

I scrambled out of the old sack and struggled to my feet, and then I started running, staggering once or twice because I was so stiff. The woman gasped and then called after me but I wouldn't stop. I couldn't get the gate open so I jumped right over it. They'd painted it green instead of black. And when I chanced one last look round I saw they'd painted the front door green too. It didn't look like my Mulberry Cottage without a butter-yellow front door. But it isn't my Mulberry Cottage any more.

I ran away, blundering down the road, round

corners, along lanes, no longer watching where I was going, not even knowing any more, just wanting to run and run. I ran right across the road and a car hooted at me and made me jump so I didn't cross any more roads for a bit and then another car hooted and I blinked at it, bewildered because I was still safely on the pavement, and it hooted again and someone shouted and I saw it was Dad. Only maybe I was still dreaming because Mum was with him too, Mum and Dad together in our car, and they stopped the car with a squeal of brakes and then they were both running towards me – and suddenly I was swept up in their arms and we were having a big hug together, Mum and Dad and me, hugging the way we used to, the three of us together. No, we used to be four. Radish!

'Oh Andy, darling, don't cry! It's all right, you're safe and we've got you back and—'

'And half the police in the country are out looking for you but we found you ourselves and just so long as you're OK—'

'Oh Andy, why did you run away? We've been so *worried*—'

'We've been going out of our minds. Everyone's been searching—'

I cried harder. 'I haven't been searching. I just gave up. And she'll be so scared without me,' I sob. 'Oh I've *got* to go and rescue Radish!'

'But you dropped her down some tree, darling, you said—'

'I know which tree. It's in a garden where I go a lot.'

'You don't mean . . . our old garden? At Mulberry Cottage?'

'No, this is a different garden. In Larkspur Lane, near my school. I was looking for it last night but I got lost and then I was back at Mulberry Cottage and you were there, both of you were, and we all had tea together and then you both put me to bed—'

'That must have been a dream, Andy.'

'Yes, I know. It wasn't ever like that, even before you split up,' I say sadly. 'But Radish isn't a dream. She really is in the tree and I must go and try to get her back.'

'That blooming rabbit,' said Dad, only he didn't say blooming. But he drove us in the car to Larkspur Lane and I pointed out the right cottage.

'It's still very early. We can't just barge into a private garden and start searching their trees,' said Mum. 'Maybe we ought to wait a while,

Andy. You're still frozen stiff. We ought to take you straight back home and—'

'And we've got to phone the police, tell them you're safe.'

'And I must let Bill and the children know. They're all so worried. Katie's been in floods of tears.'

'*Katie?*'

'Carrie and the twins are very upset too – and it's bad for Carrie to get in a state when the baby's nearly due.'

'But I've *got* to get Radish,' I said, starting to climb over the gate.

I was up and over the other side before they could stop me.

'Andy, come back!'

'We must knock at the front door first to ask permission.'

'No, we can't. I'll get into trouble,' I hissed, running across the wet grass towards the mulberry tree. 'It's OK, I know exactly where Radish is, and if you could try to get your arm down the hole, Dad, you can reach much further than me—'

But before I could get to the tree I heard the door of the house opening, and someone coming out. Two people. They'd caught us.

is for Welcome

They were two small plump elderly people, both
in their dressing-gowns. The woman was wearing a pink quilted satin affair, the man a woollen
red-and-blue tartan job. They both had those old-
fashioned slippers with pompoms. They certainly
didn't look very frightening but I was in such a
silly state I was frightened all the same.

'Please. I just want to look for Radish. I'll
only be a moment,' I stammered.

'We're so sorry to disturb you like this,' said Mum.

'I know she's very naughty playing in your garden, but my daughter's lost her toy rabbit down your tree and that's why we're here at this God-forsaken hour, you see, to try to find it,' said Dad.

'Oh, it's perfectly all right. We were expecting you,' said the old man.

'Expecting the little girl. She's our little visitor,' said the old woman. 'She comes nearly every day and we're always so pleased to see her.'

I blink at them in astonishment.

'It's been grand to see her enjoying our garden. All our grandchildren are in Australia so we've no children of our own to come and play,' said the old man.

'Of course we didn't like to intrude. We've been careful to keep our distance, but we couldn't help having little peeps at you now and then,' said the old woman, smiling at me. 'You and your little rabbit seemed to be having such fun. And yesterday you stayed such a long time and it was such a pleasure to us. But it started to get dark and we wondered if you might have lost track of the time. We hoped you might come indoors and take a bite of tea with us but when I came out to ask I must have startled you, because you ran away.'

'I'm sorry,' I said, blushing. 'That was silly. And I left Radish. I dropped her down inside the mulberry tree. Do you mind if my dad tries to get her back?'

'Not at all, my dear, not at all. Although you can easily reach her yourself, you know,' said the old man, and he gave his wife a little nudge.

'Why don't you go and look,' she said, her eyes twinkling.

So I ran to the mulberry tree. I found the little hole under the branch. But it wasn't just a hole any more. Someone had stuck some little net curtains up at the entrance, turning it into a tiny window. I peered inside – but I couldn't see Radish.

'That's upstairs,' said the old woman. 'I think she's downstairs now.'

I put my hand in the hole and felt, but the old woman was shaking her head.

'No dear, there's a much easier way to see downstairs. Run round to the other side of the tree and crouch down just a little,' she said.

I ran. I crouched. I saw another hole in the tree. There was a small doll-size doormat at the edge, with WELCOME in very tiny cross-stitch. I peeped past the mat and there was my own darling Radish stretched out happily on her own little wooden sofa, her head propped on a blue velvet cushion.

I gazed at her until my eyes blurred.

'How did . . . ?' I whispered.

'Just our little bit of fun, my dear,' said the old woman, putting her soft hand on my shoulder. 'My daughter used to play games with her little dolls inside the old mulberry, turning it into a real tree-house. Arthur and I were sure you'd be back so he did a bit of whittling and made the sofa and I did a bit of stitching to make the hole look a bit homey.'

'It looks very very homey,' I said. 'And do you know what it's called? It's Radish's own Mulberry Cottage.'

We all went inside the couple's own cottage because they were starting to shiver in their dressing-gowns, and we all had tea and hot buttered toast and Mum and Dad explained about our own Mulberry Cottage and it was all so cosy and everyone was chatting away so happily that I started to wonder if my dream might really come true . . .

But then when we were back in Dad's car he started blaming Mum for not looking after me properly when I was in bed and she got furious and started on about my not even having a proper bed at Dad's place and I clutched Radish and realized that some dreams can't ever come true.

Radish still lives with me in my pocket most of the time because I need her so much. But she has her own Mulberry Cottage too and now, nearly every day after school, I take her there. She goes boating on her lake and then she has an acorn cup of mulberry juice in her own little cottage while I have cocoa and seed cake with Mr and Mrs Peters. That's the name of the old couple. They asked if I'd like to call them Uncle Arthur and Auntie Gladys but I've got too many uncles and aunties already. Sometimes, just in my head, I call them Granny and Grandad. I never thought I'd like any old people. Mr and Mrs Peters are very old, but I like them ever such a lot.

is for Xmas

You should have seen Mulberry Cottage at Christmas. I dipped a pine cone in green paint and then I splodged on little red berries and gold stars so that Radish had her very own Christmas tree. I even made her a teeny weeny paper chain though Mrs Peters had to help me because I just kept tearing it. Mrs Peters' hands are like little claws because she has arthritis and yet she can still make them move like magic.

She gave me my own sewing-box for Christmas. It's got all these little compartments stuffed with threads and needles and a silver thimble and a tape measure that snaps back into place when you touch the button. The compartment tray lifts out and at the bottom are all sorts of materials from her own scrap bag, soft silks and velvets and different cottons with tiny sprigs of flowers and minute checks and pin-head dots, all perfect for making into dresses for Radish. She's got so many little outfits now she wants me to change her all day long so that she can show them all off.

I've made her a dance-frock that covers her paws, a velvet cloak lined with cotton wool fur, even a little sailor-suit with a big white collar and a white cap with special ear-holes. Mrs Peters had to help quite a lot with that little outfit, but I did all the designing. Maybe I won't be a fashion model after all. Maybe I'll be a fashion designer. Then I don't have to bother about getting thin. Mrs Peters is such a good cook that I'm getting bigger than ever. She doesn't mind. She says I'm a growing girl and I should eat my fill. I told Katie and she said yes I was growing all right, growing gi-normous, and she puffed out her cheeks and strutted round pretending to be me. People laughed and I wanted to cry but I didn't. I didn't hit Katie either. I just made out I didn't care and said I'd sooner be gi-normous than a silly little squirt like her, and got on with my sewing.

Mr Peters gave me a whole suite of wooden furniture to go in Mulberry Cottage. There's a big wardrobe that really opens, and a wonderful wooden trunk so Radish has got plenty of space to store her magnificent new ensembles. Mr Peters also gave me my own big penknife with a pearl handle, so that I can do a bit of whittling myself. Mum panicked and asked Mr Peters to look after the knife for me, so that I can only whittle when I'm with him. I think Mum worried that I might run amok and stick my penknife straight into Katie. I must admit it's a tempting thought. No, I'm joking, don't worry. Katie's still foul most of the time but just occasionally she's not too bad.

She gave me a little plaster ornament of Andy Pandy for my Christmas present and I was not particularly amused, especially as I'd sewn her a special velvet Alice band to tie back her lovely long hair. But then she cleared half the window-sill of all her stuff and said that it was mine now, and I could keep my

Andy Pandy ornament there. So now I own half the window-sill and Mum found the box with some of my old stuff from our Mulberry Cottage and I've got my china rabbits and a Father Christmas in a glass snowstorm to keep Andy Pandy company, and all my books and some old photos of Mum and Dad and me back at Mulberry Cottage. Dad took a special flashlight photo of Radish in her Mulberry Cottage and I've got that too, and Radish has got her own copy hanging on her wall like a big poster.

I gave Mr and Mrs Peters one of the fashion-modelly photos of me for a Christmas present. I wasn't sure they'd like it but they put it in a special silver frame and I'm in the middle of their mantelpiece with their grandchildren either side of me.

I can never get to be one on my own nowadays.

is for Yacht

My second best Christmas present was from Graham. I bet you can guess what it is. It begins with Y. Not a yak. A yacht. A wonderful, magnificent, correct in every detail Bunny *Britannia* for Radish.

Mr Peters helped Graham to make it. Mr Peters saw Radish sailing in the modest Mark One yacht and wondered if I'd made it myself.

'You've done quite a professional little job

there, Andy. You've quite a way with wood,' he said, turning the boat backwards and forwards admiringly (but making Radish feel terribly seasick in the process).

'Not me. Graham made it for me. He's my sort-of brother,' I said proudly.

'I thought you always moaned about all these sisters and brothers of yours,' said Mr Peters.

'Not Graham. We're mates, Graham and me.'

'That's good. Well any time you want to bring him along with you he'd be very welcome. Some Saturday, say?'

'Oh. Well. He's got lots of homework to do. And he shuts himself up with his computer for hours. I'm not sure he could spare the time,' I said.

Mr Peters just nodded. He didn't seem to mind either way. But I did.

I wanted to keep Mr and Mrs Peters all to myself. They'd become my sort-of grandparents and I didn't see why I should have to share them. It was enough bother having to share my mum and my dad.

And yet I liked Graham a lot. He wasn't busy *all* the time on Saturdays. He'd like to see Radish sailing his boat on the pond. He'd like Mrs Peters and her seed cake. He'd especially like Mr Peters and the little lean-to at the back of the house where he did his woodwork.

But what if it all got spoiled? What if Mr and Mrs Peters fussed round after Graham and I got left out again?

But what if it was fun? I could show Graham all my secret places in the garden and all the special things Mr and Mrs Peters had made for me and Radish, and maybe they'd fuss over me a bit while he was there so he could see they liked me a lot. And maybe Graham could do some whittling with Mr Peters while I did some sewing with Mrs Peters and then we could all join up for tea and cakes and that way no-one would be left out.

I stayed awake even longer than Katie trying to sort it all out in my head. (There was no problem about asking Katie. No way. Never.)

But the next morning I waylaid Graham on the stairs and asked him over to the Peters' place on Saturday.

'Oh, I'm not sure I could make it. I've got lots to do. No, thanks Andy, but I'd much rather not,' he gabbled.

I was mad. I thought he'd be thrilled to bits. Well, *grateful* at the very least. But it turned out I had to go down on my knees and beg before he'd agree to go with me. And even then he moaned and groaned all the way.

'This is mad, Andy. They're your friends, not mine. This old man won't really want to meet me. And I wish you hadn't shown him that boat. It was just these bits of old wood nailed together. I made it too quickly, it wasn't any good at all.'

'Well, Mr Peters thought it was *ever* so good. He's dying to meet you, Graham. He wants to show you all his woodwork stuff and you can have a go at making something together.'

'I can't do things with anyone watching. I go all fingers and thumbs. Dad says I'm useless. Oh Andy, why can't you mind your own business,' said Graham, giving me a shove.

But I didn't shove back. I understood. No wonder Graham was a bit of a wimp. Anyone would be, with the baboon for their dad. I suppose he loved Graham but he certainly didn't seem to like him. He was always nagging at him to act like a *real boy*. If the baboon was an example of a *real man* then they're a pretty duff species. My mum is *mad* wanting a bloke like the baboon. Mad mad mad. Still, I don't suppose there's any way I can like it so I'll just have to lump it. Even though un-Uncle Bill is a blooming big lump.

'It's OK, Graham,' I said. 'You don't have to feel shy. Mr Peters is ever so nice and he never ever shouts or gets shirty.'

'I don't feel a bit shy,' said Graham fiercely, going red.

He went even redder when he met the Peters. He hung his head and didn't say anything and when Mr Peters asked if he'd like to see all his woodwork things Graham just shrugged and didn't look interested. But it was all right after all. Mr Peters nodded and didn't make a big deal about it and talked to me instead and Mrs Peters talked to me too and Graham just sat and fidgeted in the armchair, but gradually his face went back to its usual pale creamy colour and his hand crept out to touch the smooth wooden fruit bowl by his side.

'Take an apple, dearie,' said Mrs Peters, but he wasn't bothered about the apples, he was looking to see how the bowl was made. And then he tiptoed over to the sideboard to have a proper look at the fancy fretwork and Mr Peters went to stand beside him and they started chatting. Graham didn't say much more than 'yes' or 'no' at first but eventually he started asking all sorts of questions and they ambled off to the lean-to together — and that was that. We practically had to drag them away when it was tea-time, even though Mrs Peters had made a treacle tart and iced fairy cakes as well as her famous seed cake.

Graham came with me to the Peters every second Saturday after that. He sometimes came over the Saturdays I was staying round at my dad's too. He and Mr Peters worked together on his Christmas present to me. My magnificent yacht. Radish can sail across her lake in seconds now. She's hankering to take to the open sea and attempt to cross the great pond in the park. She thinks her yacht is the best Christmas present ever.

Guess what *my* best Christmas present is.

is for Zoë

Carrie gave birth to my half-sister a week after Christmas. She should have hurried things up a bit so that she arrived on the proper present day but that's typical of Carrie, she's always late for everything.

It was my week to stay at Mum's but Dad came round and asked if he could take me to the hospital to see the new baby all the same. I thought Mum might make a fuss but she was in a good mood because un-Uncle Bill had got a new decorating job and they were celebrating on the sofa with drinks and chocolates and a smoochy video so Mum said yes quite happily – and she even gave Dad a little kiss on the cheek and said congratulations.

Dad looked pleased and I dared hope that they might get back together after all if they were actually kissing each other nowadays – but when I saw the way Dad kissed Carrie at the hospital I realized there are all sorts of different kisses and some mean you love someone a great deal and others mean you maybe still love someone a little tiny bit but that's all.

'Yuck yuck yuck!' said Zen, who had to come to the hospital with us. 'Do you have to do all that stupid slurpy kissy stuff?'

'I want to see my sister,' said Crystal, jumping up and down excitedly, her hair all over her face (Dad was looking after the twins single-handedly and they both looked even more ruffled and rumpled than usual).

'Here she is,' said Carrie, holding up this little bundle in a blanket.

I was right down at the end of the bed and couldn't see much. Just a tiny nose and a little red mouth. It opened and the new sister started making a lot of noise.

'She's saying hello,' said Carrie, grinning.

'Can I hold her, oh please can I hold her?' Crystal begged.

'Maybe you're a bit little,' said Dad anxiously.

'No I'm not, am I, Mum?' said Crystal, pouting.

'I think you're big enough to hold the baby – but sit on the bed and lean against me so that she can snuggle up comfortably,' said Carrie, getting Crystal and the baby carefully arranged.

'Look at me, I'm holding my sister,' said Crystal, her face bright pink with pleasure.

The baby's face was pink too because she was crying.

'I'm not big, I'm little, I'm a lickle wickle baby,' said Zen, and he started making loud *waaa-waaa* noises, imitating the baby.

'Come here, little baby,' said Carrie, and she scooped Zen up into her arms and held him as if he really was her baby again. He wriggled and protested but you could tell he liked it.

I stood watching them. Dad had his arm round Carrie, Carrie was cuddling Zen, Crystal was holding the new baby. I fidgeted in my pocket and found Radish.

Dad saw and smiled at me.

'Do you want to hold your sister too, Andy?'

'No thanks. I'm not really that bothered about babies,' I said, stroking Radish's ears.

'Why don't you take a turn? You might be able to stop her crying,' said Carrie.

'But there's no room on the bed.'

'You're big enough to hold her properly,' said Crystal enviously, and Dad handed the baby over to me.

I popped Radish back in my pocket and took hold of the baby. She was heavier than I'd thought she would be. I didn't know how to balance her at first but then her head lolled against my chest and my arms made a sort of cradle for her. She seemed to find it comfortable. She gave one last cry, several squeaks and splutters, and then quietened completely. I looked down at her. She looked up at me. She had big blue eyes but her hair wasn't fair like Carrie and Crystal and Zen. She had toffee-coloured curls. She was going to be dark like Dad. Muddy-brown like me.

I gently touched her starfish hand and her tiny fingers closed round my thumb.

'She's holding my hand!' I whispered.

'She likes you. She's stopped crying,' said Dad.

'She's so little,' I said, looking at her tiny fingernails, all so perfect in every detail.

'She's actually quite big for a baby,' said Carrie. 'Much longer and stronger than Zen and Crystal were at that stage. I think she's going to be tall.'

'She's like me,' I said.

'Well, she's your sister, so it's not really surprising,' said Dad.

'Is she still going to be called Ethel?' said Carrie.

'Yuck, Ethel's a *stupid* name,' said Zen.

I swallowed. I looked down at my sister.

'Yes, it is a stupid name,' I said. 'She's pretty. She ought to have a pretty name.'

'Well, what shall it be?' said Dad. 'We've already got A for Andy and C for Crystal. What about B for . . . Bella?'

'Belly-button,' said Zen, sniggering.

I wasn't too keen on a B name. Dad and Carrie might carry on then and have D for Dora and E for Emma and on and on all the way through the alphabet. One little half-sister was fine, but I didn't want a whole crowd of them.

'What about a Z name?' I said.

'Yeah, Z's the best. Z for Zen. That's my name,' said Zen, pleased.

'Z for . . . Zoë,' I said.

Zoë's my special favourite sister now. She really does like me. I can nearly always stop her crying. And I can give her a bottle and wash her in the bath and change her nappy, though I'm not sure that's such a treat. Mrs Peters is helping me make Zoë a little smock with a Z for Zoë embroidered on the front.

I'll maybe have to try to make something for Crystal too. She's my second favourite sister and she gets fed up quite a bit of the time because she's not big enough to do lots of things for the baby. I found her all curled up and crying in the Japanese bag the other day. I let her play with Radish for a special treat and it cheered her up a lot.

Zen gets fed up too but catch me letting Radish anywhere near him!

I like helping look after Zoë so much that I never really want to pack my things on Fridays when I'm at Dad's. But then when I get to Mum's I can pal around with Graham and Paula's given me some of her old make-up though Mum says I'm nowhere near old enough to use it yet. I look super with it on though, really grown-up. Katie smeared a whole lot of make-up on too, but she just looked silly, like a little kid with face paints. Poor old Katie.

I went to see the Family Counselling lady the other day because she wanted to know how Radish and I were getting on.

'We're OK,' I said.

'You still go to your mum's house one week and your dad's house the next?' she said.

'I've got a House A and a House B *and* a House C now,' I said. 'I go to Mum's House A one week and Dad's House B the next week and I go to Mr and Mrs Peters' House C nearly every day and Radish gets to play in her own Mulberry Cottage when she's there, though she still lives in my pocket most of the time.'

'It must take a lot of organizing,' said the lady, smiling.

'Oh it does. But I've got it under control now,' I said, smiling back at her. 'It's as easy as A B C. Really.'

THE END

The Lottie Project

Jacqueline Wilson

Illustrated by Nick Sharratt

CORGI YEARLING BOOKS

For Rupa Patel (author of The Jacqueline Wilson Quiz Book*) and special thanks to everyone at Burscough County Primary School*

SCHOOL

I knew exactly who I was going to sit next to in class. Easy-peasy, simple-pimple. It was going to be Angela, with Lisa sitting at the nearest table to us. I'm never quite sure if I like Lisa or Angela best, so it's only fair to take turns.

Jo said what if Angela and Lisa want to sit together with *you* behind or in front or at the side. I just smiled at her. I don't want to sound disgustingly boastful but I'm the one Angela and Lisa are desperate to sit next to. Lots of the girls want to be best friends with me, actually. I'm just best friends with Lisa and Angela, but anyone can be in our special Girls' Gang. Any girl. No boys allowed. That goes without saying. Even though I just did.

But guess what happened that first day of term. We got this new teacher. We knew we wouldn't be getting Mrs Thomas because when we broke up in the summer her tummy could barely fit behind her desk. Her tummy could barely fit behind

159

her *smock*. You could see her tummy button through the material, like a giant press fastener.

When I was a very little kid I used to think that's how babies were born. They grew inside the mother and then when they were ready the mum pressed her tummy button and out they popped. I told Jo how I'd got it all sussed out. Don't laugh. I was *very* little. *Jo* laughed. 'Dream on, Charlie,' she said. 'If only it were that easy.'

That's my name, Charlie. OK, my full name is Charlotte Alice Katherine Enright, but nobody ever calls me that. Jo and Lisa and Angela and all the kids at school call me Charlie. Some of the boys call me Cake or Carrot Cake or Cakehole, but they're just morons, though they think they're dead original. (Note the initials of my name. Got it?) But right since I was born, all the way through nursery and primary, no-one's ever called me Charlotte. Until this new teacher.

Miss Beckworth. She was new so I thought she'd be young. When you get a new young teacher they're often ever so strict the first few weeks just to show you who's boss, and then they relax and get all friendly. Then you can muck about and do whatever you want.

I *love* mucking about, doing daft things and being a bit cheeky and making everyone laugh. Even the teachers. But the moment I set eyes on Miss Beckworth I knew none of us were going to be laughing. She might be new but she certainly wasn't young. She had grey hair and grey eyes and a grey and white blouse and a grey skirt and laced-up shoes, with a laced-up expression on her face to match. When she spoke her teeth were quite big and stuck out a bit, but I put all thought of Bugs Bunny imitations right out of my head.

There are some teachers – just a few – who have YOU'D BETTER NOT MESS WITH ME! tattooed right across their foreheads. She frowned at me with this incredibly fierce forehead and said,

Miss Beckworth

'Good morning. This isn't a very good start to the new school year.'

I stared at her. What was she on about? Why was she looking at her watch? I wasn't late. OK, the school bell had gone as I was crossing the playground, but you always get five minutes to get to your classroom.

'It's three minutes past nine,' Miss Beckworth announced. 'You're late.'

'No, I'm not,' I said. 'We're not counted late until it's five past.'

I didn't say it cheekily. I was perfectly polite. I was trying to be helpful, actually.

'You're *certainly* not off to a good start,' she goes. 'First you're late. And then you argue. My name's Miss Beckworth. What's your name?'

'Charlie, Miss Beckworth.' (See, *ever* so polite – because I could see I had to proceed d-e-l-i-c-a-t-e-l-y.)

'Your proper name?'

'Charlie Enright.'

161

'We don't seem to be connecting correctly, Miss Enright. Charlie isn't a proper name. It's a diminutive.'

She was trying to make *me* look pretty diminutive, obviously. I tried to act cool but I could feel my cheeks flushing. I have this very white skin that can be a real problem when I get mad or embarrassed. When you have a lot of long red hair and you get a red face too you start to look as if someone's put a match to you.

'Are you *Charles* Enright?'

I can't *stand* it when teachers go all sarcastic on you. A few of the kids tittered nervously. That posh prat Jamie laughed out loud. Typical. Angela and Lisa were looking all anguished, dying for me.

'I'm Charlotte Enright, Miss Beckworth. But I've never been called Charlotte at this school, only Charlie.'

'Well, I'm going to call you Charlotte, Charlotte. Because in my class we do things differently,' said Miss Beckworth.

You're telling me we do things differently. (Well, *I'm* telling *you*, but you know what I mean!) I wasn't allowed to go and sit with Angela. She'd promised to get to school ever so early to grab the best desk (and the one next to it for Lisa) and she'd done well. The desk right next to the window, with the hot pipe to toast my toes on when it got chilly. But all in vain.

'No, don't go and sit down, Charlotte,' said Miss Beckworth. 'I was just about to explain to the whole class that while we get to know each other I'd like

162

you all to sit in alphabetical order.'

We stared at her, gob-smacked.

Miss Beckworth spoke into the stunned silence, holding her register aloft.

'So, Anthony Andrews, you come and sit at this desk in the front, with Judith Ashwell beside you, and then—'

'But Judith's a girl, Miss!' Anthony protested in horror.

'Cleverly observed, Mr Andrews,' said Miss Beckworth. 'And kindly note, I call you Mr Andrews, not plain Mister. I would prefer you to call me Miss Beckworth. Not Miss.'

'But boys and girls never sit next to each other, Miss,' said Anthony. He's as thick as two short planks – *twenty*-two – but when Miss Beckworth's forehead wrinkled he rewound her little speech inside his empty head and took heed. 'Er, Miss Beckworth, Miss. I don't want to sit next to Judith!'

'Well, you needn't think I want to sit next to *you*,' said Judith. 'Oh Miss Beckworth, that's not fair!'

Miss Beckworth didn't care. 'I said things would be different in my class. I didn't say they would be fair,' she said. 'Now, get yourselves sorted out and stop fussing like a lot of silly babies. Who's next on the register? Laura Bernard, right, sit at the desk behind Anthony and Judith, and then . . .'

I hovered, signalling wild regret with my eyebrows to Angela, who'd got up half an hour early for nothing. Angela's surname is Robinson, so obviously we wouldn't sit together. But Lisa is Lisa Field, right after me on the register, so it looked as if we were OK after all. It wasn't really fair on poor Angela if I sat next to Lisa two years running, but it couldn't be helped.

But it didn't work out like that.

'James Edwards, you sit at the desk at the back on the left,' said Miss Beckworth. 'With . . . ah, Charlotte Enright beside you.'

Jamie Edwards! The most revolting stuck-up boring boy in the whole class. The whole year, the whole school, the whole town, county, country, world, *universe*. I'd sooner squat in the stationery cupboard than sit next to him.

Jamie Edwards AARGH!

I thought quickly, my brain going whizz, flash, bang. Aha! Sudden inspiration!

'I'm afraid I can't see very well, Miss Beckworth,' I said, squinting up my eyes as if I badly needed glasses. 'If I sit at the back I won't be able to see the board. Sometimes I still have problems even at the front – so if Lisa Field can come and sit next to me again, then I'm used to her telling me stuff in case I can't read it for myself. Isn't that right, Lisa?'

This was all news to Lisa, but she nodded convincingly.

'Yes, Miss Beckworth, I always have to help Charlie,' said Lisa.

But Miss Beckworth wasn't fooled. 'I'm not convinced that you're short-sighted, Charlotte. Quick-witted, certainly. But until you bring me a note from your mother and another from your optician I'd like you to sit at the back beside James.'

That was it. I was doomed. There was no way out. I had to sit next to Jamie Edwards.

He moved his chair right up against the wall and shuddered elaborately as I flopped down furiously beside him.

'Charlie Cakehole! Yuck!' he said. But under his breath, because he knew Miss Beckworth was watching.

Jamie Edwards is the smarmiest little swot, and always wants the teachers to have him as their pet. Which he is anyway. Because he's such an infuriating Clever Clogs, always coming top top top.

Well, who on earth wants to be top of the class?

'Why can't you try harder at school, Charlie,' Jo always says. 'You're bright. If you'd only stop messing about and work hard you could do really well. You could come top if you really tried.'

I asked Jo why she always nagged so about my boring old education.

'Maybe you're not so bright as I thought you were,' Jo said. 'Can't you work it out for yourself?'

That made me feel bad. But it's hopeless. Maybe I could do better. I'm not bottom of the class, mind you. Just a nice comfy middle. But I suppose if I worked like stink then I could do better. I can generally beat Lisa and Angela if I want. Maybe I could come top of all the girls. But I couldn't ever beat Jamie Edwards. And I'd far sooner be bottom than second to Smarty Pants.

So I slid down in my seat and sulked for most of

Ooh! Please Miss Beckworth!

the morning. It was hot but Jamie kept me well-fanned, waving his hand frantically all the time because he kept wanting Miss Beckworth to pick him. Pathetic. I wouldn't put my hand up even when I knew the answers. Even in English, which is my best subject. I've always got ticks and stars and *Very Goods* all over the place for my stories.

Miss Beckworth started a poetry lesson and it was actually quite interesting and then she read this poem by some dippy American lady and you had to guess what it was about. Like a riddle. And no-one knew. Jamie guessed it might be about a river and Miss Beckworth said it was a very good guess – but it was wrong. Ha. *I* knew what it was. Easy-peasy, simple-pimple. It was a train. And I sat there with this pleased feeling throbbing through me, though I acted all cool and bored, slumped in my seat, arms folded . . . waiting. Waiting until she was just about to give up and then I was going to put my hand up after all and maybe yawn a bit or fiddle with my hair and then I was going to go 'It's a train' like it must be obvious to everyone. One up to me. And ya boo sucks to Jamie.

'Think really hard,' said Miss Beckworth. 'Can't anyone guess?'

And she looked straight at me, almost as if she could see inside my head and look at the train going puff puff puff round my brain.

I still waited. I waited just a fraction too long.

166

Because she stopped looking at me, and just as I was unfolding my arms ready to put my hand up she said, 'It's a train!'

And everyone else said, 'Oh, a train', 'Of course', '*I* get it', and Anthony and those of his ilk scratched their heads and said, 'You what?' and 'Why is it a train?' and 'I hate this soppy poem stuff.' I drummed my fingers on the desk in irritation and muttered, 'I knew it was a train.'

Jamie looked at me with those snooty eyebrows of his disappearing right up under his floppy fringe. 'Oh, sure,' he said sarcastically.

Well, I wouldn't have believed me either. But I *did* know. So I felt even less like joining in now and I drew trains all over the back of my new school jotter – large looming trains about to mash and mangle small snobby boys tied to the railway tracks.

Then we had to write our own poem about trains. I can usually write poems quite quickly so I did a silly one first on a piece of paper torn out of my jotter.

Puff puff puff
Can't stand
   this stuff
All about Trains
It gives me Pains
(Prize Pain to me
is Jamie E)

Help!

167

And Miss B is a Bore
Her train theme's a chore
Want to sit with my friend
I'm going round the bend
I feel so Blue
Choo choo choo!

I folded it up and put TO ANGELA AND LISA –
PASS IT ON – and then quickly passed it on myself
while Miss Beckworth's head was turned. It got
about halfway across the class. Miss Beckworth
looked up at the wrong moment. Uh-oh.

'Ah!' said Miss Beckworth, pouncing. 'Someone
has written a poem already, and they're so proud of
it they want to pass it round the whole class.'

She glanced at it. 'Who is the author of this little
rhyme, hmm?'

I put my hand up. I had to. Half the kids were
craning round to look at me already.

I thought I might be in dead trouble. Miss
Beckworth was such a funny old-fashioned teacher.
I didn't know what she might do to punish you.
Maybe she had a cane tucked up her skirt and she'd
whip it out and whack me one.

But all she did was crumple up my poem and say,
'I don't think this is quite Emily Dickinson standard,
Charlotte. Now write me a proper poem please.'

I decided she maybe wasn't such a bad old stick
after all – so I tried hard with my poem. I decided to
be a bit different. I chose to write about a tube,
because they're underground trains, aren't they,

168

and it was all about the dark in the tunnels and how that weird voice that says 'Mind the gap' could be the voice of the Tunnel Monster.

Jamie peered rudely over my shoulder. 'You're writing rubbish,' he sneered.

'Yours is the real rubbish,' I snapped back, reading his pathetic twee twoddle about the Train going through the Rain, in the Midst of the Storm, the Train will keep you Warm . . . Yuck!

But when Miss Beckworth walked round the class to see what we'd written so far she said he'd made a Good Attempt. And do you know what she said about *my* poem?

'Try to stick to the subject, Charlotte.'

That was *it*!

'Told you you were writing rubbish,' said Jamie.

So I put down my pen and didn't write another word. I had Angela and Lisa and all the other girls in hysterics in the cloakrooms after lunch doing my Miss Beckworth imitation. Even back in class I just had to put my front teeth over my bottom lip to have all the girls in giggles.

'Settle down, please,' said Miss Beckworth sharply. 'Now, History. I thought this term we'd do the Victorians.'

I ask you! Who wants to study the stuffy old Victorians? Well, guess. Jamie Teacher's Pet Edwards.

Miss Beckworth began telling us about the Victorians, starting off with Queen Victoria herself – that fat little waddly Queen with the pudding face

Queen Victoria

who said, 'We are not amused.' Well, I wasn't amused either, especially when Miss Beckworth started on about the Queen Vic pub down the road and Albert Park and how she lived in these old Victorian mansion flats, and did any of us live in a Victorian home by any chance?

I slumped to one side with the boredom of all this just as Jamie stuck his hand up so violently I *very* nearly got two fingers impaled up my nostrils.

'I live in a Victorian house, Miss Beckworth,' he said, showing off like mad. 'In Oxford Terrace.'

I sat up straight. I knew he was a right little posh nob – but I had no idea he lived in one of those huge grand houses in Oxford Terrace, all steps and little lion statues and incy-wincy balconies as if the people who live there might come and do a Royal Family and wave down at you.

Oxford Terrace is on our way home from the town. Sometimes when Jo and I are trailing back with our Sainsbury's bags cutting grooves in our hands we make up stuff and we sometimes play we live in Oxford Terrace and we're Lady Jo and Lady Charlie and we have champagne for breakfast and we go for a workout in a posh club every day and then we have a light lunch some-place snobby and then we shop until we drop, going flash flash flash with our credit cards, and then we eat out

Oxford Terrace. Wow!

170

and go dancing in nightclubs and chat up film stars and rock stars and football players but we just tease them and then jump into our personal stretch limousine and whizz home to our five-storey half-million mini-palace in Oxford Terrace.

'You live in Oxford Terrace???' I said.

Even Miss Beckworth seemed surprised. 'Do you live in a flat there, James?'

'No, we've got the whole house,' said Jamie airily.

'Well, perhaps you can help us understand what life was like in a big Victorian house, James.' Miss Beckworth rummaged amongst a whole box of books about the Victorians. She pounced on something about Victorian houses and held up a picture of a Victorian parlour. 'I don't suppose your house looks much like this inside, though, James?'

'Actually my mum and dad have this real thing about the Victorians and they've tried to make the house as authentic as possible, so we've got stuff like William Morris wallpaper and Arts and Crafts tiles – though we've got ordinary modern things like televisions and computers and stuff.'

I felt I was sitting next to Little Lord Fauntleroy. He carried on in this sickening fashion for ages until eventually even Miss Beckworth got tired of it.

'Thank you very much, James. If anyone wants to know more about Victorian houses then you're obviously a mine of information. Now, we'll be studying the Victorians all this term in class, but I want you all to work on your own special project at home too.'

I groaned. I hate home projects. 'You don't sound

ultra-enthusiastic, Charlotte,' said Miss Beckworth.

'Well. I don't know what to do. I don't know anything about the Victorians. Not like some people,' I said, glaring at Jamie.

'I'll copy a whole lot of suggestions for topics on the board. See if you can get your famously defective eyes to focus on them,' said Miss Beckworth briskly. 'It might be worth your while. I intend to award a prize for the best project at the end of term.'

So I copied out all her suggestions:

boring boring boring boring boring boring boring

HOME . FOOD. TOYS AND BOOKS. SCHOOL.
WORK. THE FAMILY. COURTSHIP. SUNDAY.
LAW AND ORDER. SEASIDE. CHRISTMAS.

boring boring boring boring boring boring boring

I didn't fancy any of them.

'Can we do more than one topic, Miss Beckworth,' said You-know-who. 'Can we do them *all* if we want?'

'Yes, if you like,' said Miss Beckworth.

He was quite sickening in his enthusiasm, grabbing all sorts of stuff from the book box, though he's probably got his own private library in his Victorian mansion.

'Here, it's not fair, you're bagging all the best books,' I said, trying to snatch at a book on Victorian hospitals that looked as if it might be promisingly gory.

'OK, OK. Here's one specially for you,' said Jamie – and he bungs me this book on Victorian domestic servants! 'Know your place,' he goes.

I was about to bash him on his big head with the
servant book but Miss Beckworth got narky and
told us to settle down and start the research for our
projects with the books we had in our hands. So I
was stuck with the servant book.

I flipped through it furiously – and then stopped.
There was a photo of this girl about my age. She
even looked a bit like me, skinny and pale. It was a
black-and-white photo so it was hard
to make out if her hair was red too.
It was long, like mine, but scraped
back tight behind her ears, with
a little white cap crammed
on top. She was surrounded
by little kids, but they weren't
her brothers and sisters. She
was a nursery maid. She had to
look after them. She was their
servant.

I was a bit stunned. I didn't know they used to
have children as servants. I read a bit about these
nursery maids and kitchen maids and housemaids.
They had to work all day and into the evening as well
for hardly any money. Girls as young as eleven and
twelve. No school. No play. No fun. Just work work
work.

I decided I'd do a project on 'Servants'. I was all
set to write quite a bit about it actually. I decided I'd
show that Jamie.

But Jo was already at home when I got back from

school and she had such terrible scary news I forgot all about my servant project.

I didn't remember until the next day when everyone was showing off their project books. Jamie had done ten whole pages about 'School' and he'd stuck in this old photo of kids in rows in a Victorian classroom and got his mum to do some lines of special copperplate handwriting.

'I've finished my school topic already,' he boasted.

So I whipped out an old exercise book and scribbled out a page at playtime.

'I've finished my school topic too,' I said, sticking my tongue out at Jamie.

SCHOOL

My name is Lottie. I am eleven years old. I left school today.

My teacher, Miss Worthbeck, nearly cried when I told her I could not come back. She thinks the world of me. I am her most talented pupil. I am not being boastful, this is exactly what she said:

'Dear Lottie, you are the best at English and writing and arithmetic, you know your geography and history perfectly, you play the piano well, you paint beautifully and you sing like a lark.'

There! I am also useful to Miss Worthbeck, because she is the only teacher at our school, and she has to control a class of forty mixed infants and twelve of us older pupils. I am not the eldest by any means. There is one great lad of fourteen, Edward James, but he is very slow. He is a head taller than Miss Worthbeck, and she finds it hard to control this boy. In fact many of the boys are great lummoxes, stupid and surly. Miss Worthbeck has to use her cane on them to keep them in order.

Miss Worthbeck

Edward James

I do not need to resort to the cane when I am left in charge of the boys though I take delight in swishing it in front of them! But I usually instruct the little ones, and they all try hard for me and give me apples and bites of their gingerbread and scratch 'I love Lottie' on their slates.

Miss Worthbeck has always said I am a born teacher. She has always wanted me to stay on at the school until fourteen, and then she will give me a position as a pupil–teacher, with a proper wage. But I cannot wait two years. I need to earn a proper wage immediately.

HOME

Jo and I haven't always had a home. We lived with Grandma and Grandpa at first. That was pretty bad. Grandma is the sort of lady who keeps a damp flannel neatly folded in a plastic bag and she's forever whipping it out and smearing round imaginary sticky bits. On me. Even at my age. That's nothing. She does it to Jo too.

Keep still child!

Grandma

She doesn't do it to Grandpa because he's one of those pale men in stripy suits who don't ever get sticky. I can't imagine hanging on to his sharply creased trousers or bouncing on his bony knees when I was a baby.

Grandpa

Grandma and Grandpa didn't want Jo and me around, but we didn't have any place else to go. Then we got told about the Newborough Estate and asked if we wanted a flat there. Grandma and Grandpa just about died. You've probably not heard of the Newborough Estate unless you live around here. You'll *definitely* have heard of it if you do. The police

177

get called out every night. And the fire service, because the kids keep setting fire to the rubbish in the chutes. The ambulances are always there too, because there are so many fights and people getting battered. Sometimes they come to scrape up the bodies because people throw themselves off the balconies because they're so fed up living in a dump like the Newborough Estate.

But we went to live there, Jo and me. There was this HUGE row and Grandma and Grandpa said they were really washing their hands of us this time. But Jo stood up to them. Funny that. Jo can't say boo to a goose. She lets everyone walk all over her. Especially me.

She worries terribly about Grandma and Grandpa and she tries so hard to please them. When they come over nowadays and pick faults – Grandma's the worst, pick pick pick, and Jo winces like she's scraping at her actual skin – she still stands up to them over me. It's as if it's easy-peasy, simple-pimple where I'm concerned.

I asked her how come once.

'Because you mean more to me than anyone else,' said Jo.

She does to me too. She's my mum. You guessed that, didn't you? You wouldn't guess it though if you saw us out together. Big sister and little sister, that's what you'd think. With me the big sister. No, that's just a joke. Though it won't be long before I'm taller than her. She's only little and I'm getting big.

There's only that much in it now.

There's not much between us age-wise either. She was still at school when she had me. Shock Horror Disaster!

That's what Grandma and Grandpa thought. Of course, I wasn't observing much in those days but I can imagine it all too well. Jo's told me lots of stuff anyway. They didn't want her to have me. And then after I got born they wanted Jo to put me in a Home. The sort with a capital H. So that Jo could start a new life all over again.

'This is my new life,' said Jo. 'As if I'd ever give my baby away! I'll make a proper home for both of us.'

She did too. It wasn't so bad on the Newborough Estate. Well, it was some of the time. Like when we got our door kicked in and boys wrote stuff all over the walls. Or the day this loony cornered us in the lift. Or the time our telly got nicked the day after it got delivered.

But we made some great friends there too.

It was our home, even though we didn't have any cash to do it up and make it look pretty. We were on benefit at first, and then Jo got a job once she'd got me into nursery, but we didn't spend much even then. We were saving.

Grandma and Grandpa stopped being so huffy and offered us lots of money to get us out of the Newborough Estate. I thought Jo was mad to say no. But she said we had to do it all by ourselves. To show them. Because they didn't think we stood a chance.

But we made it! Jo worked hard at her job selling televisions and washing machines and we saved like crazy and then Jo got a promotion and another and then guess what. She was made the manageress of the big branch down in the shopping centre, in charge of a staff of twelve. And so we started hanging out around estate agent windows, looking for anything going really cheap because people keep getting made redundant in our area and so they can't keep up the payments on their homes and they get taken away from them.

There were a few ex-council flats we could have managed, posher than the Newborough Estate, but Jo wasn't having that.

'We want something Private,' she said. 'Small but select.'

And that's what we've got. A one-bedroomed flat in a quiet private block with laid-out gardens. No-one tore out the roses or smashed the windows or peed in the lift. The people living there were mostly elderly ladies or young married couples or schoolteachers who don't usually tear and smash and pee publicly. They looked a bit nervously at Jo and me when we moved in – especially me – but Jo insisted we had to be on our Best Behaviour at all times.

'Well, at least till we get accepted,' she said. 'So we'll keep the CD player turned down *low*, right, and we'll smile at everyone and say stuff like Good Morning and Good Afternoon ever so polite and we won't go barging straight past someone to get in the lift first and if we're having one of our famous ding-dong rows we'll have to do it in a whisper, get it?'

I got it. I stuck to all these rules. Most of the time. And we've *got* accepted. Oh, one or two of the truly stuffy old bags have asked me pointed questions about Daddy and then they mumble with raised eyebrows, but even those ones say hello and offer me toffees and tell me how tall I'm getting. We're friends with just about everyone in the flats.

But we don't really need all the other people, of course. When we shut our blue front door (I wanted red, but Jo said we had to blend in with the others along the balcony) then we're home and it's all ours and we can be our family. Small, but select, like the flats.

We still haven't got much money to do it all up because most of Jo's earnings go on the mortgage. We've got a good telly and video and CD player and washing machine though (because Jo gets them at a serious discount) and we've painted all the flat so that it looks great. Jo wanted white for the living room (boring) but she let me choose this amazing dark red for our bedroom, and we've got these truly wonderful crimson curtains we found at a boot fair and a deep purply-red lamp and when it's a treat day like a birthday we draw the curtains and switch on the lamp and have a special red picnic in our beautiful bright bedroom. Cherries, plums, jam tarts, strawberry split ice creams, Ribena for me and red wine for Jo, yum yum.

I was kind of hoping Jo and me might be having a bedroom picnic that evening because she had an appointment with the manager for the whole of our area and she was hoping it might be about further promotion.

It was scary opening the door of our flat and seeing Jo because she doesn't usually get back from work till six at the earliest. But there she was, sitting in the middle of the living-room floor. Not doing anything, just sitting with her hands clasped round her knees.

'Jo? What's up?' She looked so small sitting there like that. I towered over her as I stood beside her. 'Jo, why are you home from work? Don't you feel well? Have you been sick?' I thought maybe that was it. She looked so white. No, *grey*, and her eyes were all watery.

'Oh, Charlie,' she whispered.

'*What?*'

'The most terrible thing's happened,' she said in such a tiny voice that I had to bend right down close to hear.

All these different possibilities came bubbling up inside my head until I felt as if it was boiling. 'Tell me,' I said.

Jo opened her mouth again but her voice was just a wisp now.

'*Tell* me, go on. You're scaring me,' I said, giving her shoulder a little shake.

I could feel she was shivering even though it was hot in the flat and she hadn't bothered to open any of the windows when she came in.

'Jo?' I sat down properly beside her and put my arm right round her.

She gave a little stifled sound and then tears started dribbling down her face.

'It can't be that bad, whatever it is,' I said desperately. 'We've still got each other and our flat and—'

'We haven't!' Jo sobbed. 'Well, we've got each other. But we won't be able to keep the flat. Because I've lost my job.'

'What? But that's ridiculous! You're great at your job. They think the world of you. How could they get rid of you? Was this the area manager? Is he crazy?'

'He's lost his job too. We all have. The firm's closing down. We all knew things had been a bit tight recently, and some of the smaller shops closed, but no-one thought . . . They've just gone bust, Charlie. They can't find a buyer so that's it. They've ordered us to lock up all the shops. I'm out of a job.'

'Well . . . you'll get another one. Easy-peasy, simple-pimple,' I said.

'I wish you wouldn't keep saying that,' said Jo, sniffing. 'It sounds so stupid. And you're being stupid. How am I going to get another job? All the electrical goods chains are struggling. There's no jobs going there. I've been to the Job Centre. There's nothing going in retail at all. There's some office work, but they want all sorts of GCSEs and certificates. Which I haven't got, have I? I'm the one that's stupid.'

'No you're not,' I said. Even though she'd just said I was stupid.

'I should have tried to keep up with my school-work. Gone to evening classes,' Jo wept.

'You had me.'

'I could have been catching up these last few years. But I didn't think I needed to. I was doing so well at work . . .'

'You'll get another job, Jo, honest you will. There *must* be shop jobs going somewhere. You'll get a job easy . . . You'll get a job, I promise.'

I promised until I was blue in the face but of course we both knew I could turn positively navy but it wouldn't make any difference.

Jo didn't come to bed till very late that night and then she didn't sleep for ages. She tried not to toss and turn but whenever I woke up I knew immediately she was awake. Lying stiff and still, staring up at our crimson ceiling. Only it doesn't look red at night. It's black in the dark.

184

I woke up very early, long before the alarm. At least the ceiling was dimly red now. Jo was properly asleep at last, her hair all sticking up, her mouth slightly open. She had one hand up near her face, clenched in a fist. I propped myself up on one elbow, watching her for a bit, and then I slid out of bed.

Jo won't let me stick any posters or magazine pictures up in the living room. We've got a proper print of a plump lady cuddling her daughter with a white frame to match the walls. I didn't want to mess up the round red glow of the bedroom but I've stuck up heaps and heaps of stuff in the loo. Want to see?

Of course, it's a bit weird with all these eyes watching you when you go to the toilet. Lisa and Angela always have a giggle about it when they come to my place.

They both like my home a lot. They've got much bigger houses but they think mine's best. They're thrilled if I ever have one or other of them to stay over. (They have to come separately – and even then Jo has to sleep on the sofa in the living room.)

Angela's house seems quite small too but that's just because she's got a big family, not just brothers and sisters but a granny and an auntie or two. It's fun at Angela's house and she's got a super mum who

185

laughs a lot and she cooks amazing food. Angela and I stayed up half Saturday night and got the giggles so bad when we went to bed that we still couldn't get to sleep for ages. I nearly fell asleep in church. That's the disadvantage of staying over at Angela's. We went to church *twice* on Sunday. I might even have had to go *again* in the evening if Jo hadn't picked me up in time.

Lisa's got an even bigger home with a huge garden and a swing. We put up this tent in her garden and camped out in it, though I'd have sooner slept in her bedroom which is pink and white and ever so pretty, with special twin beds with pink and white flowery duvets. Lisa's mum is all pink and white too and she smells very flowery but she isn't always as soft and gentle as she looks. She nags Lisa about all sorts of stuff. But Lisa's dad adores her. He calls her his little Lisalot and when he comes home from work he gives her such a big hug he lifts her right off her feet.

Lisa said it must be awful for me not having a dad. I said I didn't care a bit. And I don't. I've got Jo.

Sometimes Jo and I play this silly game that we're both male, because we've both got funny names. I'm little-boy Charlie and she's this big gruff funny bloke Jo who's my dad. We often have games together where we muck around and play at being different people. When I was little my favourite game of all was me being Jo and Jo being me, so that I was the mother and got to tell her what to do.

I wandered out of the loo and into the living room and stared at the space on the carpet where Jo had sat yesterday. I felt as if I was the mother now and she was the little kid – but it wasn't a game.

The minute Jo woke up she said, 'What are we going to do?' As if *I* knew.

I felt worried about leaving her at home when I went to school. I kept wondering if she was sitting on the living-room floor again, all hunched up. I was thinking about Jo and her job and our home so much I didn't listen in lessons and Miss Beckworth got really narked with me. So I acted cheeky and then I was in serious trouble, but I didn't really mind. That just made things more normal.

Miss Beckworth kept me in at dinner time. She didn't give me any stupid lines to write out, though. She said I could work on my Victorian project.

Boring boring boring, I thought – but better than lines. And at least I had the book box to myself. I asked for something about Victorian homes.

'Not a posh house for the rich. What about an ordinary little home for a poor family? Aren't there any books about that?'

She found me one or two pages, but there wasn't much. So I made a lot of it up.

HOME

There is nothing for it. I have to leave home.

I love my home very much, although it is only a tumbledown cottage, stifling hot in the summer and bitter cold in winter. The winters have always been the worst. Two little brothers and one infant sister died during the winter months, and Father passed away last February when the snow was thick on the ground.

I did not cry when Father died. Perhaps it is wicked to admit this, but I felt relieved. He treated Mother very bad, and though he earned a fair wage he drank a great deal of it. So we were always poor even then, but Mother kept our simple home shining bright. She made bright rag rugs to cover the cold stone flags of the floor and each bed upstairs had a pretty patchwork quilt. I cut out pictures from the illustrated papers and pinned them to the walls. I even pinned pictures out in the privy!

There was always a rabbit stew bubbling on the black—

Jessie Me Rose Frank Mother and Ada-May

188

leaded range when we came home from school..
We'd dig potatoes or carrots or cabbage from the
garden, and in the summer Rose and Jessie and I
would pick a big bunch of flowers to go in the pink
jug Frank won at the fair.

Mother always liked us to wash our hands and
say Grace at the table before eating. Father never
washed his hands or said Grace, but Mother could
do nothing about that. Sometimes Father did not
come home until very late. One night last winter he
fell coming home in the dark and lay where he
was till morning. They carried him home to us and
Mother nursed him night and day but the cold got
to his chest.

Mother used up her sockful of savings on
Father's funeral. She bought us all a set of black
mourning clothes, even little Ada-May. I thought
this a waste of money, but Mother is determined
that we stay respectable.

Our grandmother and grandfather did not want
Mother to marry Father. They thought he was a
wastrel, far too fond of the Demon
Drink. I privately agreed, but I did
not like them saying this to Mother.
They came to Father's funeral
and said it all over again. They
asked Mother how she was
going to manage now.

Mother said she would
take in washing and do fine
sewing for ladies.

Grandmother

Grandfather

189

Grandmother and Grandfather sniffed. They took
a shine to my sister Rose, who is pretty, and
offered her a home with them. It will be one mouth
less for you to feed, they said. Mother asked Rose
if she wanted to live with Grandmother and
Grandfather and she cried and said no. So Mother
said we would all stick together.

'You will be sticking together in the Workhouse
then,' said Grandmother.

Mother stuck her chin in the air and said we
would manage fine. But I heard her crying at night.
I went to comfort her. 'We will manage fine,
Mother, you'll see,' I said.

But it has become very hard. Mother
washes all day and sews half the night.
She has become very pale and thin and
coughs a good deal. I am very frightened
that she will get really ill in the winter if
she keeps working so hard. Frank and
Rose and I tried to help out this spring and
summer, running errands and selling
nosegays and sweet lemonade at the
market. But we can only earn pennies. We need
pounds to keep us out of the workhouse.

So it is up to me. I am the oldest. I must go and
earn money and send it to Mother. There is only
one job a girl my age can go for. I must be a
servant.

WORK

The phone rang. I answered it automatically. Lisa and Angela are always ringing me up – and some of the other girls in our class. I don't want to sound disgustingly boastful but I am quite popular.

But it wasn't a girl. It was Grandma.

'Hello, Charlotte dear,' said Grandma.

I told a teeny white lie to Miss Beckworth. Grandma always calls me Charlotte, pursing her lips and clicking her teeth. If you're standing right in front of her you get sprayed with spit. I found I was holding the telephone at arm's length just in case.

'Can I speak to Mummy, please?' said Grandma.

That's another weird thing she does. I've never called Jo Mummy in my life. But Grandma always does. As if Jo is *her* Mummy. Though Grandma treats Jo as if she's a silly little toddler, not a grown-up woman with a practically grown-up daughter of her own.

Grandma's voice is so loud it boomed right across the room to Jo. She shook her head in a panic. 'Say I'm not here!' she mouthed at me.

She'd been crying and she'd got to that sodden stage where everything is still dribbling. She fumbled for a tissue and blew her nose dolefully.

'I'm afraid Jo's just nipped out to the shops, Grandma,' I lied.

'Don't be silly, Charlotte. It's half past seven in the evening,' Grandma said briskly.

'There's heaps of shops still open round here, Grandma. There's the video shop, and the off-licence, and the Spar down the road—'

Grandma gave a disdainful snort. 'Please don't argue with me, Charlotte. I know Mummy's there, I can hear her blowing her nose. I want to talk to her.'

'Well, she doesn't want to talk to you,' I said – but in a little squeaky-mouse mumble as I passed the phone over.

'Josephine?'

'Hello, Mum,' said Jo wearily, sniffing.

'Are you crying?' Grandma demanded.

'No, I – of course I'm not crying,' said Jo, a tear dribbling down her cheek.

'Say you've got a cold!' I whispered, miming a major bout of sneezing.

'I've got a cold,' Jo said, nodding at me gratefully. 'Why on earth should I be crying?'

'Well, you tell me,' said Grandma. 'Your father's just read a most disturbing item on the financial page of his newspaper. It says Elete Electrical have folded.'

Jo shut her eyes and said nothing.

'Josephine? Are you still there? Is it true? Is it a

nationwide collapse? You are being kept on until they find a new buyer, aren't you? And if the worst comes to the worst, they will give you a substantial redundancy payment, won't they?'

Jo sniffed again but still couldn't speak.

'Do say something, dear,' said Grandma. 'We're very worried about you. We've always said you're in a very precarious position. How on earth are you going to keep up the payments on your flat if you lose your job? You and Charlotte can barely manage as it is. We do worry about you so.'

Jo opened her eyes. She stood up straight. She gave one last giant sniff and then spoke.

'Honestly, Mum, you do get into a silly state. There's no need to worry. We're fine. I feel I was ready for a change from Elete anyway. Of course I've known for a long time that things have been precarious with the firm – which is why I applied for my new job. I have this brilliant managerial position, and a much larger salary too – so Charlie and I are very comfortably off at the moment. I really must go now, Mum, I badly need to get a hankie, my goodness, this is a terrible cold, I think I'd better have an early night with honey and hot lemon, well, goodbye, thanks for phoning.'

She said this without pausing, absolutely gabbling the last bit and then slamming the phone down quick. Then she took the receiver off again, so that Grandma couldn't call back.

'What?' Jo said to me, wiping her cheeks with the cuff of her shirt.

'You know what! You told her one socking great lie,' I said admiringly.

'Well, I couldn't stand her going on and on like that.'

'But she'll find out that it's not true,' I said.

'I'm going to *make* it come true,' said Jo. 'You'll see.'

All the tight feeling in my tummy untwisted. It was OK. Of course Jo would get another job, easy-peasy, simple-pimple.

She was up early the next morning, hair washed, all made up, blouse fresh on, skirt carefully pressed. When I woke up she was walking up and down the bedroom, practising.

'Good morning. My name's Jo Enright. I've been the manageress of a large shop for the last year but now I feel it's time for a change. Are there any new job opportunities in your company?' she asked our bedroom wardrobe, shaking the sleeve of her dressing gown.

'Good morning. I am Mr Wardrobe. Yes, Ms Enright, you can come and manage my clothes for me and I'll pay you a million pounds a week,' I said from under the covers.

'Charlie! You didn't half give me a fright!' said Jo, finding my tummy through the duvet and tickling it.

'Don't make me laugh! I need to go to the loo. I'll wet the bed, I'm warning you,' I giggled, rolling around.

'Well, get up and go, you lazy thing,' said Jo, trying to tip me out. 'Come on, you'll be late for school. And I thought this new teacher of yours is dead strict?'

'You're telling me! Lisa and Angela and me didn't feel like playing boring old rounders yesterday so we hid in the girls' toilets. We've done that heaps of times and no-one ever thought a thing about it before, but Miss Beckworth came looking for us, right into the toilets, and when we all hid in a cubicle she peered underneath the door and said, "Will the girl with six feet please come out of this toilet immediately." We thought we were really in for it, but she said she'd hated games at school too and as she'd already picked the two rounders teams we didn't have to play just this one time and we thought *great* – but do you know what we had to do instead? Run round and round the play-ground without stopping for the entire lesson. We were absolutely *knackered*. And every time we ran past her and begged for mercy she said brightly, "Aren't you lucky to be taking part in *my* rounders game, girls?" She's so . . . slippery. You can't suss out what she's going to do next. Every time you get ready to hate her she's funny and then when you start to think she's an old softie she plays a trick on you.' I was in the bathroom by this time, sitting on the loo.

'She sounds a good teacher,' Jo called. She

followed me into the bathroom. 'Do you think I look a bit older and more professional with my hair up? Yeah, I think so. Help me pin it up at the back, eh?'

She's usually great at fixing her own hair but her hands were all fumbly this morning, and she couldn't eat any breakfast because she said she was too nervous.

'You've got to eat something. You don't want to faint dramatically in the middle of a job interview,' I said.

'Maybe I won't *get* any interviews,' Jo said. Then she stopped and took a deep breath. 'No. I've got to think positive. Right, Charlie?'

'You bet. Good luck, Jo,' I said, hugging her.

I hoped and hoped Jo would get a job that day. She went into town and she walked round in her high heels with this big bright smile on her face, going into all these different shops and introducing herself and asking and then nodding and walking out again, over and over, all day long. She came home and she kicked her shoes off and she howled. But then I made her a cup of tea and rubbed her feet and she stopped crying and the next day she tried again. And the next.

A shop selling weird way-out clothes was advertising for staff but they said Jo wasn't wacky enough. A big store wanted a sales assistant for their ladies' dress department but they said Jo wasn't mature enough. A snobby shop selling designer clothes made it plain Jo wasn't posh enough.

'This is hopeless,' said Jo, sighing.

She tried record shops, but she didn't know enough about modern music. She'd been too busy bringing me up to dash down the disco. She tried bookshops, because she likes reading,

but the only shop with a vacancy was full of all these students boys in jeans making jokey remarks, and the one with the scruffiest hair and the grubbiest T-shirt turned out to be the manager and although Jo said he was friendly it was obvious she didn't fit.

She charged out at seven in the morning on Friday to buy the local paper and she skimmed through all the small print looking for jobs.

'Nothing!' she said despairingly. 'Well, no proper jobs. There's bar work. But I'm not leaving you alone in the evenings.'

'Don't be daft. I'll be fine. Go for it, Jo! You could learn how to make all those great cocktails with the little cherries and toy umbrellas. It would be fun,' I said.

Jo went to the pub to see what it was like.

'It would not be fun,' she said. 'I wouldn't be making any cocktails there. Just serving pints of bitter to a lot of boring old men trying to look down my front. I could put up with that, but I wouldn't be free till half past eleven every night and then I'd have to walk miles home unless I forked out for a taxi – and they were only paying fifty pounds for five

197

full evening shifts. We can't pay the mortgage with that.'

Jo went back to the local paper. 'The only other jobs are cleaning,' she said.

'What do you mean, cleaning? Like at Sketchley's?' I said.

'No, not a dry cleaning shop. Cleaning ladies. You know.'

I looked at Jo.

'I can clean, can't I?' she said.

'But you hate cleaning. Look at all the fights we have over whose turn it is to vacuum.'

'OK, OK. But this is in a supermarket. You get socking great industrial cleaning machines. I quite fancy charging about with one of those.'

She didn't mean it, of course. She was just being brave.

'It's two hours every morning, that's all. Sixty-two pounds,' said Jo, tearing out the advert.

'That's not enough to pay the mortgage.'

'I know. But look, there are heaps of other adverts for cleaners. I could go after them too. Listen. "Private house, cleaning, some ironing, nine to twelve, Mondays and Thursdays, thirty pounds". And then there's this one here, they want two hours' cleaning daily plus someone to look after a little boy after school.'

'You don't want to be lumbered with someone else's little *boy*,' I said.

'I don't want to be lumbered with my own great

198

big girl if she's going to be so picky,' said Jo. 'Look, Charlie. I haven't got any choice. I'll keep on trying to get a proper job but until that happens I might as well earn what I can. It's lousy money but it all adds up. So shut up about it, OK?'

I shut up. Jo phoned the supermarket and they told her to come along for an interview. She rushed off. I sat by myself, feeling fidgety. Then I got out my notepad and a big fat felt tip pen. I wrote out my own advert.

STRONG RELIABLE SCHOOLGIRL
WANTS WORK. WILL DO SHOPPING,
RUN ERRANDS, WHATEVER YOU WANT.
APPLY MISS C. A. K. ENRIGHT,
NO. 38 MEADOWBANK.

WORK

I've got work. I earn eleven pounds a year. One pound for every year of my age.

I did not tell anyone my real age. I swore I was thirteen, going on fourteen. I do not know whether anyone believed me. I put my hair up and lowered the hem of my skirt as far as it would go. At least I looked respectable in my mourning clothes.

I went to a domestic service agency in town. They said they had just the job for me. But when I went to the house and saw the cross sulky face of the Mistress I wasn't so sure. I did not find out what the Master did for a living, but it was easy to tell he was not a gentleman. They wanted a maid-of-all-work and I could see at once I'd be toiling all day long and well into the night, and scolded all the time no matter what pains I took. I am willing to be a servant but I will not be a slave.

I went back to the agency and said the first position wasn't suitable. They seemed astonished at my effrontery, but sent me after another position. I thought at first this was more likely. It was in a grand house with six servants. I was to be the nursery maid, helping the upper-nurse care for a little boy.

I do not care for little boys. My brother Frank has always been a great trial to me. I believe he takes after Father. I certainly did not care for this little boy, who stuck out his tongue in a very rude manner and then kicked me hard upon the shin. I did not care for the upper-nurse either, who had a face like a boot and long nipping fingers like button hooks. But I would have taken the position even so, if it weren't for the Master of the house. He was a widower, and I was all prepared to feel sorry for him if he were still mourning his late wife. Ha!

This gentleman patted me at the interview and said I was a fine-looking girl fresh from the country. His eyes slid sideways and I detested the way he was looking at me. He might be a gentleman but he didn't act like one. I knew he would be quick to take liberties and if I complained I would be sent packing with no reference. I am young but I am no fool.

I went back to the agency yet again and said the second position wasn't suitable either, and I said why, too. This time they were appalled at my impertinence. How dare I criticize my Betters? But they gave me one last chance. I knew I had to take it this time.

I do hope it is third time lucky. I am employed by a mistress who wants a young nurse for her three children, Victor who is six, Louisa who is four, and baby Freddie who is still in petti- coats. I did not meet the Master, but I shall have to hope for the best. There are two other servants in the household, a cook and a housemaid. I hope they will be friendly.

I am not sure about this mistress. She does not look cross but she seems very firm. She told me my duties in great detail. I must light the fires when I get up and dust the day nursery, I must dress Louisa and help Victor with his boots and buttons, I must attend to the baby, and then we have breakfast. Victor and Louisa are then to be sent down to their mother while I wash and dress baby Freddie and give him his bottle and put him back in his cot. I must then clean and tidy the night nursery and then dress the children in outdoor clothes and take them for a walk. They will have a rest on our return while I brush their clothes and clean their boots, and then I must get them ready for their dinner. We are to take another walk in the afternoon when possible, and then after a light tea I must put baby Freddie to bed while Victor and Louisa go downstairs. Then I must put them to bed and tidy the nurseries and eat my supper and then go to bed myself.

'Do you feel you can manage all this?' she said. 'You look very little.'

'But I am strong, Madam. I will manage,' I said determinedly.

'Very good. You can start on Monday. I will give you the print for your uniform and a bolt of cotton for your apron and caps. I hope you are satisfactory at sewing, Charlotte?'

I blinked at her. 'Charlotte, Madam?' I said fool—ishly.

'That is your name, is it not?' she said.

'No, Madam. I am called Lottie, Madam. It was the name of Mother's doll when she was small. No—one's ever called me Charlotte.'

'Well, I do not think Lottie is a suitable name for a servant. You will be called Charlotte whilst you are working for me.'

FOOD

Jo phoned me from the town.

'Guess what! I've got the job.'

'Great!'

'Well. It's not really. It wasn't even a proper interview. It obviously doesn't matter what you're like when you're a cleaner.'

'Still. I bet you're going to be the best-ever squeakiest-cleanest cleaner they've ever had,' I said.

'The start of a whole new career,' said Jo. 'Do you think I'll make it to the Champion Floor Cleaning Polish trials, hmm?'

'You bet. So you'd better get into training quick. When do you start?'

'Tomorrow.' I heard Jo gulp. 'At six. In the morning. Oh, Charlie, I must be mad. I could claim income support and lie in bed till noon.'

'Still, you don't have to fib to Grandma any more. You really have got a job.'

'I can just imagine what she'll say when she finds out I'm a cleaner.'

'No, you're not a *cleaner*. You're . . . you're a state-of-the-floor supervisor, right?'

'You're a sweet kid, Charlie.'

'I was a snotty kid earlier. You coming home then? I'm starving.'

'Yes, I've just got to buy something for tea. I hoped I might get staff discount at this supermarket but that's only for the women working the tills.'

'Get some red treats for a bedroom picnic to celebrate your job.'

'Hey, we're economizing.'

'Very cheap red treats?'

'Do you think baked beans could be called red?'

'Just. Get some red plums for pudding.'

'Or red apples. And a block of raspberry ripple ice cream?'

'Yes! And what about a strawberry gâteau?'

'I think that's coming it a bit, old girl. Beans, plums and ice cream, that'll do. I'll be home soon then. You get the trays ready.'

I padded about the kitchen thinking we really should have a cake to celebrate properly. I remembered this ancient packet of cake mix I'd won on a tombola at the school fête donkey's years ago. I had a poke around the kitchen cupboard and found it crumpled behind some tins of soup. Jo didn't go in for making cakes and the only sort I'd ever made were pretend pink dough ones when I was a little kid, but this packet sort looked a doddle. You just had to add an egg. I found one egg in a box at the back of the fridge. I thought back to when we'd last had scrambled eggs and it was only about a fortnight ago so it should be all right.

I tipped the contents of the cake mix packet into

205

a bowl, swished the egg around until it was all sticky, scooped the lot into the tin and shoved it in the oven. Easy-peasy, simple-pimple.

'What's that lovely smell?' said Jo when she came in the door.

'A surprise. Hey, congratulations.'

'I've got *two* jobs! I phoned the number where they want someone to look after the little boy as well as do a bit of cleaning. That's in the afternoon, so it'll be easy to fit that in too.'

'Where are you going to look after this little boy then? Not round here, I hope,' I said. 'I don't want him messing up all my stuff.'

'He sounds a nice sensible little boy, though he's very shy. I spoke to him on the phone. And his dad sounds nice too, though ever so sad. His wife left and he's trying to cope on his own.'

'We cope fine on *our* own,' I said. 'Look, you're a cleaner now. Why don't you just stick to cleaning jobs. You don't want to be a nanny too.'

'It's seventy-five pounds a week. That's not bad. If I could find just one more job like that to fit in mid-morning then we'd be laughing,' said Jo. 'Hey, is your surprise all right? It's not burning, is it?'

It had burnt just a little bit, but only around the edges. I decided to cut them off – and then I went on cutting and trimming, turning the round sponge into two letters, a big 'J' and a small round circle for the 'o'. We didn't have any icing so I smeared some

206

strawberry jam on the top and then studded both letters with Smarties.

'That looks wonderful,' said Jo. 'Hey, you're really good at this.'

I don't want to sound disgustingly boastful, but it really wasn't bad for a first attempt.

I added a line to my work advert:

MAKES EXCELLENT CAKES.

I didn't show Jo my advert. I wanted to surprise her. But when I took my advert into the newsagent's and asked Mr Raj to put it in the window he shook his head.

'You can't work. You're just a little girl,' he said.

'Girls work just as well as boys. *Better*,' I said indignantly.

'It's not because you're a girl. You're too young. You couldn't do any proper work.'

'Yes I could! Look, a hundred years ago I could work full time as someone's servant. I could be scrubbing all day. I'm doing this project about it for school, see.'

'That's what you should be doing at your age. Concentrating on your school work.'

'You don't get paid for doing school work.'

'You kids. Just wanting money money money. What do you want? A bike? Roller blades? A computer? My kids want all these things, nag nag nag. If the boy don't turn up to deliver the newspapers and I ask my boy to help me out then it's "How much money will you pay me?"'

'*I'll* do a newspaper round,' I said.

'You can't. You're too little. It's against the law, see. Times have moved on since your history project. Kids aren't allowed to work.'

I could see I was wasting my time. I tried the newsagent's down in the town but he said the same. So I decided to use my initiative. I'm quite good at that. I spent most of my spare cash photocopying my advert and then I went round sticking them through people's letterboxes in our flats and the flats over the road and half the houses down the street.

I'd put my phone number, so I sat by the phone and waited. And waited. And waited.

'What's up with you?' said Jo.

'Nothing.'

'Come on. Are you waiting for a phone call?'

'I might be.'

'Don't play games with me, Charlie, I'm feeling too dopey to work it out,' said Jo, yawning.

She'd started her job at the supermarket and was finding it an awful struggle to get out of bed at five.

'Look, why don't you go to bed now, get a really early night. You look exhausted,' I said.

'Why do you want me out the way? Who is it who's going to phone, eh?' Jo's sleepy eyes suddenly sparkled. 'Hey, it's a boy!'

'What?'

'You're waiting for some boy to phone you!'

'I am not.'

'Yes, you are. You've got a boyfriend,' said Jo, giggling.

'Don't be so stupid. I hate boys.'

'So you *say*. I know. It's . . . what's-his-name? The one you keep going on about at school. The one you sit next to.'

'Jamie Edwards! You have to be joking. I can't *stick* him. Sitting next to him is driving me absolutely crazy.'

I couldn't believe Jo could be so crackers. I truly detested that Jamie. He was just the most annoying person in the whole world to have to sit next to. He waved his hand in the air so often to answer Miss Beckworth's questions that I was in a permanent breeze. And every time he got the answer right – which was nearly flipping always – he gave this smug satisfied little nod, as if to say, see, what a super intelligent smartie-boots I am.

I hated the way when Miss Beckworth set us some work he'd start straight away, his posh fountain pen bobbing up and down as he wrote, while the rest of us were still scratching our heads and ruling margins and looking at our watches to see how long it was till playtime.

I hated the way his work came back from Miss Beckworth, tick tick tick at every paragraph, and *Well done, Jamie!* written at the bottom. I got lots of crosses and *You could try much harder, Charlotte,* and *Tut tut, this is very shoddy work,* and *You can't fool me by making your writing enormous and widely spaced. You can only have spent five minutes on this work at the most. This is not good enough!*

I didn't want to be bothered with anything else but learning about the Victorians. I was starting to kind of enjoy writing my project. It was weird. I read stuff in books and then started writing and it was as if this other girl entirely was scribbling it all down. The servant girl. Lottie the nursery maid. She'd started to feel real, like I'd known her all my life. I knew her better than I even knew Lisa or Angela. I just picked up a pencil and all *her* thoughts came rushing out on the paper.

I couldn't stand the thought of Miss Beckworth speckling it with her red biro. It was private. At least we didn't have to hand our projects in till they were finished, and we had weeks yet.

Of course You-know-who had practically finished his project already. He didn't want to keep *his* project private. He kept flashing it around at every opportunity. He even took it into the canteen with him at dinner time. Well, he did that once. I just happened to choke on a fishfinger and so needed an immediate drink of Coke and in my haste I happened to tip the can over and the merest little spitty bit of froth spattered Jamie's precious folder. Only the outside. But he declared the posh marbled paper was all spoilt. The next day he carted his project to school, completely re-covered with repro-Victorian wrapping paper, all fat frilly girls in bonnets and soppy boys in sailor suits, yuck yuck. And inside there was page after page of Jamie's neat blue handwriting with his own elaborate illustrations, carefully inked pictures of railway engines and mineshafts and factory looms, but he didn't have any train drivers or miners or factory hands because he can't draw people properly.

'I'll draw them in for you, Jamie,' I offered.

He turned down my generous offer. He didn't trust me. I wonder why!

He had lots of proper pictures too, cut out of real old illustrated Victorian papers, and samples of William Morris wallpaper, and photos of Victorian families standing up straight in their best clothes, and real Victorian coins carefully stuck in with Sellotape. Jamie's file was bulging already. My notebook was small and slim and there were still only a few pages of writing.

'You haven't done much yet, Charlie,' said Jamie, snatching it up and rifling through it.

'Give it *back*,' I said, trying to grab it.

'Why have you done it in this funny pencil writing? What's all this stuff? It's like a diary. "Well, I do not think Charlotte is a suitable name for a servant." What are you on about?' said Jamie, holding it just out of my reach.

'Don't you *dare* read it!' I said, and I gave him such a smack on the head he dropped my book instantly.

'Ooooow! What did you do that for?' he gasped, clutching his head.

'I warned you,' I said, clutching my book to my chest.

'You're mad! If you weren't a girl I'd sock you straight back,' said Jamie.

One side of his face was bright red and the shape of my hand. There were tears in his eyes. I felt a bit worried. I hadn't meant to hit him quite as hard as all that.

'You can try hitting me back but I wouldn't advise it,' I said. 'Just stop messing about with my private stuff, right?'

'It's just your Victorian project, for goodness' sake. And you're doing it all wrong, not a bit the way Miss Beckworth said.'

'I'm doing it *my* way,' I said.

'You'll get into trouble.'

'See if I care,' I said.

Miss Beckworth came into the classroom just then. She gave us all one quick glance – and then fixed her gaze on Jamie.

'What's the matter with you, James?' she said.

I held my breath. It looked as if I was in trouble right that minute. I expected Jamie to blab. He looked as if he were going to. But then he shrugged and shook his head. 'Nothing's the matter, Miss Beckworth,' he said.

I was amazed. And even more astonished when Miss Beckworth didn't pursue it. She just raised her eyebrows as if to say 'You can't kid me,' but then she sat down at her desk and started the lesson.

Jamie started working right away, one cheek still scarlet. I watched him for a while. I struggled with myself. Then I leant towards him. He flinched, as if he was scared I might slap him again.

'Why didn't you say I slapped you?' I whispered.

Jamie blinked at me nervously. 'I'm not a sneaky tell-tale,' he said.

'Well. Thanks,' I mumbled.

He didn't say anything back but his other cheek went red too.

So perhaps Jamie isn't one hundred per cent revolting and disgusting and infuriating. Just ninety-nine per cent. But as if I'd ever sit chewing my nails waiting for his phone call!

Nobody rang. Not a single soul required the services of the strong reliable schoolgirl.

'Why don't you ring him?' said Jo, still dopily deluded.

But the next day Miss Pease from downstairs waylaid her as she was stumbling back from her morning shift at the supermarket.

'Yes, Miss Pease wanted a little word about you, Charlie,' said Jo, hands on her hips.

'If she's nagging on about my music again she's nuts. I keep it turned down so soft I can barely hear it myself. She must have ears like Dumbo's,' I said, munching toast.

Jo snatched half of it from my plate. 'Here, spare a crumb for your poor hardworking mother,' she said. 'I'm starving.'

'So am I. You make your own. I've got to go to school.'

'Yes, well, you can wait a minute. Miss Pease says you've been soliciting.'

'I've been *what*?' I said.

'Well, that's the word she used,' said Jo. She was trying to sound stern, but she looked as if she might giggle any minute. 'Yes, that's what she said. "I really must bring this to your attention, Josephine. Charlotte has been soliciting."' Jo's voice wobbled.

I chuckled tentatively. It was a mistake.

'No, it's not funny, Charlie. What have you been playing at, posting all these little letters in people's flats offering to do work?'

'I was wanting to help out.'

'Oh, Charlie. You are a nutter. Miss Pease is right for once in her long and boring life. You can't advertise yourself like that, especially when there are such loonies around. Some weird guy might have read about this little schoolgirl wanting work and got some terrible ideas.'

'I'm not little, I'm big. And strong. But I take your point. Still, you don't have to fuss. No-one's phoned. Not a single sausage, and after all that money I spent on photocopying. It's daft. The whole idea was to *make* a bit of money.'

'Don't worry. That's my job. And anyway, it has worked in a way. Miss Pease says she's got a job for you.'

'Really?' I tried to feel pleased, but Miss Pease is such a pain. She's the sort of old lady who pats you on the head like a puppydog and relentlessly asks you how old you are, as if you might have aged five years since the last time you told her a week ago. Still, work is work.

Only this work was worse than most. You'll never guess what she wanted me to do. *Read* to her.

I don't really like reading aloud at the best of times. I don't like hearing my voice go all silly and showing-off. And that's when I can pick and choose my own book. Miss Pease wanted me to read her library book, one of those large big-print books that make your arms ache when you hold them up. My arms ached, my back ached, my head ached, my throat ached, my entire body was in ache overdrive after I read to Miss Pease for a whole hour.

It was this terrible stupid story about some dippy woman who kept being pursued in the desert by this total nutcase in a striped nightie. Well, that's what he was wearing on the book jacket. Instead of telling him to get lost sharpish the heroine simpered and swooned into the sand. I kid you not. And Miss Pease obviously adored this utter rubbish. She sat back liter-ally licking her chops. Mind you, that might have been because of all the Cadbury's Milk Tray she was eating. She got through a good half of the box.

'Of course I'd offer you one, Charlie dear, but you can't really read with your mouth full, can you?' she said.

'I can try,' I said hopefully.

She thought I was joking. And *I* thought she was joking when she handed over my wages for the reading session.

'Here you are, dear,' she said, fumbling in her purse. She handed me a ten-pence piece.

I stared at it. Had she mistaken it for a pound coin? Even so, what a totally mingy rate of pay!

'Pop it in your money box, dear,' said Miss Pease. 'And come back and read to me tomorrow.'

Not flipping likely! I was dead depressed, and annoyed when Jo just laughed and found it funny. But she was in a good mood because she'd got herself *another* job, cleaning this big posh house three days a week from ten to twelve.

'*Three* jobs!' she said, and she sent out for pizza with three extra toppings to celebrate.

'You'll exhaust yourself,' I said. 'What with getting up at five and doing the supermarket and then looking after the silly little sprog in the afternoons.'

'I'll be OK. And this new job's a doddle. The house is big, but they keep it very tidy. She's ever so worried about the idea of employing another woman to do her dirty work. I bet she runs round with the vacuum before I get there.'

'Where is it?' I asked, my mouth drooling cheese fronds.

'Oxford Terrace,' said Jo.

I stared at her, so shocked that my half of the pizza slipped out of my fingers onto the floor. I didn't care. I wasn't hungry any more.

216

FOOD

Oh, how I long for Mother's cooking. One of her
meaty stews, bubbling with
barley beans and carrots.
Or rabbit pie. Mother has
such a light touch when it
comes to making pastry.
Her fruit lattice pies are
famous all over the village.
And her suet puddings. If I
could only have a plateful of Mother's jam suet
pudding and custard! Or even a big doorstep slice
of bread and dripping . . .

I have to slice up the bread so thin here I slice
my fingers too, and Louisa won't eat her crusts
even then. The baby likes his bread pounded into
mush with warm milk. Mother would never dream
of pampering us so. We always ate what we
were given and chewed it cheerily. Well, mostly. But
Louisa always plays around with her food and
cries and complains something chronic, and Victor is
extremely pernickety for a boy, fuss fuss fussing if
he swallows a little lump in his custard. Sometimes
it's all I can do not to grab their plates and eat it

up for them because I'm so hungry. I have to
manage on nursery food too, no meat at all during
the week, and just one slice off the roast on
Sundays. I am allowed one egg a week too, but
it's a pale watery thing compared with the
deep gold yolks laid by our hens at
home.

I have to make do with this niminy-
piminy fare with the merest scrape of
butter. The only food that is plentiful is
milk pudding. I shall start mooing before long.

'We don't want you to fall ill with too rich a
diet,' says the Mistress, as if servants have
different stomachs from posh folk.

Mrs Angel the cook and Eliza the maid are
supposed to survive on this frugal diet too, but they
eat their meals down in the kitchen and Mrs Angel
is adept at keeping back the choicest portions for
their own plates before Eliza serves the Master
and Mistress in the dining room. I have my meals
in the nursery so I miss out on these perks. Mrs
Angel and Eliza treat me like one of
the children anyway. They whisper
and have secrets and laugh unkindly
at the things I say. They are
excessively tiresome. They are the
childish pair. I do my best to ignore
them, but then Mrs Angel calls me hoity
toity and Eliza pulls my hair so that it tumbles
down out of my cap. It is hard to bear sometimes.
At home I was always a favourite. At school I

218

was definitely Miss Worthbeck's pet. All the children loved me. Even the boys. Yes, even that great lummox Edward James. But now I am openly despised and it makes my heart sore. At night I cry into my pillowcase, the sheets pulled right over my head so the children will not hear me.

Victor sees my red eyes in the morning and says that I have been blubbing.

'Nonsense,' I say firmly. 'I have a slight cold, that is all.'

Perhaps that was tempting fate. Now the whole household has gone down with colds, even little baby Freddie. Mrs Angel has taken to her bed and Eliza is trying to take charge of the kitchen, but with very bad grace. The Mistress says her ailing children must have calves' foot jelly served to them at every meal. I ask Eliza to prepare it but she utterly refuses, saying she has her work cut out as it is and she cannot abide messing around with lumps of messy meat.

So I have to make the jelly. The whole kitchen reeks and the walls glisten as the calves' feet boil and boil and boil, and I skim and skim and skim, and then when I go to strain the liquid through the jelly bag my hands slip and . . . disaster! By the time I have run out to the butcher's for six more calves' feet and started the whole business in motion all over again I am in such savage spirits that I would cheer if a whole herd of calves stampeded through the house and trampled everyone within it with their poor feet.

TOYS AND BOOKS

I was so scared! Jo could be cleaning Jamie Edwards's house. I could just imagine Jamie lounging on a velvet chaise-longue in his posh William Morris-papered parlour, snapping his fingers imperiously at Jo.

'Hey, you! Cleaning lady! Get me another cushion,' he'd command. 'I've spilt crumbs all over the carpet so get cracking with the hoover. And don't sigh like that or I'll dock your wages.'

Get a move on, chop, chop!

Yes sir, sorry sir

I could see it as clear as anything. Poor Jo would have to wash Jamie's clothes and tidy Jamie's bed and dust all Jamie's pos-

sessions. Maybe Jamie had a brace of younger brothers just as bratty as him, and she'd have to wash their clothes and tidy their beds and dust their toys. If he had a baby brother she'd maybe even have to wash and tidy and dust *him* down.

'It's not your Jamie Edwards's house,' said Jo. 'This is the Rosen family, Mr and Mrs, with two teenage daughters.'

I practically passed out with relief.

'Are you disappointed?' said Jo. 'Did you hope I'd get to go in your Jamie's bedroom, eh, to tell you all about the posters on his wall and whether he still has a teddy on his bed and maybe even have a sneaky peek in his diary to see if he ever writes anything about you?'

'He's not *my* Jamie!' I shrieked. 'You are so nuts, Jo. I keep telling you, I can't stick him.'

Jo wasn't the only one who teased me about terrible Jamie Edwards. Lisa and Angela had started up this stupid game too. I was starting to get seriously annoyed with them. I didn't know what had got into them this year at school. Last year we were the three leaders of nearly all the girls and we had this special club badge with GAB on it, short for 'Girls Are Best', and we all called each other Gabby and we had this cheerleader chant I made up: 'Girls are best, Never mind the rest, Boys are a pest, So *Girls are best!*'

Some of the other girls got a bit fed up and drifted away but Lisa and Angela and I kept up our special girls' gang all the time, and the three of us always went yuck and pulled a face whenever any of the boys spoke to us. I wanted to extend the rules to cover men too, but Lisa said that was daft because her dad was a man and she loved him better than anyone else in the whole world, and Angela was equally awkward and got this immense crush on this pop star and squealed whenever she saw him on the telly and she stuck hundreds of pictures of him all over her bedroom walls and kissed every one of them goodnight when she went to bed and she did inky designs of his name entwined with hers all over her school books and her ruler and her bag and even on the sleeve of her jacket, though her mum got very narked about that.

Lisa and I thought Angela had gone incredibly crackers because this guy she likes is *pathetic*. Angela agrees with us now, and she's torn down all his pictures and crossed out his name and she's got a new jacket – but she's in love with another pop group now, *all* of them, and she's forever striking up these boring boring boring conversations about what she'd do if she could only get to meet them.

I knew that if only I'd been able to sit next to Angela at school as I'd planned then I'd have been able to be a good influence on her and keep her under control. She was starting to get on my nerves so much I was wondering about whittling my best friends down to one. But then Lisa fell in love too. And that was worse. Because she started to go crazy over David Wood – and he's certainly not a famous star in a band, he's just this ultra-boring boy in our class at school.

'He's not ultra-boring!' Lisa squeaked. 'He's dead cool. I love the way he does his hair. And his eyes. And he looks really old for his age, doesn't he, because he's so tall.'

'He might look old but he acts like a

222

toddler,' I said, disgusted. 'Didn't you see him in the canteen throwing his lunch around?'

'That was just his bit of fun,' said Lisa. 'One of his chips landed right in my lap!'

'Oh wow! How could you contain your excitement,' I said, dead sarcastic.

'She ate it too!' said Angela. 'After he'd drooled all over it.'

'I wouldn't mind if he drooled all over *me*,' said Lisa.

'Oh shut *up*,' I said. 'Honestly. I think you had a lobotomy in the summer holiday.'

'A lobby-what?' said Lisa.

'It's an operation they perform on your brain,' I said. 'Don't you know anything?'

'I know one thing, Charlie Enright. You're getting a right pain, always showing off and looking down your nose at other people. You're getting just like Jamie Edwards.'

'Yeah, maybe it's rubbing off on her because they sit together,' said Angela, giggling in this particularly irritating way. 'Hey, Lisa – Charlie and Jamie, what a pair, eh?'

'They're always yacking away together, certainly. Miss Beckworth had to tell them off the other day, they were getting so carried away,' said Lisa, giving Angela a nudge.

'You're the one who's in danger of getting carried away – in a body bag,' I said, giving them both a simultaneous example of *my* sort of nudge. I have very very sharp elbows. 'I hardly *ever* speak to Jamie

Edwards – and when I do it's just to have a ferocious argument with him.'

However, I needed to speak to Jamie in a dead-casual, almost-friendly way to find out exactly where he lived in Oxford Terrace. He knew what Jo looked like. We'd both been going to this school since we were practically babies. For years and years our mums had delivered us or collected us. I had noticed that Jamie's mum was plump and beady-eyed like him, with lots of hair and jazzy jumpers and coloured tights and bright boots, none of them matching. He had probably noticed that Jo was much younger than the other mums, and dyed her hair to match mine and wore high heels to make her just a tiny bit taller.

It's awfully hard to strike up a dead-casual, almost-friendly conversation with someone you can't stick. We're barely allowed to breathe in Miss Beckworth's classes anyway, let alone converse. But at playtime I took ages putting away my books and let Lisa and Angela go off by themselves. Jamie always took his time too, not at all keen to go out into the playground. He's not the outdoor type. He's hopeless at football and he can't even run properly, his arms and legs go every which way. He isn't bullied by the other boys because he can be quite quick and cutting with what he says, but he's not exactly number one popular person with his peers. (Not like *some* people I could mention if I wanted to be disgustingly boastful.)

He generally slopes off into a corner by himself and reads a book. I watched him take one out of his satchel. It was covered in the Victorian wrapping paper so you couldn't see the title.

'What's that you're reading then, Jamie?' I asked.

He looked at me suspiciously. 'Why?'

'I just want to know, for goodness' sake,' I said.

'With you it's usually for badness' sake,' said Jamie.

'Let's have a look, then,' I said, reaching for it.

He hesitated, holding it away from me. 'Are you going to hit me again if I don't let you?' he said.

'That was different. That was *my* book. So what's yours? Why have you got it all wrapped up like that? Hey, it's a dirty book, that's it, isn't it! Shock, scandal, swotty old Jamie's reading a rude book. And you didn't want anyone to see you're reading it. What is it, eh? Show me!'

'Get off!' said Jamie, trying to push me away, but he was still wary of me. I snatched his book easily and opened it.

'"Esther Waters",' I read, flicking through the pages. 'Oooh! What a swizzle. It's just some boring boring boring old Victorian book. Typical you, Jamie Edwards. You're just doing some extra swotting up for your project, aren't you?'

'The Victorians thought it was a rude book,' said Jamie. 'They were ever so shocked when it came out.'

'Well, they were shocked by anything. They were

225

so stupid they even covered up their piano legs! If a woman raised her skirt a few inches above her ankles the chaps practically fainted dead away,' I said scornfully. 'So what does this Esther Waters get up to, Jamie? Is she so dead brazen she flashes her kneecaps?'

'Oh, ha ha,' said Jamie, sighing.

I saw he had his bookmark more than halfway through.

'Gosh, have you read all that? It looks *terribly* dull and difficult. You're mad,' I said.

'It's a good story actually,' said Jamie. 'It's about this girl Esther—'

'No!'

'—and she's a servant and—'

'She's a servant?' I said, stopping messing about.

'Yes, and she goes to this big place in the country and this footman chats her up and she doesn't really want to go out with him but he forces her and she ends up having a baby and she doesn't know what to do because she's young and she's not married and she's lost her job . . . Why are you staring at me like that?' said Jamie. 'What is it?'

'Nothing. It just doesn't sound quite as boring as I thought. Maybe I'll borrow it after you, OK?'

I mostly stuck to reading horror stories, the spookier and scarier the better, but I wanted to find out more about this Esther.

'What happens to her? Does she keep her baby?

Does she get a job? She doesn't get married at the end, does she?'

'I haven't got that far yet. OK, you can borrow it after me. Or some of my other books if you want. I've got a whole lot of Victorian ones sorted out because of my project.'

'Oh, Jamie, you would!' I said. Then I suddenly realized this was my golden opportunity. 'So, I might come round to your famous Victorian house some-time and see your books. What number Oxford Terrace, eh?'

'Number sixty-two,' said Jamie.

I felt my stomach squeeze. Number 62. Jo's Rosen family lived at Number 58, next door but one to Jamie. What if he saw her going into their house? What if Jamie's mum nipped along the road to have a cup of coffee with Mrs Rosen when Jo was dashing around with a duster? What if Jamie's mum thought Jo looked dead handy with a hoover and offered her a job? I was proud that she was working so hard but I couldn't *stand* the idea of her cleaning all Jamie's junk.

'Has your mum got her own cleaning lady?' I blurted out before I could stop myself.

Jamie blinked at me, baffled. 'What? Why? Are you scared you'll get all dusty if you come round to my house?' he said.

'Does your mum do her own dusting?' I persisted.

'No. Mum's hopeless at any sort of housework. We did have a cleaning lady once but then she got ill and—'

'You're not looking for another one, are you?' I asked, horrified.

'My dad does the housework now. The hoovering and that. Mum might do the bathroom, and I'm supposed to do some stuff, me and my brother, only we skive off mostly. *Why?*'

I shrugged elaborately. 'I – I've got interested in the whole idea of housework and stuff because of my servant project,' I said.

Angela and Lisa put their heads round the classroom door.

'Come *on*, Charlie. Playtime's nearly over. What are you doing?' said Angela.

'Of course, we don't want to interrupt anything if you and Jamie are *busy*,' said Lisa, giggling.

'I'm *coming*,' I said, charging over to them.

 But then that idiotic Jamie put his great big foot in it. 'So, you're coming round to my house after school tonight, right?' he said, in front of Lisa and Angela. Their mouths dropped open. Mine did too.

'Wrong!' I said, and rushed off.

Lisa and Angela rushed too.

'We were just kidding you before. But you really have got a thing going with Jamie, haven't you?' said Angela.

'You're going round to his *house*!' said Lisa. 'Oh, I do wish Dave would ask me round to *his* house.'

'I'm not *going* round to Jamie Edwards's house,' I insisted. 'He was just going on about these boring

boring boring Victorian books and he seemed to think I was mad enough to want to look at them, that's all.' My heart was thumping a bit as I said it. I knew I was kind of twisting the truth. But I had to stop Lisa and Angela getting the wrong idea once and for all.

So all that day I sent them notes under the quivering Beckworth nose as often as I dared, with silly caricatures of Jamie and rude little rhymes about him. Jamie saw his name and must have thought I was writing a note to him. He peered over my arm and read it. I'd just written a *very* rude bit about him. (Sorry: far too rude to be repeated where adults like Miss Beckworth might whip this book out of your hands at any minute!) Jamie read the very rude bit. He blinked. He didn't look baffled this time. He looked upset.

Still, it was his own fault, wasn't it? He shouldn't have been nosy enough to read my private note. I passed it to Angela and she cracked up with silent laughter and then she passed it on to Lisa and she read it and snorted out loud and had to protest to Miss Beckworth that she had a horrible cold and couldn't help it. Lisa and Angela and I all fell about helplessly when we came out of school.

I certainly didn't go round to Jamie's house after school. Lisa and I went round to Angela's house first because her big brother had just got some dead flash roller blades for his birthday and we were hoping we'd get to her home from our school a good half-hour before he got back from *his* school, so we could all maybe have a sneaky go on his blades. But he'd got wise to Angela's wily ways and installed a brand-new padlock on his bedroom cupboard. We found his old skateboard stacked in a corner but we weren't really into skateboarding any more, and anyway, one of the wheels was all wobbly.

Angela's mum was doing a day shift at the hospital so she couldn't fix us anything exciting to eat so we all went round to Lisa's instead. That was far more promising, because Lisa's mum was being a hostess for a jewellery party that evening and so she was making all these fiddly little vol-au-vents and tarts. She let us sample them while she got busy icing a cake. Lisa wanted us to go straight up to her bedroom, but I hung around her mum for a bit, watching how she did the icing with this natty little squeezy bag.

'I always wondered how people wrote those little messages,' I said. 'Is it difficult?'

'No, pet, it's easy as anything,' said Lisa's mum, and when she had finished she let me practise icing these cookies she'd baked. I iced my name and then Lisa's and then Angela's. That was dead crafty, because we got to eat them!

I asked Lisa's mum how she made the cake and she thought I was angling for a slice of that too.

'Sorry, pet. I'm saving it for the ladies at my party. Hey, maybe your mother would like to come?'

She hesitated. 'I mean, just for the chit-chat at the party. I know she's not really in a position to buy any jewellery right this moment.'

'She goes to bed really early now. Because she has to get up at five for this new job,' I said.

Lisa's mum's smooth face went into a crease of pain.

'Oh my goodness. She's being so *brave*,' she said, as if Jo went and wrestled with a pit of poisonous snakes instead of one unwieldy industrial cleaner.

'But I really would like to know how to make a sponge cake like that. We don't make cakes at home,' I said.

'Well, it's so simple. And really not very expensive. Tell your mother you just need to put the butter and the sugar and the flour in the blender and—'

'No, we haven't got a blender.'

Lisa's mum stared as if I'd said we hadn't got a *kitchen*.

'Oh. Well. I suppose you could mix it all by hand. I know!' She went to her shelf of cookery books beside the spice rack and pulled out an old fat book; the pages had gone a little yellow. She flicked through it.

'Aha! This was *my* mother's cookery book. She certainly didn't have a blender. Yes, there's a whole section on cake-making. Do you think your mother would like to borrow it?'

'It's not for Jo, it's for me. I'd *love* to borrow it,' I said eagerly. 'I want to suss out how to make cakes. Proper ones, not the packet sort.'

'Well, good for you. I wish my Lisa would get interested in cookery. You're a strange girl, Charlie. You've always seemed such a tomboy. I never thought you'd get keen on cake-making. Still, you're all getting older. It's only natural you're changing.'

'I'm not changing,' I said quickly.

'What's that saying? "Too old for toys but too young for boys." Though my Lisa has certainly started on boys already. It's Dave this and Dave that until we're sick of the sound of him! Which boy do you like, Charlie?'

'None of them,' I said firmly.

'Give it another six months,' said Lisa's mum, smiling at me.

I had to stay polite because she'd just lent me the cookery book but when I got home to Jo I moaned like anything.

'She's treating me like I'm retarded or something,' I said. 'Like I still play with my Barbie dolls.'

'What's wrong with Barbie dolls?' said Jo.

She used to buy me lots of Barbies with all their different outfits and we'd dress them up and drive them round in their Cadillac and take them to the disco and make them bop up and down on their tiny high heels. I think Jo liked playing Barbie games just as much as I did. If not more. I wanted to chuck all mine out ages ago but she wouldn't let me.

'Store them in a drawer and keep them for *your* daughter,' she said.

So they're stored. I took off all their glitzy little outfits and laid them on their backs in my underwear drawer and covered them with bits of old pillow case, playing one last ritual game with them. Mortuaries.

Jo got totally unnerved when she opened the drawer looking for spare socks.

'Have you come to view the corpses?' I said.

'You are a seriously weird child.'

'It's coming from a single-parent family,' I said. 'I'm seriously deprived. It's no wonder I'm weird.'

I was only joking of course. I *like* being a select family of two. Jo and me. And that's the way it's always going to be.

TOYS AND BOOKS

I cannot believe the toys the children have here!
Victor has a dappled rocking horse as big as the
old pony in the field behind our cottage at home.
It's such a splendid creature, with a curly mane
and a long tail of real horse's hair, a red saddle
and reins and great green rockers. Louisa begs and
begs Victor to let her take a turn but he will
rarely agree. Once when the children were
downstairs with the Mistress I stood staring
at the rocking horse. Before I knew what I
was doing I had hitched my skirts above
my knees and clambered into the
saddle. I fingered the curly mane and
stroked the smooth shining wood,
and then I dared lean forward and
rock once, twice, three times. The
rockers creaked and I did not dare
persist in case they could hear me down
below.

Louisa's china doll seemed to watch with her
blue glass eyes. Her painted red lips were open as
if she might tell. But I must not be fanciful. She is
only a doll. But a beautiful doll all the same, with

golden ringlets and three sets of fine clothes. She
even has little lace mittens for her tiny china
fingers, imagine! I have had to help Louisa on and
off with those clothes, stripping the doll right down
to her white silk drawers. She has three petticoats,
two silk and one flannel, and white cotton stockings and little soft kid shoes, three pairs,
in black and grey and pink for
parties. Three pairs of shoes
for a doll that cannot
walk. Rose and Jessie
and I have never had soft
shoes. We'd run around barefoot
in the summer and plod in our old boots
throughout the winter. How Rose and Jessie would
love Louisa's dolls, and the dolls' house with all the
furniture — little chairs and tables, a four-poster
bed no less, and even a miniature mop and mangle
in the scullery!
   We had our own halfpenny dolls at home,
      one each in our Christmas stockings, and
      we'd sew them little dresses and make
         them a home in an old
         wooden crate, the
         same crate that was
         once our Frank's boat
         and carriage. Sometimes I
         gave baby Ada–May a
         ride in that old crate and
         she crowed with delight . . .
         Oh, how I miss her. How I miss Rose

and Jessie. I even miss Frank. I miss dear Mother
most of all. I write to her once a week,
unburdening my heart. I hope Rose reads my letters
properly to Mother. She can read well enough when
she wants, but she hurries so over the words.
Mother was kept at home as a child to mind her
own young brothers and sisters so she never
learnt to read. She used to marvel after I went to
the village school and learnt to spell out words.

Miss Worthbeck let me read aloud to the
children on Friday afternoons from wonderful
story books, *Alice* and *The Water Babies* and some
of Mr Dickens's books. I do not wish to boast but
she once said I had Shining Intelligence.

My Shining Intelligence is tarnishing rapidly now I
am a nursery maid.

FAMILY

It was Grandma and Grandpa's Pearl Wedding anniversary in a couple of weeks.

'We're not having a party,' said Grandma. 'That's not our way.' She spoke as if parties were incredibly vulgar, on a par with naked mud wrestling in pig sties. 'We thought we'd like to celebrate the occasion with a special Sunday lunch.' She paused. 'Just for the family.'

She meant Jo and me. Once she was off the phone we moaned and groaned, trying to think up wild excuses to get out of it. We don't like going to Grandma and Grandpa's at the best of times.

'And this will be the worst,' said Jo. 'They'll talk about their wedding and their anniversaries, all thirty of them. Grandma will fiddle with her wedding and engagement and eternity rings. She might *even* get out their wedding album. Oh help, she might even delve in the trunk upstairs and come out with this truly horrible yellowy-white lace veil and then her voice will go all shaky when she says she kept it specially for me to wear at my wedding. And then she'll stop and sigh because I didn't ever have a wedding. Watch out, Charlie. She'll be

237

saving it for you now.'

'*I'm* not going to get married!' I insisted. 'I'm going to stay here with you. I look old for my age and you look young so by the time I'm grown up we'll just be like two sisters. I'll be earning too so it'll be easy-peasy, simple-pimple paying that old mortgage.'

'I wish!' said Jo.

We didn't have any spare cash for Pearl Wedding presents so we had to be inventive. Jo bought a half-price droopy pot plant and fed and watered it until it stood up straight and grew new glossy leaves. She bought some pearl-white ribbon and then tied thirty tiny bows all over it.

'There? Do you think it'll do?' she said, tying the very last bow.

'It looks lovely.'

'It's nowhere near as impressive as your cake.'

Yes, I'd made Grandma and Grandpa a proper cake! I used Lisa's mum's recipe book. I couldn't do a fruit cake because the ingredients were too expensive. I just did a sponge. Well, I did three sponges if you must know. I didn't quite get the hang of it the first time and failed to realize you had to mix it all like crazy until your arm practically falls off. There was just this surly sulky crust at the bottom of the tin when I took it out of the oven. The second go was better, but I was too eager, opening the oven door a couple of times to see how it was getting on.

It didn't rise properly and so I left it in longer and then it got a bit burnt. I cut off the burnt bits and made it into a trifle, but even so, I was starting to think I was squandering money instead of saving it. Jo said I should have one more go and *this* time it was third time lucky. My sponge was *perfect*.

Now I could get started on the best bit. I covered it with apricot glaze to stop any crumbs getting mixed up with the icing. Then I piped *Happy Aniversary* across the top of the icing and made little rosettes all the way round and studded it with tiny pearly balls. It took ages but I was so proud when I'd finished. Jo looked worried when I showed it off to her.

'What?'

'It's beautiful,' she said. 'They'll love it.'

Ha! They didn't love it. Or Jo's plant. Grandpa nodded and said, 'How delightful. Thank you so much. How thoughtful of you. But you really shouldn't have.'

That sounds OK down on paper. But my grandpa speaks in this slow serious voice with hardly any expression. He doesn't go *Wow!* or hug or kiss. If he ever touches me accidentally he wipes his hands on his hankie afterwards, as if I'm sticky.

Grandma uses enough expression for two. 'Oh, darlings, we weren't expecting *presents*. Especially in your current circumstances. Josephine, I've been very worried about your new job, you've hardly told me anything about it.'

'Look at the cake Charlie's made you. She did it all herself. It took her ages,' said Jo.

'Yes, it's *lovely*, dear. Yum yum. We'll all have a slice for tea.' But Grandma sighed. 'What a pity!'

'What?' I said.

'I can't wait to sample this cake,' said Jo quickly. She was sending signals with her eyebrows to Grandma. Grandma ignored them.

'It's such a shame you left out the "n", dear.'

I'd left out one of the 'n's in *Anniversary*. Even though I *knew* how to spell it. I couldn't stand it. I'd thought it really was perfect.

'As if that matters,' Jo said, furious with Grandma for pointing it out.

'Well, as a matter of fact, I *do* think spelling matters although I know they don't pay much attention to it in school nowadays,' said Grandma, putting my cake on her kitchen table. She took the pot plant to the sink.

'It doesn't need watering yet. I did it yesterday,' said Jo.

'I just want to perk it up a little,' said Grandma.

She should have watered Jo and me. We were visibly drooping. I can never work out if Grandma knows what she's doing. She's certainly an expert at chewing you up and spitting you out in tiny pieces. No wonder it took Jo months and months before she dared tell them she was going to have me.

Grandma and Grandpa still treat her like a schoolgirl in disgrace. Grandma kept on and on about her old job while she put the vegetables on to cook, prodding Jo as sharply as the potatoes. Jo lied a lot but she's not as good at it as me. Grandma didn't even shut up when we started eating.

'What do you *mean*, Josephine? What does this new supermarket job entail?' Grandma attacked her grapefruit, jabbing at it with a serrated spoon. 'You're being deliberately evasive. Are you sure you're not working as a cashier on the tills?'

Jo suddenly flung down her own spoon, going as red as the glacé cherries Grandma used for decoration. 'I am not a cashier,' she said. 'I am a cleaner at the supermarket. So now you know.'

Grandma sputtered like the hot fat cooking her roast beef. She gave Jo a roasting all the while we chewed on our meat. She told Jo it wasn't a suitable job when she'd been a manager for nearly a year, as if Jo had deliberately turned down umpteen other manager's jobs just to be contrary. She told Jo she was being an irresponsible mother going out early in the morning and leaving me, and that made me so mad I had to put in my two-pennyworth.

'I think *you're* being the irresponsible mother to Jo, telling her off and being so horrible when Jo's tried so hard to sort things out. I think she's wonderful to get up so early and trudge off like that. *I'm* OK, I'm still in my bed. Jo has to get up early every single morning except Sunday, and she should be having a lovely long lie-in today, but she couldn't, because we had to get the train and the

241

bus right over to your place to wish you a Happy Anniversary – *two* 'n's – only you're just mucking it all up.'

They were all staring at me. 'That's quite enough, young lady!' said Grandma.

'You're not my mother so you can't tell me off,' I said. 'Jo? Do you want me to shut up?'

'Yes!' said Jo. 'Come on, Charlie, we'd better go home.'

'Now don't be ridiculous. We haven't even started on pudding yet,' said Grandma.

'Why don't you all do a lot more chewing and a lot less yapping,' said Grandpa, calmly working his way through his second helping of roast beef.

So we sat still and no-one said anything. Jo and I left a lot on our plates. So did Grandma. But Grandpa didn't even leave a glisten of gravy.

I didn't think I'd be able to eat pudding. It was pineapple upside-down cake and my own stomach felt upside-down too. But I tried a tiny bit and it was actually good, so I ate a bit more, and then a bit more still, until I'd finished it all up.

Grandpa nodded in approval. He finished his last mouthful too.

'Now that you've all calmed down, perhaps we ought to discuss your financial situation, Josephine,' he said.

I wanted to tell him it was none of his business. But even I didn't quite dare cheek Grandpa.

Jo stammered a little as she told him that we were managing, and she'd sorted things out with the building society to give us a little leeway, and she didn't just have the one job, she had three, and she was still looking for another supervisory position all the time. She said it all as if he was giving her a formal interview. Grandpa nodded, occasionally easing the collar of his shirt where it rubbed his neck. He never wears casual clothes, not even at weekends. I couldn't remotely imagine him in something like a T-shirt. I can't even picture him in his under-wear. I don't think Grandpa has an ordinary body at all, he's just hard smooth plastic underneath like a Ken doll.

Grandma wanted to know all about the other cleaning jobs. She raised her eyebrows and looked pained when Jo told her about the Oxford Terrace job, but she actually leant forward and looked interested when she heard about Robin, the little boy Jo picks up from school.

'So what's his father like?' said Grandma, suddenly all ears. I could actually see them getting pink underneath her neat grey curls.

I sighed and flopped back in my chair. This was so *typical* Grandma. She can't even get it into her head that Jo *likes* being a single mum and isn't remotely interested in meeting any men. Grandma used to keep trying to introduce Jo to all these

243

creeps, and she nagged her to join a Singles club and she even once advertised Jo in a Lonely Hearts column. She did, I kid you not. She thinks if she can only get Jo married off then she won't have to be ashamed of us any more.

I waggled my eyebrows at Jo, expecting her to wink back. But she wasn't looking at me. She wasn't looking at anyone. She was staring at the shiny yellow pudding on her plate as if Robin's father was reflected there.

'He's very nice,' she said. Her tone was brisk – but she blushed.

I stared at her. Grandma was staring too.

'Very nice?' said Grandma impatiently. 'What *sort* of very nice? What job does he do? What does he look like? What's happened to the boy's mother?'

'He's very nice – what more can I say?' said Jo. 'He's something in the Civil Service.'

'Which grade?' said Grandma.

'As if I know!'

'Is he good looking?'

'I suppose so. In a kind of lean, lost sort of way,' said Jo.

'Mmm!' said Grandma. 'And is he a widower?'

'No. His wife left him. She had custody of Robin at first, but he didn't get on with the boyfriend, so now he's back with his dad.'

'And Dad doesn't have a girlfriend?'

'No. Well. He could have. But he hasn't mentioned one,' said Jo.

'She's just his cleaner,' I said crossly. 'She doesn't have anything to do with him, do you, Jo?'

'No. That's right. Yes,' said Jo, sounding muddled.

I frowned at her. What was she on about? And why did she have that stupid little smile on her face? I suddenly got terribly anxious. What was going on?

Jo hadn't ever said anything about this man to me. Well. She'd said he was nice. Very nice. But that's such a limp nothing sort of comment that I didn't even notice it at the time.

I didn't have a clue what he was really like. I'd never met him. I had met Robin. It was easier for Jo to bring him round to our place after she'd met him from school.

'It's so I can be here for you too, Charlie. We can all have a snack together,' said Jo. 'Then I can take him home and do a spot of cleaning before his dad gets back.'

I wasn't at all keen on this idea, but I couldn't really object much to Robin. He wasn't like an ordinary boy of five at all. He was very little, with a long thick fringe and huge dark eyes in a white face. He gnawed nervously at his bottom lip all the time, and he trembled for the first few visits. He was like one of those small furry nocturnal creatures you see in the zoo, hunched at the bottom of their cage.

Robin

He certainly didn't run amok, messing up all my things. He sat where he was put, picking anxiously at the scabs on his bony bare knees, going nibble nibble nibble at his lips. Jo brought him books and he looked at them obediently. Jo found him paper and crayons and he drew neat square houses with a mummy on one side and a daddy on the other and a very tiny Robin in the middle, under the house. He wasn't any good at perspective so it looked as if the house was falling on him, about to crush him completely. Or maybe that was really how he wanted it to look, I don't know. I asked him but he wouldn't talk properly. He'd just nod if I said, 'Is this your mum?' I'd only got him going once. I noticed he had a little pocket in his school sweatshirt that he patted every now and then. I thought he was checking up on his handkerchief. Robin was the sort of little boy who always breathes heavily and has a runny nose. He kept sniffling one afternoon so I told him rather sharply to use his handkerchief.

He looked stricken. He didn't move.

'Your hankie! Your nose is running. Yuck!' I said.

He shrivelled away from me, practically going inside the neck of his sweatshirt.

'Stop nagging him, Charlie. Here, we've got some tissues somewhere,' said Jo.

'But look, he's got his hankie with him,' I said, putting my hand in his pocket and pulling something out.

It wasn't a hankie. It was a little fluffy toy.

'That's mine! Give him back!' said Robin, and he darted forward, grabbing.

'Hey, OK! Don't get in such a flap. Here's your

little toy. What is it?' I said, peering.

Robin held it tight against his chest.

'Is he shy, your little animal?' I said. 'Oh yes, he is, isn't he? Sorry. Didn't mean to frighten him. He's looking at me with one big beady eye. I think he really wants to make friends. Are you going to get him to say hello to me, Robin?'

Robin didn't seem sure. He fidgeted, not meeting my eyes – but he seemed almost to be joining in the game.

'Hello, little shy animal,' I said into Robin's clasped hands.

'He's not an animal,' said Robin. 'He's a bird. He's Birdie.'

Birdie edged his beak into the air so that I could see.

'Oh, so he is! Hello, Birdie. Can you fly?' I said.

Robin nodded, and made Birdie nod too.

'I don't believe you,' I said.

'He can!' said Robin, and Birdie's beak went up and down.

'No. I'm sure he can't possibly fly,' I said.

'Yes, he can, I'll show you,' said Robin, and he unclenched his fist so that Birdie's woollen wings flapped free. Robin stood up and skipped round the kitchen, making his arm swoop up and down. Birdie flew along with him. He had two black bead eyes, a yellow beak, and big brown wings, carefully scalloped at the edge. He wore a bright-red knitted waistcoat.

Birdie

247

'I get it! Birdie's a Robin, like you,' I said.

Robin nodded happily, and Birdie flew faster.

'Did your mum make him for you?' I said without thinking.

Robin stopped. Birdie lost height rapidly and landed. Jo frowned at me from across the kitchen. Robin went and sat on a chair without saying another word. I didn't know whether his mum had made Birdie or not.

'I'm sorry, Robin,' I muttered.

I wondered what it would feel like if your mum didn't really want you. I knew what it felt like not to have a dad, but then that was OK. I didn't want one. Certainly not one like mine. When I was really little, younger than Robin, Jo used to tell me all these fairy tales about a lovely daddy who was so sad he couldn't see me, but I soon twigged she wasn't telling the truth. I asked her straight and so she told me straight. My dad was Jo's first boyfriend. She loved him like crazy but he was never so keen on her. Then when she found out she was going to have me she told him and he didn't want to know. 'That's your problem,' he said. I've been Jo's 'problem' ever since but we manage just fine.

Robin doesn't look like he's managing very well, even if he's still got this very nice dad. If he *is* very nice.

I don't like the sound of him.

FAMILY

It is our Jessie's birthday today. She is five years old, quite the little lady. I have been fretting over what to send her for a birthday present. Louisa has so many discarded toys in her trunk. There's a little china tea—set our Jessie would adore. Louisa packed it away so carelessly all the little teacups fell out of their cardboard setting and the lid of the sugar pot seems to be lost for ever.

'I don't care about that old tea—set, not now I have my new willow—pattern set,' said Louisa.

I very nearly asked her if I could have it for my little sister. Louisa might have said yes, but I didn't think the Mistress would like it. There are many many many things the Mistress doesn't like!

I did not risk taking so much as one tiny teacup for Jessie's present. I cut up one of my old black stockings that had worn away to holes and sat up sewing half the night, turning it into a little toy monkey like the one that sits on the organ—grinder's shoulder. I wanted to give him a little jacket and cap too, so I cut a square out of my red flannel petticoat. It will not show, after all. The monkey looked splendid in his fine red clothes. My eyes were red too the next day from sewing by candlelight and I was desperately tired, but I did not care for once. I wrapped the monkey in a piece of last week's newspaper and tied it with string and inked the address really large and clear upon the front and posted it off in plenty of time.

I felt happy for the first time since I have been working here. But now I feel sad, because I cannot see Jessie opening her present. I cannot give her a birthday kiss. I am so scared Jessie might forget all about me as I can only go home one day a year, on Mothering Sunday. Baby Ada-May will think me a total stranger. It makes my heart break.

The Mistress came into the nursery unexpectedly and found me weeping with my head in the wardrobe.

'Whatever is the matter, Charlotte?' she said. 'You are not ill, are you?'

'No, Madam.'

'Then why are you crying? Make haste with Miss Louisa's dress, or the child will get a chill.'

'Yes, Madam. Sorry, Madam. I'm just sad because I miss my family so.'

'You are part of this family now,' said the Mistress.

She said it as if she were granting me an immense

250

privilege. But I do not care for this family. How can I be part of it when I can never answer back or say what I really think? How can I feel really close to these children when I have to call them Miss and Master? I have to look after them all the time but there is no—one to look after me.

COURTSHIP

'I look such a mess,' Jo wailed.

'You look fine,' I said. Though she didn't. She had two spots and her hair needed washing and her sweater had shrunk and her leggings were all baggy at the knee.

'I'm going to have to change,' said Jo, diving into the bedroom. 'Keep an eye on Robin for me.'

I frowned after her. I went and fetched a drawing pad and felt tip pens. I put them in front of Robin on the kitchen table.

'Right. You can do a drawing with my own personal set of super felt tip pens – so long as you promise not to press too hard on the points, OK?'

'OK,' said Robin eagerly, because I didn't often let him borrow them. He was used to making do with his own little-boy wax crayons.

He picked up the red, ready to draw his usual neat square house.

'Don't draw any of that boring old house and mummy and daddy stuff. Why don't you pretend

252

Birdie's grown ginormous and you get on his back and you both fly away to a Magic Land where anything can happen. Draw that.'

Robin blinked at me doubtfully.

'Go on,' I said, giving him a little nudge. 'I'm just going to go and have a talk with my mother, OK? Do not disturb us unless it's a dire emergency like you've been seized with an uncontrollable desire to stick two felt tips simultaneously into your eyes and you need immediate medical attention.'

Robin nibbled his lip, glancing nervously at the tin of felt tips as if they might spontaneously attack him.

I sighed and marched into the bedroom. Jo had pulled off her old cleaning clothes and was standing in her underwear, making faces at her clothes in the wardrobe.

'Yuck,' she said. 'They're all old and grotty and rubbish.' She scratched her head. 'Double yuck. So am I. I've *got* to wash my hair. I was going to do it yesterday but I was so blooming tired and then there wasn't time to do more than splash my face this morning. Oh God, I think I'll climb into the washing machine at the Rosens' tomorrow morning and give myself a good soaping . . .' She went burbling on like this, to herself rather than me, as she made for the bathroom in her knickers, remembered Robin, went back for her tatty old dressing gown, and then stripped off and stepped into the bath. 'Do you think we'll ever have enough spare cash to have a shower installed?' she shouted over the roaring taps. 'Pass us that Snoopy mug, Charlie

253

– and the shampoo. What is it, eh? 'Cause I'm in a tearing hurry.'

'Why are you fussing about what you look like?' I said, sitting on the loo.

'What?' Jo said, tipping water over her head.

'Why are you washing your hair *now*?'

'Oh, for goodness' sake. My hair's all lank and disgusting, that's why,' said Jo, exasperated. She lathered shampoo in and then wiped the bathroom mirror clear of steam and looked at herself. '*Look* at me. Spots all over the place. And huge great bags under my eyes. It's not fair. I thought all this hard work would make me super fit at the very least and yet I look a wreck.'

'Why does it matter so much?' I said sternly.

'Of course it matters,' Jo snapped, rinsing. 'I haven't quite given up on myself yet. I don't want to go round looking so dirty and disgusting that people in the streets run away from me screaming.'

'You don't mind what you look like when you go out to the supermarket,' I said.

'Well at that time most people have their eyes tightly closed – even the ones that are up,' said Jo, sluicing more water over herself and then getting up. 'Pass us that towel and stop being so stupid.'

'You're the one that's being stupid in my opinion,' I said. 'You don't care what you look like when you go to the Rosens' either, you just wear any old gungy thing. You don't care what you look like when you go and collect Robin from school and bring him back here. But suddenly, when it's time to take him home to his dad, it's flap and fuss and you getting worked up into a right flap-doodle.'

'I don't know what you're on about,' said Jo, towelling herself dry.

'Yes you do. What's the matter with you, Jo? Why are you trying to impress that wimpy little kid's father, eh?'

'I'm not. I just want him to see he's got a competent and reasonably clean person looking after his son. Stop looking so *fierce*, Charlie.'

'But you like him, don't you?' I asked.

'I don't even know him properly. He's just my employer.'

'You're not going to do anything really gross and go out with him, are you?' I said.

'Oooh, now, that's a great idea,' said Jo. 'And you and your Jamie could come too on a double date, how about that?'

'You shut up teasing me. I'm serious!' I said. 'I'm having grave doubts about you, Loopy Mum. We don't like men, remember? *Especially* the lean lost ones. Honestly! What a description. You are a *fool*.'

'Don't you tell me I'm a fool. I'm your mother!' said Jo, trying to act all dignified. 'Now go and keep an eye on poor little Robin and stop bugging me. Do as you're told!'

'Who's going to make me? You and whose army?' I said, standing my ground.

'Go!' said Jo, giving me a push.

'No!' I said, giving her a push back.

'You do as I say,' said Jo, pushing with both hands.

'I don't want to,' I said, pushing back.

We went on pushing and shoving and Jo's towel fell off and she tried to grab it and I snatched it first and slipped on the bath mat and Jo fell on top of me and we rolled around, starting to giggle as we wrestled.

'Oh!' said a little voice.

 We looked up and there was Robin at the bathroom door, his mouth open in astonishment.

'Sorry, Robin!' said Jo, grabbing the towel back and wrapping it round herself.

'Are you fighting?' Robin enquired timidly.

'Yes,' I said.

'No, of course we're not,' said Jo. 'Take no notice of Charlie, Robin. She's a wild child, totally out of my control.'

'Grrrrrr!' I said, baring my teeth dramatically.

'Will she fight me?' Robin asked.

'No, of course she won't, she's only teasing,' said Jo.

'Yes, I will,' I said, and I swooped on him and picked him up under his armpits and swung him round wildly so that his spindly legs kicked in the air.

He squealed noisily but he seemed to be enjoying it.

'Stop being so rough with him,' Jo called, pulling on her clothes in the bedroom.

'Is he lean and lost like his daddy then?' I said, setting Robin back on his feet. His face was flushed robin red, his eyes dark with excitement. He took a step and staggered. I caught hold of him.

'It's OK, you're just giddy,' I said as he clung to me. His hands were like little monkey paws. I wondered if he'd ever clung to his mum the way he was clinging to me.

'Giddy,' Robin repeated. This was obviously a new experience for him. He moved tentatively.

'There, it's getting better, isn't it? Hey, did you put all the tops back on my felt tip pens, yeah?'

'Oh yes. Honest,' said Robin.

'Did you do a drawing?'

'I started.'

'Let's see then.' I walked him over to the kitchen table. He'd drawn a very big Birdie as I'd suggested, with a tiny Robin clinging to his back. They were just landing in the Magic Land, Birdie's wings outstretched. I touched the strip of green below Birdie's claws. 'Is this the Magic Land then?' I asked.

Robin nodded. 'Yes! Shall I draw it for you, Charlie?'

'OK. Go on then. What's in your Magic Land, eh? Pink candy-floss trees and rivers with tame dolphins and unicorns you can ride and it's never ever bedtime?' I suggested, trying to conjure up a dinky little Magic Land that might take his fancy.

Jo and I elaborated endlessly on our own Magic Lands. It was one of our favourite games. Jo's current Magic Land was a huge turquoise swimming pool and she'd float endlessly on a white lilo sipping champagne and eating white cream chocolates all day long.

My special Magic Land was an immense jungle and I'd hack my way through, not the slightest bit scared even when huge pythons wound themselves round my waist or tigers roared at me or elephants suddenly charged. I'd whistle a magic tune so that the python swayed in a hypnotic trance, I'd roar right back at the tiger, and I'd catch hold of the elephant's trunk and get him to lift me up on his head between his mighty ears and we'd thunder across the land together.

I started drawing my own Magic Land, concentrating on the immensely tall trees, home of great gorillas and hairy orang-utans and tribes of funny furry monkeys, and I was Queen of all the Apes and swung through the trees faster than any of them.

'Look, this is my Magic Land. See the monkeys?'
I said, showing Robin.

He was kneeling up on his chair, drawing intently,
his tongue sticking out he was concentrating so
hard. I peered at his picture.

'That's not a Magic Land!' I said. 'You're just
drawing your mum and your dad again.'

'Yes, they're in my Magic Land, and we all live
there and it's magic,' said Robin. He bent his head
very near his drawing, as if he was trying to step
inside it.

'It's nearly time we were off, Robin. We'll show
Daddy your lovely picture, yes?' said Jo.

That wasn't all they were going to show off to
Daddy. Jo was wearing her shortest skirt and
her little angora wool jumper. I usually call her
Fluffy Bunny when she wears it. I didn't at all
feel like flattering her with babyish nick-
names now. What was she *doing*, getting
all dolled up to deliver little Robin back
home? She was supposed to do some
housework when she was there too, so
why dress up like she was going dating,
not dusting?

'What?' said Jo, all wide-eyed, as I glared at her.

'You know what,' I said.

She was hours getting back home too. Well, an
hour late. Just over half an hour. But she was still
late.

'What are you playing at, eh?' I said furiously.

Jo burst out laughing.

259

'It's not funny!' I exploded.

'Yes it is. Talk about role reversal. Watch it, Charlie. You're starting to sound just like Grandma. "Why are you so late back, Josephine? This simply isn't good enough. And wipe that smirk off your face, it's not funny."'

'Well, maybe if you'd listened to Grandma instead of thinking you knew best then you wouldn't have ended up as a single parent having to go out cleaning for other people to keep a roof over our heads,' I said.

There was a sudden silence. We were both shocked. Jo's never minded if I shout back at her but I've never tried to hurt her like that before. I put my hand over my lips to try to get them under control.

Jo was struggling too, no longer laughing. 'OK. Maybe that's a good point – if a cheap one. Though I'm glad I made that major mistake because I got you out of it. And you're the best thing that's ever happened to me, even if you're acting like a right old ratbag at this present moment in time,' said Jo. 'I'm sorry if you were worried I was late. I didn't realize. Mark and I just got talking and—'

'So it's Mark, is it?'

'Oh come off it, Charlie. He's not the sort of man you call Mr Reed.'

'No, he's the little-boy-lost type, yeah?'

'I don't know why you're being so *stupid*,' said Jo. 'You're acting like I'm going out with him or something.'

'Well – don't you want to?'

'Of course not. He's my employer. He's a nice quiet friendly man who adores his son and he's still hurting after the break up of his marriage and he's lonely and he just likes to talk a bit, that's all. And – and – I like to talk to him too.'

'Why? You're not lonely. You've got me.'

Jo looked as if she might giggle again. 'You're sounding like my husband now!'

'Well, why do you have to get all prettied up in your best clothes just to talk to this Mark?'

'*Definitely* like a husband. Oh, Charlie!' Jo put her arms round me, her angora tickling my cheeks.

'Get off. You're getting fluff all over me,' I said, sneezing.

'Well, stop being such a prize berk, eh? Look, if it keeps you happy I'll tell Mark tomorrow that I'm not allowed to say another word to him because it annoys my fierce bossy man-hating daughter.'

'Right, you do that,' I said.

I knew I was being ridiculous. But I couldn't help it.

I was fed up at school too. Angela and Lisa were being stupid stupid stupid. Angela had joined this dippy fan club and had a special magazine and a signed photo of her new favourites and a T-shirt with all their heads on which she wore every day under her school shirt. She endlessly read aloud the most amazingly trivial facts about her new darlings, like one had a thing about red-and-white striped toothpaste and another

261

had a wacky Scottish auntie and another fell about laughing every time he saw Bugs Bunny. Well, so what??? But Angela kept giving great excited whoops and yelling, 'Listen to this, listen to this!'

Lisa was getting pretty cheesed off with this too, but she was just as bad over Dave Wood. Worse even. She went bright red whenever he came remotely near her, and when one day in singing the music teacher had her standing right next to Dave, Lisa was so overcome she couldn't sing a note, she just opened and shut her mouth like a goldfish.

'I was so *embarrassed*,' she kept saying afterwards. 'I mean, we were practically touching.'

'Yuck! I wouldn't touch Dave Wood with a bargepole,' I said.

'Oh *you*,' said Lisa. 'Look, do you think Dave likes me?'

'*I* don't know,' I said impatiently. 'Why don't you ask him?'

'I can't *ask* him! No, I've got to find some subtle way of finding out.'

'I'll ask him, if you like,' said Angela, reaching down her school blouse and blowing kisses to the faces on her T-shirt.

'No, that's not subtle enough,' said Lisa.

'Angela, stop doing that, it looks seriously weird,' I said. 'And you're trying to be so subtle it's just a waste of space. Never mind whether that twerp likes you. He most likely doesn't have a clue that *you* like *him*.'

262

'Well, I can't tell him that!' said Lisa.

'Why not? Though *how* you can like him I just can't fathom. I can't stand the way his hair flops forward into his eyes so that he has to keep flipping it out the way!'

'I think that's seriously cute,' said Lisa.

'Yuck!'

'Yes, double yuck,' said Angela, giving me hope, but then she started on about the hairstyles of all her pop darlings until I was ready to tear out *my* hair. In fact I got so seriously bored that I stalked off by myself.

I was feeling so fed up that when some stupid boys kicked their football and hit me right on the head I found I had tears in my eyes. I blinked rapidly, horrified. I never ever cried at school, no matter what. Even when I was a little kid right back in Year One and some big boys gave me a Chinese burn I didn't cry.

SMACK!

'Watch it, you stupid idiots,' I said, and I took their football and threw it as far away as I could, right over behind the bike sheds.

'Oh, you rotten pig, why did you go and do that?' they groaned. 'What's up with you, Cakehole? Just because you've had a tiff with your little girly gang there's no need to take it out on us.'

I responded with a very rude gesture. Miss Beckworth was on playground duty. I hoped she hadn't seen. I made off sharpish in the opposite direction, dodging behind the Portakabins.

Jamie Edwards was sitting on the steps, head deep in a book. He looked startled when he saw me – but he smiled nervously.

'You still reading about that Esther?' I said.

'I finished that book ages ago. I read ever so quickly,' said Jamie, unable to resist a little boast.

'So what you reading now then, eh?' I peered at the densely printed pages. 'It looks even worse. Ever so hard.'

'Ever so Hardy,' said Jamie, chuckling, showing me the spine.

'*Tess of the D'Urbervilles* by Thomas Hardy – oh, I get you, ha ha, very droll. It sounds awful! Is it French with that funny name?'

'No. It's English, about this girl Tess and she goes to work on a farm and this man has his wicked way with her,' said Jamie, eyes gleaming.

'Oh, another one of *those*. You are awful, Jamie.'

'And it's ever so sad, because Tess has a baby and then she falls in love again but it all goes wrong and I know it's not going to have a happy ending.'

'Oh, hang about! I've seen it on the telly, I think. There's a bit about Stonehenge at the end – I watched it with Jo and we both wept buckets.'

'Is Jo your sister?'

'No, my mum.'

'And you're allowed to call her by her first name?'

'I can call her whatever I like,' I said.

264

I felt like inventing some new and incredibly nasty names for her because I was still so annoyed with her. I kept thinking about her with this creep Mark. I didn't know what he looked like, so I imagined him like Robin but big. A *total* wimp. So why why why did Jo want to bound round to his house in her bunny jumper and twitch her nose at him?

Mark?

'Are you planning to go round to Lisa's or Angela's on Friday night?' Jo said that evening.

'Maybe. I don't know. I've got a bit fed up with them recently,' I said gloomily, chucking my school copy of *Victorian Life* on the floor. None of Miss Beckworth's books went into the sort of detail I wanted. 'I might just go round to Jamie's house because he keeps telling me he's got all these Victorian books he'll lend me.'

'Oh, round to Jamie's house, eh?' said Jo.

'So?' I said fiercely. 'It's just to borrow a book.'

'OK, OK. But if you stay for tea or anything, can his mum or dad run you home? I can't come and fetch you because . . . I'm babysitting for Robin.'

I stared at her. So Mark was going out?

'Who's this Mark going out with?' I asked.

Jo shrugged uneasily. 'I don't know. Look, he just asked if I could – could come round and babysit, so I said OK, but I won't be back late, and I can always say no if it's not all right with you, Charlie.'

'It's fine with me,' I said. It obviously wasn't fine with Jo. I felt a bit sorry for her. But I was also thrilled for me. The wimp had got himself some girlfriend so he couldn't be interested in Jo. He just wanted her to look after little Robin.

Or so I thought.

I was so stupid! I didn't twig at all. Not that first Friday, or even the Friday after. I was so pleased and relieved I was extra nice to Jo.

We had a wonderful Sunday, having a really long lie in and then a dozy hour or two snuggled up in bed playing Magic Lands and then, when we eventually got up, I made us special little fairy cakes. We ate them hot out of the oven for breakfast and then later when they'd cooled down I iced them pink and then changed to white in my little icing bag and piped funny messages over them – HELLO and I LIKE YOU and FUNNY FACE – like those little love heart sweets.

I took them to school the next morning. There was a lot of silly teasing about Cakehole making cakes – but everyone seemed dead impressed when they saw them. Everyone wanted one, but they were only for a select few. I gave Lisa an I LIKE YOU and told her what to do with it. She giggled and blushed and protested and wouldn't give it to Dave Wood outright – but he saw her leave it on his desk, so the message got through.

I gave Angela another I LIKE YOU and she pretend-fed it to the grinning faces on her T-shirt and then gobbled it up herself.

266

I gave more cakes to the girls I'd liked best in our old gang, and then Lisa and Angela and I had another two each. There was just one left by the time we went back into school.

'Did you make those little cakes yourself, Charlie?' Jamie asked.

'Yup.'

'They looked ever so nice. Really tasty,' said Jamie wistfully.

I looked at him. And then I sighed and reached in the tin and gave him the last one. It didn't say HELLO. It didn't say FUNNY FACE. It said I LIKE YOU.

COURTSHIP

It was bitterly cold in the park today. Louisa cried
because she could not feel her feet inside her boots
and baby Freddie's nose kept running in a most
unattractive way. Victor ran ahead with his hoop
to get warm, so I stuck Louisa into the pram
beside Freddie and ran too. We raced all the way
home, careering round the corner and practically
running over the butcher's boy. He did not seem to
mind.

'Whoops—a—blooming—buttercup!' he said. 'Mind
what you're doing with that perambulator, Miss. It's
a dangerous weapon!'

No—one has ever called me Miss before. I must
admit I liked it, though I stuck my nose in the air
and called the butcher's boy a saucepot.

Trust Victor to hang back at that precise moment. 'What were you saying to that errand boy, Charlotte?' he enquired.

'It's none of your business, Master Victor,' I said haughtily.

'Is he going to be your gentleman caller?' Victor asked.

'Certainly not!' I said, and I took Victor's hoop and bowled it so hard he had to run like the wind to stop it going into the road and under a carriage.

That settled his hash. He well knows that his mamma does not allow the servants to have gentleman callers. I had to protect Eliza when she was canoodling in the kitchen with her current sweetheart, the draper's assistant, who had come to deliver the Mistress's new shawl and gloves. In finest cashmere. If only I had a warm woolly shawl and mittens! I have chilblains that throb and itch like the devil.

Anyway, I was down in the kitchen fetching the children's hot milk and biscuits when I heard the Mistress clip-clopping down the stairs in her neat kid boots.

'Quick, Eliza, the Mistress is coming!' I hissed, and then I bounded *up* the stairs and waylaid the Mistress by telling her a very long story about Miss Louisa–not-drinking-her-milk-even-though-it's-so-good-for-her, and by the time I'd done and the Mistress had made her way down to the kitchen Eliza had had time to bundle any number of gentlemen callers out of the back door.

She didn't say anything to me, but Eliza and Mrs
Angel stopped calling me Baby and laughing behind
my back — and yesterday when the children were
asleep Eliza slipped into the nursery with a bowl of
Mrs Angel's special sherry trifle for my supper.

Mrs Angel is Mother's age but she has
gentlemen callers too! The fat policeman
for the street calls on a regular basis for
his piece of pie and Mrs Angel's patter. I
was astonished to see a woman so old go rosy-
cheeked and chuckle when he praised her pastry.

I received a letter from Rose today and now I
am starting to worry that Mother herself might be
courting!!! Rose says that Mr Higgins from the Dog
and Duck brings Mother a jug of ale from time to
time, and in return she cooks him a meal. I do not
like the sound of this!

Rose's letter makes me feel *so* homesick. It is a
poor ill—spelt half—page but I have read it as avidly
as if it were a masterpiece by Mr Dickens. Rose
has never tried hard enough at school. She
writes that Miss Worthbeck sends her
kindest regards and can scarce manage
without me. And a certain Edward
James sends a most impertinent
message to Dear Little Lottie. Hmm!

SUNDAY

I found it seriously weird going round to Jamie's house. I mean, this was Jamie Edwards, the worst boy in the whole class, old chubby-chops super-swot wimpy-wuss Jamie. I made pretty sure all the boys in our class treated me with respect but I wanted a capital 'R' from Jamie.

Yet in his huge great famously Victorian villa he was so different. As if he'd grown to fit his fourteen-roomed house. (I counted.) And I felt different too. As if I'd shrunk considerably. It felt strange just going into his house through that dark-blue front door with the big brass lion knocker. I felt as if I should slink round the back or down the basement steps like my Lottie.

If Jamie and his family had lorded it over me I'd somehow have felt easier. I could just dismiss them as horrible snobs and sneer at them. But they were ever so friendly. Even Jamie's elder brother Jules.

Elder brothers are usually a race apart. Angela's elder brother charges straight past you without

271

even bothering to say hello. He doesn't even mean to be rude, it's just that you don't register with him. But Jules said Hi and chatted like I was his age and he made me and Jamie a toasted sandwich. We ate it in the kitchen – but *what* a kitchen! I stared round, scarcely able to swallow.

There was a shelf of cookery books and I had a quick peer but I couldn't see anything special on cakes. When Jamie's mum got home much later I saw she wasn't really a cake-maker. She came in clutching all these files and folders, her cardie falling off her shoulders, her scarf trailing on the ground. She said hello as if she was really pleased to see me, and then she unpacked some shopping and made us an amazing treat of cream cheese and smoked salmon in a strange round roll. (No wonder Jamie is chubby round his chops with all these delicious snacks on offer.) Jules had one of these bagel things too, and then went up to his room to get on with his homework.

All Jamie's family are seriously brainy. Jules is going to take *twelve* GCSEs, and then there are two older brothers, both at university. Jamie's mum and dad *lecture* at the university. He teaches French, she teaches Politics and Economics.

'The Economics is a bit of a laugh,' said Jamie.

272

'Mum can hardly add up. She's meant to pay me when I do stuff like vacuuming and that, two quid an hour, plus appropriate percentage for ten minutes extra, say, and *can* she work it out? Nope! Clueless, aren't you, Mum?'

I didn't think his mum clueless at all, paying Jamie a measly two quid per hour when the rock-bottom going rate was £3.50 and the Rosens right next door paid Jo a fiver an hour – dead Economical! Things got a bit awkward when Jamie's mum started chatting about how she remembered me from way back when I had my hair in a pony tail (yuck!) and then she said: 'And you always looked so cute because your big sister had a pony tail too, so you both walked along to the school, hair bobbing away.'

I smiled in a strained sort of way and decided to keep my mouth shut. But Jamie didn't.

'Oh, Mum, honestly! That wasn't Charlie's sister. She's her mum.'

Jamie's mum looked startled. 'Good Heavens! Oh Charlie, what a lovely young mum you've got! Not an old bag like me, eh? What does your mum do?'

I swallowed. 'Well . . . she used to be sort of a lecturer like you.' It was true in a way. She was always having to give her staff a right lecture in her shop.

'So now . . . ?'

'Now she's – well, she's been made redundant, I mean, it's not her fault, she didn't get the sack or anything, it's just—'

'Oh, tell me about it! We're in a sticky situation at

273

the moment too. We're all very worried. So has your
mother found another post at all?'

'Well. Not – not lecturing. She's having to do
temporary work.'

'I see. Well, I do hope things sort themselves out
soon for her. Is it . . . ?' She paused delicately, trying
very hard not to put her foot in it again. 'Is it just your
mother and you at home?'

'Yes.'

Just Jo and me in a home we're hanging on to by
the skin of our teeth. If Jamie's mum loses her posh
job then they'll maybe have to swop from smoked
salmon to tinned, but they'll still be able to live in
their huge great house. OK, they have actually got
a couple of lodgers right upstairs, two students from
the university. They've got a bedroom each, a
shared living room and kitchenette, and their own
bathroom and loo. The students' rooms are bigger
than our flat.

It still leaves the Edwards with so many
different rooms. This includes a *library*.
They've got books in absolutely every room,
even the downstairs loo, and there are shelves
in the hall and the living room downstairs, but
there's this huge great room on the first floor
absolutely crammed full of books, and there
are shelves and shelves of Victorian stuff.

'See,' said Jamie proudly, pulling various
volumes down and displaying them in front of
me.

I saw. No wonder Jamie's Victorian project was

274

so brilliant. Still, he was letting me look at the books if I wanted.

'You've still got time to do a proper project instead of that old diary thing,' he said. Unwisely.

'Cheek! I don't want to do a boring old project. Who wants to be like everyone else? I'm doing my diary – and yes it is "old", it's *supposed* to be old, it's meant to be written by a Victorian, for goodness' sake.'

'OK, OK. You don't have to get all heavy with me,' said Jamie. 'You're so fierce, Charlie.'

'Fierce?' I said. I said it again, savouring the word. I felt as if he'd paid me a real compliment.

'So don't you want to borrow any of the Victorian books, then? Because we can go and play a game on my computer if you want. Or I'll show you my dinosaur stuff. Or we can play War.'

'War? You mean fight?' I said, grinning. 'I know who's going to win.'

'No, it's a game, with all these little soldiers – *they* fight, and there are little guns and land mines and all that stuff. It's great to play but Jules won't play it with me, neither will Mum or Dad or anyone because they're all pacifists.'

'I'm not. I'll play you. But just let me look at this book a tick.'

I'd found a whole set of Victorian girls' books. I wanted to see if there might be any Lottie could have read. There was one huge fat annual with lots of pictures, like a magazine. There was one coloured picture of a huge table groaning with wobbly jellies

and puddings like castles and all sorts
of dinky sweets and teeny sandwiches . . . and fancy cakes.

'Hey, look! I just want to take a
couple of notes, OK?'

'OK. Though why don't you borrow it?'

'You mean I can take it home with me?'

'Sure.'

'Oh. Well. Great.' I tucked the huge book under
my arm. 'So let's play War.'

We played War for hours. It was a great game. And
guess who won!

Jamie's mum ran me home in her car. I was
worried she might object about the book
because it was probably valuable as
it's so old but she didn't turn a hair.
Her hair is already grey. I wonder
what it's like to have a mum old
enough to be your granny. I think it's much more fun
to have a mum young enough to be your sister.

'We've heard so much about you, Charlie,' said
Jamie's mum.

I blinked.

'You've made a big impression on Jamie,' she said.

I thought about it. I'd made a *literal* impression on
Jamie several times.

'We're going to the V and A on Sunday afternoon,'
she said.

'The what?'

'Sorry. The Victoria and Albert Museum. I know
Jamie would love it if you'd come with us – and it

276

would be very useful for this famous Victorian project.'

'Well. Thank you very much. But Sunday is sort of special. Jo and I do things together.'

'She's very welcome to come too.'

'Thanks, but . . . I don't think we can.'

'Well, another time maybe. And do come round to our house any time you want. It'd be lovely to see you,' said Jamie's mum.

I was a little bit dubious. Did Jamie have an actual thing about me? He hadn't acted all lovey-dovey when we were in his room. The mere thought of Jamie Edwards acting lovey-dovey was enough to crease me up. Just let him try! And anyway, I didn't want to go to some stuffy old museum on a Sunday. Like I said, Sundays were just for Jo and me.

So I was utterly shocked and stupefied when Jo dropped this ginormous bombshell.

'We're going out on Sunday,' she said.

'Oh yeah?'

'How would you like to go to Red River Theme Park?' she said.

I stared at her. I'd been wanting to go to Red River ever since it opened. Lisa had promised she'd get her dad to take Angela and me for her birthday treat, but that wasn't until next year. And it wasn't a certainty anyway, because it cost a fortune to get into Red River.

'We can't afford it,' I said to Jo.

'We're being taken out,' she said. 'Isn't it great?'

'*Who's* taking us out?' I said, starting to smell a rat. A great big rat with twitchy whiskers on its lean lost face. And I was spot on.

'Mark was talking about taking Robin this Sunday and he thought it would be so much more fun if we all went together. He's paying, and I'm getting a picnic together. It's going to be a fantastic day out.'

'We don't have days out on Sundays. We have days in. Just you and me. As a matter of fact, *I* was asked out on Sunday, the Edwards family asked me, they wanted to take me out for this bumper day in London, a drive all round the sights and lunch in Planet Hollywood and then this museum for Victorian stuff and then tea at one of those really posh hotels, scones and cream cakes and all that, and then – then we were going for dinner at the Hard Rock Café and – and *then*—'

'Then you were going to be violently sick, I should think,' said Jo. She reached out and ran her finger up and down my lips, the way you do a baby to make it go wibble-wibble-wibble. 'This is a bad mouth,' said Jo. 'It is telling fibs.'

'They did ask me out on Sunday, honest,' I insisted.

'Well, you can't, because I've already said we're going to Red River with Mark and Robin,' said Jo. 'Come *on*, Charlie! You've been desperate to go to Red River for ages. I thought you'd be over the moon. I think it's absolutely great of Mark to invite us.'

278

'Why us, though? Why isn't he going with this girlfriend of his?' I said.

'What girlfriend?' said Jo. She frowned.

'The one he's started seeing on Friday nights when you babysit,' I said.

'Oh. I see. Ah,' said Jo.

'What?' I said. '*What?*' Although I suddenly *knew* what.

'I think you maybe got hold of the wrong end of the stick,' said Jo. 'I never said Mark had a girlfriend.'

'So where did he go when you went round to babysit?'

'Well . . . the first Friday he was going out, just to see this film he fancied, but we got chatting, and then we watched this film together on the telly instead, so—'

'So you're the one who's been telling dirty great lies,' I said.

'No I'm not!'

'And *you're* his girlfriend now, aren't you?' I said.

'Of course I'm not. Don't be so silly. I'm not Mark's girlfriend. I work for him. I've only known him a few weeks. Oh, Charlie, don't be so difficult.'

I felt like being difficult. I was Mega Mad. No-one seemed to understand why. Lisa and Angela and I went round the shops on Saturday afternoon and they thought I was completely nuts.

'Can't you get this guy to take us too?' said Lisa hopefully. 'Say we're your all-time best friends and you can't go without us. After all, I promised I'd get my dad to take you two on my birthday.'

'This guy isn't my dad though. He isn't anything. He's just this creep who's started chatting up my mother.'

'Still, who cares if he's a creep? You still get to go to Red River,' said Lisa.

'Yeah, I'll go in your place if you don't want to,' said Angela. 'I just go to church on Sundays. You count yourself lucky, Charlie.'

'No, you've got to be a good girl and go to church,' said Lisa. '*I'll* go instead of Charlie. I just have to go to all these boring antique fairs with my mum while my dad plays golf, it's not fair.'

'Neither of you are going,' I said. 'And *I'm* not going too.'

I told Jo that on Saturday evening, while she was busy getting all this picnic stuff together.

'OK,' said Jo, mashing up hard-boiled eggs.

'I really mean it. I'm not going. And you can't make me,' I said.

'Right,' said Jo, mashing harder.

'So that's settled,' I said.

'Yep,' said Jo, pounding so hard that the bowl rattled.

'I'm not going to Granny's or anything. I'll just stay here. By myself. I'll be fine,' I said.

'Aha,' said Jo, and her hand slipped and she banged it hard on the edge of the kitchen top. She bent over, clutching her wrist.

'You're not supposed to mash like that. You're hopeless when it comes to cooking,' I said. 'Jo?'

She didn't answer this time. Her head was so bent I couldn't see her face for hair. I went over to her. I saw a tear trickling down her cheek.

'I've really upset you, haven't I?' I said.

'No. I've just hurt my wrist, that's all,' said Jo.

She can be as stubborn as me sometimes. Her wrist wasn't really hurt. And she stopped crying when I put my arms round her and told her that I would go to Red River on Sunday if she really really really wanted me to go.

I even made some more little fairy cakes for the picnic. With messages.

Mark was exactly how I imagined him. No, worse. The sort of bumbling Bambi-eyed boy-man that makes some women go bananas. He had a tuft of hair sticking up on top and little round glasses and a big check shirt and faded jeans and one of his socks was black and the other was navy. *Pathetic*. Mark almost made little Robin look macho. He was ever so scared of me. 'Hi, Charlie,' he said, trying to sound dead casual, but he stuttered – and when he attempted this silly little wave, spreading his fingers, I saw his palm was all sweaty. Yuck.

But there was something far far worse. Jo. She was better at acting cool, of course. If you didn't know her you'd think she was dead relaxed, making a fuss of Robin and flappy little Birdie, chatting nineteen to the dozen to Mark, telling some silly story about her supermarket job, the day her machine ran away with her and attacked a pile of loo rolls. I don't think it even happened, she was just making it up as she went along, but it made Mark laugh and even little Robin tittered behind Birdie's wing. But she was just pretending all the time, her voice too high, her eyes blinking, her hands gesticulating wildly. She was like a clockwork toy that had been wound up too tightly.

I yawned and started humming to myself while she was in mid-flow to show her I wasn't impressed. I hardly said a word the entire car journey to Red River Theme Park. Jo was going jabber jabber jabber so there was no point anyway.

Mark seemed so impressed that he could barely keep his eyes on the road ahead. 'Yeah? Mmm? *Really?*' he'd go, and every so often he'd crack up laughing.

I slumped back in my seat, weary with this deeply disgusting performance. Mark caught sight of me in his driving mirror. 'Are you all right, Charlie?' he said.

I didn't bother to reply.

'She's not feeling sick, is she?' Mark asked Jo.

Jo turned round. 'Stop being a pig,' she mouthed at me.

I gave one small snort for her

benefit. Robin blinked at me in surprise.

'She's OK,' said Jo.

'And you're OK too, Robin?' Mark asked. 'You don't feel sick or anything?'

'I don't think so,' Robin mumbled. 'But maybe Birdie does a bit.'

Oh great. I didn't care for the idea of Robin chucking up all over me.

'Talk to Robin, Charlie,' said Jo. 'Take his mind off it.'

I didn't want to talk to Robin. Or his dad. Or my stupid mother, all got up in her fluffy pink top and her tiny skirt. To match her new shrunk tiny brain and her fluffy pink persona. Bimbo Mum. Out with Bambi Man and Birdie Boy.

'What's *up* with you, Charlie?' Jo said, her voice sharp.

There was nothing up with me. I was the only person in the car acting anywhere near normal.

'She's shy,' said Mark.

Me, shy! I snorted again.

'She's not shy,' said Jo. 'Are you, Charlie? I'm the one who always gets into states about things and can hardly say boo to a goose. Charlie's always had far more guts than me. She was born a fighter, eh, Charlie?'

She was sucking up to me now. It was sickening. Robin seemed to find it sickening too. Literally.

'Birdie's starting to feel *very* sick,' he gasped, his face pale green.

I snapped into action mega fast, opening his

window and sticking his little head out just in time. He was sick all over the car, but at least it was outside, not inside. We had to pull up in a lay-by and get him mopped up and the car wiped down. I backed away from both these proceedings. As Mark had to deal with the car Jo had to sluice the sicky dribble off Robin. She's always had a weak stomach. Still, she was the one who wanted to play Happy Families. Let her be Mother.

Robin started wimpering that he smelt, and eventually Jo had to waste a bottle of the picnic water washing him. Then Robin snivelled that Birdie smelt too, because one tiny tip of his wing had got stained. Birdie had to have a regular little bird-bath too.

I was practically at screaming point by the time we drove off in the car. The day didn't improve. The world and his wife had decided to visit the Red River Theme Park. We were not the world and we certainly weren't ever going to be anyone's wife, but we were stuck in their traffic jam. It took hours before we got there, and then there was a huge queue to park and by the time we staggered through the entrance we felt as exhausted as if we'd already had a day out.

Still, I decided I might as well make the most of this opportunity and I clamoured straight away to go on the really scary famous Red River Run.

'Let's go a bit gently first,' said Jo. 'Robin still looks a bit pale. What would you like to go on, Robin?'

He twittered and skittered and eventually decided

284

he wanted to try the Treetops ride because Birdie might see a lot of big birds up there. I was getting heartily sick of all this twee Birdie nonsense by now. I wished Birdie would flap his wings and fly away, sharpish.

We went on this Treetops ride and it was a bit babyish because you rode round this aerial scenic railway ever so slowly, absolutely no swooping up and down or looping-the-looping. Big birds were very few on the ground too. Well, few in the air, shall we say. I'd have stuck stuffed parrots to every branch and dangled a few eagles in the air just to make the view a bit livelier. You couldn't rely on the real birds to put on an entertaining aerial display. A few sparrows flapped far away and that was our lot.

It was all very tame. For me. Not for Robin. He went a familiar pale green.

'Put your head over the side of the truck,' I said quickly.

But when he did as he was told he looked down *through* the treetops and got so scared he couldn't even be sick (which was just as well for all the unsuspecting folk wandering around underneath!) Robin just opened his mouth and screamed.

'Hey, Robin! It's OK, son. Don't yell like that. It's meant to be fun,' said Mark, turning round and trying to put his arms round him.

'Don't look down, Robin.

285

Look up at the trees. Look, there's a pigeon,' said Jo.

'Can't anyone shut him up?' I said. 'Robin, you're giving Birdie a headache. Look, he's had to put his head under his wing. Shut up, OK?'

It wasn't OK. He didn't shut up until we'd finished the ride and hauled him off. Mark picked him up and he buried his head in his shirt and gradually adjusted the scream to an intermittent sob.

'Well, he's having a whale of a time,' I said.

Jo gave me a shove. 'Will you stop being so hateful?' she hissed. 'Poor little Robin.'

'Yes, poor little wimpy-pimpy,' I said. 'Come on, Jo. He's not a baby. He's five, for goodness' sake. In Victorian times he'd be old enough to shove up a chimney.'

'I wish I could shove you up a chimney,' said Jo. 'Look, he acts like a baby because his mum's cleared off and he feels like his whole world has fallen apart. Can't you understand?'

I was starting to feel that way myself. Like my own mum had cleared off. Jo turned her back on me and started fuss fuss fussing over Robin, and all the time Mark was looking at her with this sickening soft expression so that now I was the one who felt like throwing up.

Robin wouldn't go on any other rides, apart from a twiddly little roundabout for tiny tots. He sat bolt upright in a little car and held on to that steering wheel so tightly his knuckles were practically bursting out of his skin. Jo and Mark waved like crazy every time he came round but he never once looked at them. He stared straight ahead, as if he were watching the road.

He wanted another go. And another.

'Look, this is loopy,' I pointed out. 'It costs a fortune to get in and you're supposed to go on all these incredible rides and all we're doing is watching Robin go round and round a roundabout that would only cost fifty pence at a summer fête.'

'At least he's liking it,' said Jo.

'But this is his last go. I agree with you, Charlie. Hey, we'll go on the Red River Ride, eh, you and me?' said Mark.

I couldn't stand the way he was trying so hard to get on with me.

'I'll go on my own, thanks,' I said.

But for some infuriating reason they didn't let kids under twelve ride on their own.

'You come, Jo. Go on. Please,' I said, practically begging.

But it was no use. I ended up surfing the Red River with Mark. It spoilt it all utterly. People seeing us together might have thought he was my *dad*. I sat as far away from him as I possibly could. He kept yelling, 'Isn't this fun! Isn't this great!' though he'd gone almost as green as his son. When we lurched up to the very top and then swooped down like crazy he screamed so that I could see the fillings in his back teeth. When we got to the last and largest hill of steel before the watersplash he actually tried to put his arm round me.

'Do you mind?' I said, and I wriggled as far away as I could just as we went over the top. My head jerked forward as I hurtled down and I banged my nose hard on the safety bar. Pain exploded in my head as water splashed right over us and soaked us to the skin.

OW!

'Wow!' said Mark. 'Hey, Charlie, what's up? Did you bump your head? Your poor nose is all red.'

'No. I'm fine,' I said thickly, trying to blink my tears back.

I didn't want his soggy sympathy. Even though it was all his fault. Him and his silly snively son.

Jo was still so busy fussing over Robin that she didn't even *notice* that my nose had suddenly turned into a tomato. So I decided I wouldn't bother to tell her. Even though it was more than likely broken, and my looks would be marred for all time.

We went to the picnic area but I wasn't really hungry. My nose throbbed so much and chewing aggravated it. The picnic wasn't up to much anyway. The sandwiches had gone limp inside and hard out because Jo had made them the night before. She'd packed the crisps under the cans of Coke so that they were all broken into little bits. The grapes had got so squashed that one more trample would have turned them into wine.

The only good part of the picnic were my fairy cakes which I'd packed myself in a nest of paper tissues inside a big tin. They were delicious. And carefully iced with witty messages. I handed them round so that everyone got the right one.

Mine said HEY, BEAUTIFUL.

Jo's said TRAITOR.

Mark's said DEADLY POISON.

Robin's said GET LOST.

'What does it mean, g-e-t l-o-s-t?' said Robin, licking his message tentatively.

'Oh, it's just Charlie being silly,' said Jo, glaring at me. She didn't even touch her cake. Mark gave a great false roar of laughter and ate his in two gulps.

'Yum yum, delicious,' he said, and then he gasped and pretended to choke.

'Daddy?' said Robin.

'It's OK, Daddy's just dying,' I said.

'It's a silly joke, Robin,' said Jo, cramming the lid back on the rest of the cakes. She looked like she wanted to cram me inside too. Without any airholes. 'How would you like another go on that little round-about, Robin?'

He had many more goes. And I went on some other rides too, but somehow they all seemed a waste of time. My whole head was hurting now, not just my nose. Sometimes I went on the rides with

Mark while Jo looked after Robin. Sometimes I went on the rides with Jo. That wasn't any better, because we weren't speaking.

Then we got to the Stardust Sparkle ride. It was all pink glitter and hearts and flowers outside.

'That's pretty,' said Robin.

'Pretty yucky,' I said.

'Would you like to go on the Stardust Sparkle ride, Robin?' said Jo. 'We could all go on it, eh?'

Robin watched the ride warily. A couple got into a pink pretend Cadillac and it drove through a door in the shape of a big heart. You couldn't see inside the door. It was all dark.

'No,' said Robin. 'Too dark. I don't like the dark.'

'Surprise surprise,' I said. 'Well, *I* certainly don't want to go on the Stardust Sparkle ride either, if anybody's interested. Not that anyone is.'

'I'd like to,' said Mark. 'Come on, Jo.'

I stared at her. But she didn't even look at me.

'Look after Robin, Charlie,' she said, and she rushed off with Mark.

The two of them together. In a pink Cadillac. Disappearing through a big heart into the dark.

'They've gone,' said Robin.

'Too true,' I said.

'They'll be back soon?' Robin asked.

'How should I know?' I said.

The ride was mostly enclosed, but the first couple's Cadillac suddenly shot through a door overhead and rode through the air in full view of everyone for several seconds. The couple didn't seem to realize. They were kissing.

'Look!' said Robin, giggling.

The first couple disappeared through another dinky door. We waited for the second couple. We waited a long time, and then suddenly they burst through the overhead door. They rode through the air in full view of everyone. They didn't realize either. They were kissing.

'Look!' said Robin, giggling again. And then *he* realized. 'It's Daddy and Jo!'

I didn't say anything. My nose was still hot but the rest of me had turned icy cold.

'But they were kissing. Why were they kissing? They don't kiss,' said Robin, sounding perplexed. He rubbed Birdie's wing against his cheek like a cuddle blanket.

'Looks like they certainly do kiss,' I said. 'So there you go, Robin. Your dad. And my mum. Well, he's not going to be my dad. And she's not going to be *your* mum.'

'I've got a mum,' said Robin.

'Yes, but she doesn't want you any more, does she?' I said.

'Yes, she does,' said Robin uncertainly. 'Daddy said. It's just her new man who doesn't want me.'

'Well, my mum's obviously got herself *her* new man. So she doesn't want me. And your dad's got himself his new lady. So he won't want you either now. Tough, isn't it?'

It made the pain ease just a little if I made Robin

291

smart too. His face crumpled as he clutched Birdie.
I started to get scared.

'Hey, don't cry again. I was only joking,' I said.
But we both knew I'd been serious.

SUNDAY

Sunday is meant to be a day of rest. Well, ha ha.
There's no rest as far as I'm concerned. Baby
Freddie wakes up screaming just the same as
always and I have to crawl out of my warm bed
and change his napkins and
give him his bottle, and by
the time he's settled
Louisa comes trailing in
clutching her doll and
Victor leaps up and starts
bouncing on his bed in his
nightgown and I have to
do my best to quieten
them, because it's Sunday.

They have to wear their Sunday best,
even the baby, and by the time I've got all three
laced and buttoned and booted, my chilblains throb
so bad I can barely do up my own clothes. It's my
Sunday best too, though my hideous servant
uniform is nothing to show off about. We all have
to go to church after breakfast. Louisa and Victor
are supposed to sit still in the pew, but of course
they swing their legs and nudge each other and

giggle and I get the
blame. If Freddie cries
the Master and
Mistress glare at me
and expect me to
stop him — but if he
really gets going then I'm allowed to take him out
of the church to carry him around outside. When
the Vicar is droning on and on I sometimes feel like
giving baby Freddie a sly pinch just to escape!

We were never really church folk at home. When
Father was alive us children were sent off to
Sunday School every week — but I think that was
just so Mother and Father had a bit of peace and
quiet without us. I liked Sunday School well enough,
because you were given a book every year if you
attended regularly. I liked singing the hymns too,
though the words sometimes made me ponder. 'All
things bright and beautiful' is pretty enough, but I
do not care for the part where it says God made
us high or lowly and each to our estate. In other
words, us servants must know our place.
Fiddlesticks!

I talked about this with Mrs Angel and Eliza
when we were having a cup of cocoa together at
the end of the long day. Eliza
giggled but Mrs Angel was
shocked. She said I was being
bad and blasphemous and
shooed me out of her kitchen.
But Mrs Angel was in a bad

294

mood anyway because she was so tired. Sunday is such a long boring day that everyone wants to eat all the time and she is forever serving meals, her huge roast beef and Yorkshire, with three puddings to follow, and scarcely have they eaten the last morsel than they're ringing the bell for afternoon tea.

The children are bored silly too, because they are not allowed to play with their usual toys. I am supposed to lock away Louisa's favourite doll and bring out her grand Sunday doll with her golden curls and cream silk clothes from France. Louisa admires this doll but does not dare carry her around for fear of mussing her. Victor is not allowed to play any rumbustious boys' games. He is supposed to occupy himself with a suitable Sunday story book, all instruction and no adventures. Victor finds this very dull fare.

It is usually easy to get the children to go to bed on Sundays because they are so eager for it to change to Monday!

I have been tormented these last few Sundays thinking of Mother. Mr Higgins closes the Dog and Duck on a Sunday. I have a terrible feeling that they might be stepping out together. I shall not be able to bear it if Mr Higgins becomes my new father. I did not care for my old father, but I shall care for this one even less.

LAW AND ORDER

We were all very quiet in the car going home. Jo and Mark kept giving little quick glances at each other. I couldn't stand it. They both seemed to have forgotten that there were passengers in the back.

I started singing stupid songs as loudly as I could.

'Charlie!' said Jo. 'For heaven's sake, you can't even sing in tune.'

'It's fun to sing in the car,' said Mark. 'Let's all have a sing-song, eh? What about "Ten Green Bottles"? We know that one, don't we, Robin?'

Robin didn't reply. He was scrunched up with Birdie's wing right over his face.

'Are you feeling sick again, Robin?' Jo asked, peering round at him.

No response.

'Is he asleep?' she whispered to me.

'I don't know,' I said, taking a deep breath for my next song.

'Shut up,' said Jo. 'Don't you dare wake him up.'

He wasn't actually asleep. Whenever we were on a brightly lit road I could see the gleam of his eye.

And when I went quiet I could just hear his snuffling above the car engine.

I should have reached out and given him a cuddle. I should have told him that he mustn't worry, of course his dad would still want him. I should have told Mark and Jo that he was crying.

I didn't. Oh, how I wish I had. But I didn't. I stayed hard and hating.

Mark dropped me and Jo off outside our flats.

'Thank you for a fantastic day out,' said Jo, putting her head so close to his that I thought she was going to kiss him again right in front of me. But she straightened out and he started to wind up his window.

'Say thank you, Charlie,' said Jo.

'Thank you,' I said, with absolutely no expression, total Dalek daughter.

'What the hell is the matter with you?' Jo exploded, the moment we were inside our own front door. 'You've been foul the entire day.'

'I'm surprised you noticed. You've only had eyes for one person all day long. Oooh Mark, how lovely, what a treat, gee-whizz how fantastic,' I said, imitating her gushing tone.

She blushed, but she tried to stare me out.

'Grow up a bit,' said Jo. 'You're acting like a toddler whose mum has started to talk to someone else. Surely you don't seriously mind that I've made one nice friend all by myself? You've got hundreds of friends, you always have done, and I've been thrilled you've got such a good independent social life. I've always been useless at making friends. And now for the first time ever I've found someone I get on with, why do you have to make all this fuss?'

'But he's not just a friend, is he?' I said.

'Yes, he is!'

'Don't give me that rubbish. I don't go round snogging my friends.'

'What?'

'You heard. I saw you. On that stupid Stardust ride.'

She went redder than ever, and now she couldn't meet my eyes.

I couldn't stand to look at her either. She looked so stupid and flushed and girlie, like Angela swooning over her beloved rock group or Lisa dithering over Dave Wood. But she was Jo. She was my mother. She was mine.

I didn't say another word to her all evening. We both went to bed early but we didn't sleep. We tossed and turned separately, a great gap in the middle of the bed.

It still seemed like night-time when the phone rang. Jo sat up, looking dazed. 'Have I slept in for work?' she said.

I peered at the alarm clock. 'It's only three o'clock. So who on earth's phoning . . . ?' I said, as I jumped out of bed and ran into the living room. 'Hello?' I said, as I snatched up the phone. 'Hello, who is it?'

'It's Mark here, Charlie.'

I couldn't believe it!

'Can I speak to Jo, please? It's urgent.'

I dropped the receiver as if it were burning me. Jo came rushing into the room.

'Who is it? What's going on?'

'It's only your *friend*,' I said. 'And he says it's *urgent*. Well, would you mind asking him to save his urgent little lovey-dovey messages till it's actually daylight. I'd like to get some sleep before I go to school, if it's all the same to you two lovebirds.'

'Do shut up, Charlie,' said Jo, picking up the receiver. 'Mark? What is it?' She was silent for a few seconds.

I started to do a mime of exaggerated kissing and then pretended to puke. But then I saw the shock on her face and I stopped the pantomime.

'What's happened?' I said.

'It's Robin,' said Jo. 'It's little Robin, he's gone missing.'

The words sizzled in my brain like an electric shock.

'Missing?' I whispered.

Jo was asking Mark heaps of questions, and I could hear the frantic tone of his answers.

'You're *sure* he's not just hiding somewhere? Under his bed? In one of the cupboards? Let me come over and search,' said Jo.

More talk.

'No, I want to come anyway. I'll be with you in ten minutes,' said Jo, and hung up.

She ran to the bathroom. I followed her.

299

She was on the loo, cleaning her teeth at the same time, shaking her head to wake herself up. She shook it again at me.

'Look, Charlie, I can't take any sneering from you just now. This is nothing to do with Mark and me. It's serious.'

'I know,' I said, biting my knuckle. 'Has Robin really run away?'

'I don't know! Mark woke up and he just popped his head into Robin's room to check up on him – he'd been a bit funny when he put him to bed after the day out – and – and he wasn't there. Mark says he's searched everywhere. I don't see how Robin could have got out the door and run off somewhere, I mean, he's such a timid little thing – oh God, I keep thinking of awful possibilities . . .' Jo was nearly in tears as she rushed round the bathroom and then ran back into the bedroom, pulling on jeans and a jacket over her nightie.

I started yanking on my own clothes too.

'Charlie? Look, you'd better not come. Go back to bed. Maybe you could phone the supermarket later if I'm not back. And you get yourself off to school and—'

'No! I'm coming too! Oh, Jo, something awful will have happened to him, won't it?' I clung to her as if I were a tiny kid myself.

'Hey, hey. We'll find him. He'll be OK,' said Jo, although neither of us believed it. 'Someone will have found him wandering about and—'

'But that's what I'm scared of. What if some really

creepy pervert gets hold of him and—'

'Don't. No. Look, he'll have just wandered down the road – maybe sleepwalking, something like that – and he'll be curled up in a doorway somewhere, perfectly safe, sound asleep.'

'But it's cold out – really cold for a kid like Robin. And if he was just wearing his pyjamas . . .'

'Mark said his school jumper's missing too – and his slippers.'

The thought of Robin setting off in his new too-big school jumper, his pyjamas and his scuffed slippers made me bite my knuckle almost to the bone.

The lights were all on in Mark's flat – and there was a police car outside.

'There! They've found him,' said Jo, taking my hand and hauling us both up the stairs.

But they hadn't found him. Mark had called the police and was telling them over and over again how he'd looked in on Robin's room, and he wasn't in his bed, and he'd gone to the bathroom, he'd gone to the kitchen, gone round and round every room in the house, calling and calling . . . His voice was hoarse now, and his face looked dreadful, pale grey and shiny. He caught hold of Jo but this was different; he was just so desperate to get Robin back safe and she might be able to help.

I might be able to help.

I had to tell them.

I opened my mouth but I couldn't get the words out.

'Don't worry,' said this young policewoman, patting my shoulder. 'We're doing our very best to find him. We've sent out his description and everyone's searching. Children go missing every week – and they nearly always turn up safe and sound.'

'Not kids as little as Robin. It's all my fault,' I said. 'I made him run away. I even gave him that little cake with GET LOST on it.'

'Oh, come on, Charlie – that was silly, yes, but that's got nothing to do with it,' said Jo.

'But I said . . . I said all this hateful stuff . . . when we saw you kissing . . .' I waited.

Mark put his hands on my shoulders. His hands dug right into me. 'What did you say, Charlie?'

'I – I – it was so awful . . .'

'I don't care how awful. You've got to tell us. It might give us some clue where he's gone. I've been running round the streets this past hour, everywhere he goes, down to the shop on the corner, up the road to the park, he's not anywhere – I've looked, I've called – and yet how could he have got further, just wearing his slippers, and he hates going for walks, and he'd never go off willingly without me . . .' Mark's voice cracked.

'I told him you wouldn't want him any more,' I whispered. 'I didn't really mean it, I said I was joking, but – but it was a horrible thing to say to him, I'm so sorry, it made him cry in the car going home

302

and I didn't tell and it's so awful and if anything's happened to him—'

'Nothing will have happened to him,' Jo said, putting her arm round me. We're nearly the same height and yet I seemed to have shrunk and she'd become a great big enveloping mother. 'We'll find him, I promise you, we'll find him.' She was promising Mark too, saying it over and over, trying to convince us.

'What did Robin say when you said all this?' Mark persisted.

'He mentioned his mum. Could he have run away to see her?' I asked.

'She lives in Manchester. How could he possibly . . . ? But I know he's been missing her ever since his last visit. Though he always said he wanted to stay with me when I talked to him about it. Oh, Charlie, *how* could you tell him I didn't want him?' said Mark, tears running down his face.

He wasn't angry with me. Yet. This was far worse. I started to cry too.

'It was a terrible thing to say but you were angry and upset,' said Jo. 'Everyone says terrible things when they feel really bad. Stop it Mark, she's only a kid herself. Can't you see how desperately sorry she is? Don't blame her, blame me. I forced her into that day out. She wasn't ready for it. We've been too close . . .'

I listened to Jo sticking up for me, making all these excuses. It made me feel worse, the worst person in the whole world.

303

Messages kept crackling over the police radio clipped to the policewoman's shoulder. We froze each time – but it was never to say they'd found him.

'I've got to go and search for him again myself,' said Mark.

'It'll be light soon. I should wait till then,' said the policewoman.

'But Robin's frightened of the dark—'

'He's probably tucked up in a corner somewhere, fast asleep. We've alerted everyone available. They're all searching. We've got the helicopter up too. It's got this special thermal imaging sweep that works even in the dark. The scanner picks up heat from the body—'

'The body?' said Mark, his voice cracking.

'From the person, from your little boy, and it gives off a green image. It's an amazing invention; we've had great success with it.'

But Mark couldn't wait, couldn't stay still, so he went off in one of the patrol cars cruising the area. Jo and I waited in his flat with the policewoman. She made us a cup of tea but when I drank it down it made me feel so sick I only just got to the toilet in time. I splashed cold water on my face afterwards and stared at myself in Mark's bathroom mirror. I felt I was looking at a murderer.

I've never really felt bad about myself before. I could be cheeky, I could be bossy, I could be fierce – but I'd always thought I was one of the good guys. If any little kid at school was getting bullied I'd always charge in and send the bully flying. If anything needed sorting out then all the other kids would turn to me. Everybody liked me. Even the boys.

But now I'd done the meanest thing in the whole world. It didn't matter that I was sorry. Robin had run away and maybe he was going to be lost for ever.

I felt myself folding up so that I was crouching on the bathroom floor, my head banging against the cold edge of the bath. I shut my eyes tight, banging and banging, trying to knock myself backwards, trying to make time tick backwards, so that I could undo and unsay everything. But no matter how I tried I couldn't stop the hands on my watch moving forward, and every minute Robin was still missing.

I heard the whirr of the police helicopter overhead. I wondered if they'd be able to spot Robin staggering along a grass verge, crouching down beside a hedge, curled beneath a tree. He might look up and show Birdie this immense mechanical relation . . . No, if he heard the whirling noise he'd probably be frightened and hide in a doorway, a cardboard box, behind a dustbin, and then he'd never be spotted.

I could see him so vividly in my head, crying, shivering with the cold, clutching Birdie desperately. And then I saw a sinister shadow beside him, someone reaching out and grabbing him, a hand over

305

his mouth so that he couldn't scream . . .

'Charlie? Charlie, let me in.' It was Jo, knocking on the door.

But I needed to stay in there by myself. I scrunched up tight into a ball and I closed my eyes and I mumbled, Please let Robin be all right, Please let Robin be all right, Please let Robin be all right, over and over, until the words concertinaed. I didn't dare stop even for a second – not until I heard the front door bang.

I rushed out of the bathroom. More police. And Mark – holding something small and shabby in his hands.

'Robin?' I whispered.

Mark shook his head. 'I went to the park,' he said, his voice breaking. 'It's still too dark to see properly, but I thought I'd check the pond – I always take him there to feed the ducks. And he's not there – no sign of him – but over by the gate the police officer stood on something. He thought it was a dead bird . . .'

Mark held out the cloth wings and the stained scarlet chest. Birdie.

LAW AND ORDER

Oh my Lord! Baby Freddie is missing and I fear it is all my fault.

I was worn out and near to despairing with all three children. Freddie kept me up half the night wailing and whimpering, then Louisa would *not* wear her proper day dress and insisted on putting on her party silk — and then spilt her porridge all down the front. Victor gave me cheek all morning and when I remonstrated he kicked me hard upon the shin.

I was so cross with my disagreeable and disobedient charges that when we were in the public gardens together I parked the perambulator and stormed off for a few moments by myself, calling all three children as many bad names as I could think of under my breath. When I had calmed down a little I went back again. There was no sound from the perambulator so I assumed baby Freddie had gone to sleep at last. Louisa was over by the pond, feeding the ducks with crusts of stale bread begged from Mrs Angel, while Victor bowled his hoop round and round the pond, singing a vulgar song at the top of his voice.

I told him to hush and begged Louisa to take
care because she was standing right on the edge.
Louisa took no notice and hurled a crust wildly,
lost her balance and toppled over into the water!
The pond is not deep but Louisa went headlong. I
had to hitch up my skirts to wade in and grab her.
Louisa clutched at me wildly, convinced she was
drowning — and over I toppled too.
Victor shrieked with laughter
at the pair of us. I had duck-
weed streaming from my hair
when I struggled out at last,
Louisa under one arm. We
were both sopping wet.

'Quick! Home at once before
we catch our death of cold,' I
said, shivering, conscious that we
made a right spectacle. I took hold of the
perambulator handle — and peered at the
pillow. No baby Freddie! I pulled back the blankets
frantically, tossing the pillow to one side.
He was gone! I ran desperately
around the perambulator,
wondering if he could possibly
have clambered out by himself.
I wondered if Victor was
playing another prank on me
but one look at his white face
made me see that this time he
wasn't joking.

Someone had snatched baby Freddie and stolen

him away! I stopped passers-by and asked them if they had seen the little mite. Someone said they'd seen an infant in the arms of some scoundrelly looking creature and I started shrieking. I ran home with Victor and Louisa, pushing the empty perambulator. I had to tell the Mistress. I could scarce get the words out. She had a fit of the vapours at the terrible news and Eliza had to fetch the smelling bottle. Mrs Angel ran down the road to find her policeman friend and he took all the particulars. He swears he will search every thieves' den in the town, for he thinks Freddie has been stolen to be held to ransom. He is going to write to the police station in the neighbouring district, and a piece will be put in the *Police Gazette*.

He said that once he catches the varmint responsible he will have him publicly flogged and if he has harmed the baby then he will hang by the neck until he is dead.

Oh my Lord, I am so scared. If only I hadn't stormed off like that. If only I had kept a watch on the perambulator all the time! If only, if only, if only!

SICKNESS

'They'll find him,' Jo kept saying. 'He'll be in the park. Or nearby. They'll find him when it's light. He'll have just fallen asleep now, Mark, that's all.'

'The helicopter hasn't tracked him down. And we've looked everywhere. All over the park,' said Mark, hugging Birdie to his chest. 'We called and called. They're still there now, calling. If he was asleep he'd wake up and hear. He could be in the pond – they're going to dredge it. He could be lying in a ditch somewhere—'

'Don't think like that, Sir. There's no reason to think the worst,' said the policewoman. 'I've been with parents so many times, and they've been going through agonies like this but it's always turned out well in the end—'

'That's right, Mark. We've got to be positive,' said Jo, putting her arm round him. She held her other arm out to me. 'Come here, Charlie.' But I couldn't go. I felt too ashamed. Police came, police went. The phone rang but it was Mark's ex-wife, ringing from an all-night motorway café. She was on her way here with her

310

new man, desperate to know if there was any further news. The policewoman made more tea, endless cups, although no-one took more than a few sips of each fresh brew. Someone switched on the radio at six and tuned it into the local station.

'*A five-year-old boy is missing from his home in Newcombe Way,*' said a voice. '*Little Robin West is small and slight, dark hair, dark eyes, believed to be wearing nightclothes and a grey sweater . . .*'

It made it all so horribly real hearing Robin's name on the radio. Everyone's head jerked at the sound.

More news bulletins kept tuning into my head. Imaginary ones with terrible news. I put my hands over my ears, but I couldn't block out the sound of my own thoughts.

Then the police radio crackled again, and the policewoman answered it.

'You're sure? He's OK?'

We all stared, hardly daring to hope.

'Robin?' said Mark, springing up.

'Yes, I think it is!' said the policewoman. 'Small boy, dark hair, found at the railway station. He'd crawled behind a whole pile of parcels awaiting delivery, so no-one spotted him at first.'

'He's all right?' said Mark, tears pouring down his face.

'I think so, Sir – but freezing cold, so they're taking him straight to the hospital. We'll take you there right away.'

311

'We have to go too,' said Jo, pulling me up.

I didn't dare believe it until we got to the hospital. I kept thinking it would be some other little boy – it couldn't be Robin because I was so sure he was lost for ever now, and that it was all my fault, and that I would hate myself for the rest of my life.

Jo knew, and held my hand very tight all the way there, and when Mark ran forward at the hospital Jo elbowed our way through too.

'She has to see him, just for a few seconds,' she said when nurses tried to catch hold of us.

There was something so commanding in her voice that they let us through. There were more nurses at a bed, a doctor with a stethoscope, a policeman, all circling a narrow bed containing a small tinfoil parcel like a chicken ready to be roasted for Sunday dinner. A flushed face peered out of one end, a smaller bird than a chicken. A Robin.

'Oh, Robin!' I whispered. 'It really is you!'

He didn't hear me. He was too busy blinking up at Mark.

'Daddy!' he said. 'What are you doing here?'

'What are *you* doing here, you silly sausage?' said Mark, and he bent and kissed the tiny bit of Robin that was exposed. 'Oh, Robin, you've led us a merry dance! What did you run away for? We've been so scared.'

'I was scared too. I wanted Mummy—'

'Mummy's coming. She'll be here soon. And you can see her for as long as you like. But Robin, you do know we *both* love you and want you. You're the most important little guy in my life. I was so frightened when I found your bed empty.'

'I had a nasty dream and I wanted Mummy so I got Birdie and we thought we'd go and see her.'

'In Manchester? But Robin, how could you possibly think you could walk to Manchester?' said Mark.

'You get the train. You took me once. We went through the park to the station so that's what we did, Birdie and me, but when we went past the pond the ducks woke up and quacked at us and scared us and then . . . and then . . .' Robin burst into tears.

'You dropped Birdie – but look, Robin, look!' said Mark, producing Birdie, who flew down onto Robin's chest, one wing touching his cheek. 'Birdie's got more sense than you, Robin. He flew home to Daddy.'

I wanted to talk to Robin myself, to tell him how sorry I was.

'Not now,' said Jo, pulling me away. 'He just needs Mark. And we don't want to be here when his mother comes. We'll go home.'

It seemed extraordinary to be back at our flat, having breakfast at the usual time. Whole weeks seemed to have gone by since yesterday.

'You ought really to go back to bed,' said Jo. 'You look exhausted.'

I was far too wound up to sleep. 'I still can't believe he's safe!' I said.

'I said he would be!' said Jo, hugging me.

'Don't, Jo. You've been so nice to me. When I was so wicked.'

'But you didn't mean it.'

'I should still be terribly punished.'

'Well, what do you want me to do? Whip you? Shut you up in a cupboard for a week? Shave all your lovely long hair off and paint you purple?'

'I mean it, Jo. I feel . . . bad. Robin *will* be all right now, won't he?'

'Yes, of course. Once they've got him all warmed up and checked over then I'm sure he'll be able to go home.'

'And can we go round and see him straight away?'

'Well, not if his mother's there too. I don't want to look as if I'm butting in. And maybe this might bring them back together again as a family . . .'

I didn't dare ask her if she'd mind terribly.

Jo went off to the supermarket to explain why she was so late – and I went to school.

Lisa and Angela came charging up to me the minute I set foot in the classroom.

'Hey, Charlie! Did you hear on the radio? That little boy who went missing, Robin. Isn't he the one your mum looks after?'

So I had to say yes, and then when I told them we'd been with Robin's dad half the night and that I'd actually seen Robin in the hospital they asked me dozens of questions, and practically all the class gathered round wanting to hear. So I had to turn it into a proper story and spin it out a bit while they all gasped and exclaimed. They didn't even quieten down when Miss Beckworth swept into the room and told everyone to go to their seats.

'Miss Beckworth, Charlie's practically headline news, she helped find that little boy. Tell Miss Beckworth, Charlie!'

So I told the story all over again, though I was starting to tire of the whole tale. It didn't seem right that even Miss Beckworth seemed mildly impressed. But then she asked the one question I was dreading. Trust her.

'Why did the little boy run away, I wonder?'

I just shrugged and backed away to my desk, sharpish.

Jamie stared at me, looking a little puzzled. 'I love the way you tell things, Charlie. Making it ever so exciting and funny,' he said.

I made little slurpy noises with my lips, to show I thought he was sucking up to me.

'But did it all really happen?' Jamie persisted.

'Yes! What do you think I am, some kind of nutter with a compulsion to tell blatant lies to everyone?'

'But how come your mum looks after this little boy? I thought you said she was a lecturer, like mine?'

315

I took a deep breath, thinking hard. A blatant lie indeed. Well, call it an elaborate evasion. It was time for another.

'She lost that job, right? So for the moment she . . . she teaches little Robin.'

I had to tell my story all over again at playtime to kids in different classes, and they went off and told other kids, so that by dinner time it was all over the school. There were many different versions by this time. Some assumed that my mum and Robin's dad were already a definite item, which infuriated me.

HERO!

Others gave me an even more prominent role in the story, so that I'd gone out in the early morning and tracked Robin through the park to the station all by myself. It was starting to turn into a story about how I'd saved little Robin's life.

It was a relief when school was over at last. I went rushing straight home, wondering if Jo would be round at Mark's place with Robin.

But she was at home, looking tired out herself, pulling fluff out of her bunny jumper, pick pick pick.

'Is Mark's ex-wife round at his place then?' I asked delicately.

'I think she's at the hospital. With Mark,' said Jo.

'What? Is Robin still there then?' I paused. 'He is OK, isn't he?'

Jo's fingers fidgeted down the sleeve of her fluffy jumper. 'Well, I'm sure he's going to be OK, yes, but . . .'

'But what? Tell me!'

'I don't really know much. Mark only had ten pence for the phone. He just said that the doctor was a bit worried about Robin's chest—'

'His chest?'

'Apparently he's always been slightly asthmatic, and he did get very chilled, so now he's got a touch of pneumonia.'

'Pneumonia! People die of pneumonia!'

'Now calm down, Charlie. There's no need to get yourself all worked up. I promise Robin's not going to die—'

'You promised he'd be as right as rain, out of hospital as soon as they'd got him warmed up.'

'Well, he *will* be as right as rain. They'll just need to give him some antibiotics.'

'And people always get completely better after pneumonia if they take antibiotics?'

'Well, nearly always. How do I know anyway?'

'Let's go and see him now.'

'I shouldn't imagine he can have too many visitors. He'll need to be kept quiet. He's got his dad – and his mum.' Jo's jumper was going to be picked bald quite soon.

'Couldn't we go to the hospital just to ask if we could see him for two minutes?' I said.

'No, we can't just keep pushing in,' said Jo.

I kept going on at her. I can always wear her down. I had to see Robin again. I hadn't been able to talk to him when he was trussed up in tinfoil like a tiny turkey. I had to tell him something.

317

But I still didn't get a chance. We found our way to the children's ward and it was still visiting time so we walked the long length of the polished floor, looking for Robin. There was no sign of him.

We walked back again, pausing at every bed. There was one empty one and I suddenly took Jo's hand.

'Can I help you?' said a nurse, hurrying past.

'We're looking for Robin West,' said Jo anxiously. 'He's the little boy who was lost.'

'Yes, I know. He's in the side ward up at the end – but I'm not sure he should have any more visitors,' said the nurse.

'There, Charlie,' said Jo. 'I told you.'

'Couldn't we just put our heads round the door to say hello?' I pleaded.

'I suppose you can take a quick peep, if you promise to be quiet,' said the nurse.

'As a mouse,' I said.

When we got near the side ward we walked on tiptoe, though the polish made our shoes squeak like real mice. We were still hand in hand. Our clasp was clammy.

I put my head round the door first. There was Mark, sitting right by the bed, his head in his hands. A pretty blonde woman with a pinched face was wiping her red eyes. And there was Robin lying very still in bed, his face milky white, his eyes closed. Birdie was on his chest, wings spread.

'He's dead!' I burst out, forgetting all about my promise to be quiet.

Robin stirred and whimpered.

'Who on earth . . . ?' said the blonde woman, glaring at me.

'What do you want, Charlie?' said Mark, standing up. His grey face was going patchy red with anger. 'Haven't you done enough?'

'I just wanted to say . . . I'm sorry,' I said.

'Oh, that makes all the difference in the world, does it?' said Mark.

Jo was tugging at me to get me to go. 'We shouldn't have come. We were both just so worried about Robin,' she muttered. 'Come *on*, Charlie.'

'He is going to get better, isn't he?' I said desperately.

Mark ignored me but touched Jo on the shoulder to reassure her. The blonde woman tightened her eyebrows.

'He's still got a high temperature but they're pumping him full of antibiotics and they keep saying he'll be fine,' he said. Then his eyes swivelled to me. 'No thanks to you.'

I let Jo tug me out of the doorway and out of the ward. We had to wait a long while for a bus outside the hospital and then it was a twenty-minute walk home. Jo kept talking to me but I hardly said anything.

She thought it was because I was scared of crying

in public. When we got home at last she put her arms round me and said, 'Right, you can let it all out now. Have a really good cry and then you'll feel better.'

I did cry a bit. Jo did too. I don't know whether she felt better. I didn't.

I felt really bad at school the next day. Angela and Lisa still kept on about Robin, asking if I'd seen him and how he was, wanting me to tell them all about it.

'Look, I don't really want to talk about Robin,' I said.

'What are you on about? You did nothing *but* talk about Robin yesterday,' said Lisa.

'OK, OK. That was yesterday. This is today, right? Let's talk about something *else*,' I said.

Angela immediately started burbling about the birthsigns of her beloveds and I groaned and pretended to gag.

'There's no need to take that attitude,' said Angela, hurt. 'You told me to talk about something else, so I did. There's no pleasing you sometimes, Charlie.'

'Hey, my dad says he's still taking us to the Red River Theme Park for my birthday,' said Lisa. 'Which rides are the best, Charlie? Come on, you didn't get a chance to tell us yesterday.'

'No!' I said fiercely.

'You can be a right pain sometimes, Charlie,' said Lisa huffily. 'There's me inviting you out on my birthday treat and yet you just shout at me.'

'Yeah, I can't stick it when you throw a moody like this,' said Angela. 'You think you can treat us like dirt, Charlie Enright, but we might just start to get fed up with it. Isn't that right, Lisa?'

'You bet,' said Lisa. 'Come on, Angela.'

They walked off across the playground arm in arm. I was left all by myself.

I decided I didn't care a bit. There were lots of other girls desperate to be my friend. Or even boys. Like Jamie.

I went and found him in his usual place, head deep in a book. Still *Tess of the d'Urbervilles*, but he'd nearly finished it, even though it's hundreds and hundreds of pages long.

'You'll go cross-eyed reading so much,' I said, flopping down beside him. 'Are you really enjoying that?'

'It's great,' said Jamie. 'Here, Tess murders this guy at the end, the one who had his wicked way with her – Alec.'

'The one she had the baby with?' I said. I tried to remember the film, but I just had this hazy picture of pretty girls in white frocks doing a dance, and afterwards Jo and I had done our own dance in our white nighties. 'Did Tess have a daughter or a son?'

'A little boy.'

'So what happens to him? I don't think there was a little boy in the film.'

'No, he dies when he's a baby.'

'What of?'

'I don't know. I don't think it says.'

'Babies don't just *die*.'

'They did then. Especially little puny ones. They just need to get a little cold and then it develops into pneumonia or something—'

'Shut up!' I shouted.

Jamie jumped. 'What's up?' he said. 'Hey, Charlie – where are you going?'

I didn't know where I was going. I wanted to get away from him, away from Lisa and Angela, away from the whole school . . .

I made for the gate, deciding to make a dash for it and bunk off school for the afternoon. But Miss Beckworth was on playground duty and her eagle eyes were beady-bright.

'Charlotte Enright! Where on earth do you think you're going, young lady?' she called.

I was so desperate I kept on running but I collided with a bunch of little kids coming back into school after going home for dinner. I tripped as I dodged them and fell flat.

I heard them squealing excitedly. Ominous footsteps paused by my side. I didn't try to get up. I just lay where I was – and cried.

'Out of the way, children. There's no need to gawp. Off you go. Shoo!' said Miss Beckworth. She seemed to be bending down beside me. 'Charlotte?'

I howled harder.

'I need to know if you've really hurt yourself badly and need medical attention,' said Miss Beckworth. 'Can you try and sit up so we can examine the damage?'

So I had to sit up, snivelling and snorting. I'd cut my knee and grazed the other, but it was nothing much. Certainly nothing to cry about. Though I was spouting like a fountain.

Some other kids were coming nearer, eyes popping at the sight of Charlie Enright bawling her eyes out.

'Will you go *away*, please?' Miss Beckworth said briskly. 'Charlotte, you'd better come with me.'

She put her hand under my armpits and got me to my feet. She walked me across the playground, shielding me from the stares. She took me right into school and sat me down in the empty classroom.

'There.' She looked at me, and felt up her sleeve for a tissue. 'Use this.'

I blew and mopped.

'That's better. Now. What's the matter?'

'I'm not crying because I fell over,' I said.

'I realize that.'

'And I'm not crying because I shouted at Jamie. Though I feel bad about that.'

'I expect Jamie's used to your shouting at him,' said Miss Beckworth drily.

'And I shouted at Lisa and Angela too and I think they've broken friends with me, but I'm not crying about that either,' I said.

'So . . . what are you crying about?'

I said nothing.

'The little boy who was lost?'

I nodded. 'He's ill. He's got pneumonia. Everyone says he's going to be all right, but I'm so scared that maybe . . .' I cried harder.

'Now, calm down, Charlotte. I haven't got any more tissues! You mustn't worry. Look, I've had pneumonia myself and I recovered perfectly. I know you're obviously very fond of this little boy—'

'No, I'm not! I've been horrid to him. *That's* why I'm crying. You think I'm being all kind and concerned but it's because I've been so bad.'

'Oh dear,' said Miss Beckworth. 'Go on. I think I'm pretty shockproof after twenty-five years of teaching. So tell me.'

So I did. All of it. And stuff about Jo and me from way back. Stuff I'd never dream of telling anyone – let alone *Miss Beckworth*.

She listened to it all – and then she put her arm round me and let me cry on her shoulder even though I was all slurpy and snotty.

'I know you think you're all-powerful, but the little boy didn't run away *just* because of you,' said Miss Beckworth. 'You're only a little part of all this. You were a bit silly and spiteful but you're truly sorry now – and you certainly didn't mean any of this to happen. I'm sure the little boy will get better.'

'You're really sure?' I said, sniffing. 'Because you're never wrong about anything, are you?'

324

'That's right!' said Miss Beckworth. 'Now, you'd better run along and wash that poor old face. Try to cheer up, Charlie.'

It wasn't until I was right along in the girls' cloak-rooms that I realized. Miss Beckworth had called me *Charlie*!

SICKNESS

He's been found! I can scarcely believe it. Little
Freddie is back with us — though we are all still so
worried about the poor lamb because he is sick.

   He wasn't taken by thieves and robbers. It was
a woman half-demented because all her own
babies had died. She watched us in the public
gardens, she admired Freddie's chubby cheeks and
golden curls — and when Louisa fell in the pond
and I rushed in after her this woman snatched our
Freddie and made off with him.

   She was all set to make him her child, but her
brain was so addled she scarcely fed our poor
little boy and left his napkin unchanged. She
covered him with just one thin sheet at night and
of course the poor child caught a chill. She took
fright as he grew dangerously sick and eventually she wrapped him in her cloak and left
him on the doorstep of the
foundling hospital. (She was
observed and followed, and is
now in police custody.)

   The Master and Mistress were sent
for when Freddie was found and great was their

rejoicing — but their joy turned to terror when they saw the state of their poor darling. They took him home and we put him straight to bed and called the doctor. He listened to Freddie's rasping breathing and felt his fevered brow.

'There is nothing I can do', he said sorrowfully. 'Keep him warm, feed him sugared water, and let us hope the Good Lord sees fit to spare him.'

The Mistress and I have been taking turns to nurse him. For once we are not like Mistress and servant at all. We are more like sisters, united in our desire for Freddie to recover. I feel as much for Freddie now as little Ada—May at home.

Victor and Louisa are being as good as gold. Eliza is looking after them, while I nurse Freddie. Mrs Angel is forever bringing him bowls of nourishing broth but the poor mite is too poorly to even suck the spoon.

Oh, please let him be saved!

SEASIDE

We were back to Charlotte the next day. We had English first lesson, one of those boring writing exercises – a formal letter of apology. It seemed a perfect opportunity to make things up with Lisa and Angela. (I didn't need to go to letter-writing lengths with Jamie as I was sitting right beside him. I could just give him a nudge and mumble, 'Sorry I yelled at you to shut up. You can tell me to shut up some time if you want.' Jamie blinked at me. 'I'd have to make sure you were in a good mood first!' he said – displaying his famous intelligence.)

Anyway, I got cracking with my apology letter. I think I did it beautifully, in my very best hand-writing, no blotches, no smears. I put my address at the right-hand corner, I remembered the date, I flaunted an amazingly varied vocabulary, I didn't make a single spelling mistake, I signed off appropriately, and I even personally decorated my piece of paper. You look:

My Desk
Miss Beckworth's Class
Avondale Junior School

Truly Terrible Tuesday

Dear Lisa and Angela,
   Do not rip this letter up in disgust when you see
it's from the appalling, beastly, crosspatch, dolthead,
egotistic, foul, gross, horrible, irritating, jealous,
knavish, loathsome, mangy, nerve—wracking, odious,
presumptuous, quarrelsome, ratty, spoilt, terrible,
unkind, verminous, wicked, X—rated, yucky, zero
   called Charlotte Alice Katherine Enright
       (commonly known as Charlie), who used to
       be your friend. No wonder you both broke
       friends with me! I have been Utterly Foul
       (though with just cause seeing as I've had
       Terrible Things on my Mind) but that is no
       excuse to be hateful to you two, who are the
dearest sweetest kindest friends any girl could
ever wish for. And if I had a wish it would
be this: Please will you make friends with
me again?
   Yours utterly sincerely — and with
lots of luv and XXXXXXXX
   Charlie

UTTERLY FOUL

wish wish wish wish

   Jamie read my letter over my shoulder (I let him
because I was trying so hard to be a new sweet
person) and he cracked up laughing.

329

'That's a merry sound, James – but a little in-appropriate in a classroom,' said Miss Beckworth. 'Please tell me why you're laughing.'

Jamie had long since stopped laughing. He had gone red and stammery. 'I – I was just clearing my throat, Miss Beckworth,' he said.

'I not only have all-seeing eyes, James. I also have all-hearing ears. You were not clearing your throat. You were laughing. Why?'

Jamie shifted desperately on his chair. He's so weird, he gets so worried the rare times he gets told off. I expected him to blurt out that he'd laughed because of my letter but he kept his lip buttoned to try to keep me out of trouble. Which was sweet of him, but a total waste of time.

Miss Beckworth was looking at me, eyebrows raised, one arm extended. 'Bring me that piece of paper, Charlotte. How dare you mess around instead of getting on with your set written work.'

'It *is* my written work, Miss Beckworth,' I said, taking it out to her.

She read my letter. For one second her lips twitched – and I thought I was going to be OK. No such luck.

'This is *not* a formal letter of apology, Charlotte,' said Miss Beckworth.

'It *is* – sort of,' I insisted unwisely. 'You know what I'm like, Miss Beckworth. I always have to do things my way.'

'I appreciate that, Charlotte. There is just one small point you seem to have missed. This is my class, not yours. In my class we do things *my* way. And you will do me a proper sensible sticking-to-the-rules formal letter of apology now, and you will write out another *five* formal letters of apology, all different, at home tonight. That might make you reflect a little and learn that it makes more sense to do things my way right from the start.'

That was the most amazingly atrocious punishment of all time – especially as I wanted to do something extremely important and very time-consuming that evening. But even I realized it would be unwise to argue further. It seemed utterly unbelievable that such a cruel unbending beastly teacher could have let me cry all over her jumper just yesterday, but there you go.

The one weeny good thing was that she gave me my original letter back, so I could give it to Angela and Lisa at playtime. They laughed too. Lots. And we're best friends all over again, so at least that's something.

I got started on my five foul letters the minute I got home. It took me ages but I knew it would be foolish to fudge them. I actually wrote a sixth letter, just a little one.

Dear Miss Beckworth,

This is partly yet another formal letter of apology. I am sorry I mess around at everything. I will truly try to do things your way. Though it will be very very difficult.

This is also an informal letter of thanks. Thank

you for letting me say all that stupid stuff on Monday. Sorry I used up your tissues! And you were right, because Robin is lots better!

Yours sincerely,
Charlotte

Mark might have made it plain that he wanted nothing to do with me, but he phoned Jo to tell her that Robin's temperature had gone down, his chest was clear, and the antibiotics were obviously doing their job well.

'So is Robin properly awake now, sitting up and able to look at things?' I asked.

'Yes, but I'm not taking you to the hospital again, no matter what you say,' said Jo.

'It's OK. I can see we can't go. Mark really hates me now, doesn't he?' I said.

'No, of course he doesn't. He's just still terribly wound up and anxious over Robin,' said Jo.

'And he blames me.'

'He wasn't thinking straight.'

'Look, *I* blame me. But it's just sort of weird. Being hated by someone.'

'He doesn't hate you, I keep saying that. And anyway, it doesn't even matter if he does because you don't have to see him ever again. He probably won't want me to work for him any more, let alone . . .' Jo's voice tailed away. She looked so miserable I couldn't bear it.

'Jo? I'm sorry I've mucked things up for you and him,' I mumbled.

Jo gave me a push. 'What rubbish! You're not the slightest bit sorry about that, Charlie! You did your level best to spoil things right from the start. And I don't know why you're carrying on about Mark not liking you, because you made it amazingly plain that you hated him.'

'Yes, I know. I couldn't stand it when he smarmed all over me, and kept trying to take my side. But now . . . I still don't like him but I want him to like me.'

'That's just typical of you, you spoilt brat,' said Jo. 'Have you finished all your letters? Shall we go to bed and watch telly for a bit?'

'*You're* the one that spoilt me! Not that I blame you, of course. Seeing as I'm so chock full of charm.'

'Ha! Come on, I can't be too late. I daren't mess them about at the supermarket after missing my Monday shift.'

'I want to do a bit of drawing first. You go. I promise I won't wake you if you go to sleep first, I'll creep in ever so quietly.'

I sat up for hours doing my drawing. I drew a bed in the middle of the page, with a pale little boy and a tiny toy bird propped up on the pillows. Then in all the rest of the space I did an immense flock of birds come to wish Robin and Birdie better. I did great eagles and albatrosses swooping round the ceiling, parrots and cockatoos and canaries singing silly songs, soft doves fanning him with their feathers, lovebirds billing and cooing above his head, tiny wrens whizzing every which way while swallows flitted in strict formation, ostriches and emus picking their way cautiously across the polished floor, little fluffy chicks cheeping in clumps, proud peacocks spreading their tails as screens around the bed.

I coloured it all in as carefully as I could, until my

eyes watered and my hand ached. But it was done at long last – and I just hoped Robin would like it.

Jo came rushing in to tell me *she* liked it at half past five in the morning.

'Hey! I didn't wake you up last night,' I grumbled under the covers. 'Can you stick it in an envelope and post it to Robin at the hospital?'

Jo said she would – but when I got home from school that day she told me she'd taken it to the hospital herself.

'It would have spoilt it, folding it all up to fit into an envelope. So I took it to the hospital after I'd been to the Rosens'. I was just going to give it to one of the nurses but then I bumped into Mark quite by chance . . .'

'Oh yeah!'

'What are you looking at me like that for? Anyway, he seemed quite happy about me having a peep at Robin, and he's doing wonderfully. They think he can come out of hospital by the end of the week. And I showed him your picture and he just loves it, Charlie; he spent ages and ages looking at all the different birds and now he's got it pinned up on the wall beside his bed. Mark was so pleased. He looks a bit better himself now that Robin's recovering. He's taken the next week off his work too, and he's talking about taking Robin to the seaside.'

'With Robin's mum?'

'Ah. No. She's had to go back to Manchester – when she knew Robin was going to be all right.'

'Has that upset him?'

'Well. He obviously misses his mother a great deal, but Mark was always the one who looked after him most even when they were together.'

'She looked a right cow to me,' I said.

'Charlie!' said Jo. But she looked pleased.

'What about Mark? Does he miss her too?'

'Well . . . He doesn't seem to, no. He said things were never very good between them, and they had all these rows—'

'Yeah, listen and proceed cautiously, Josephine! *That's* what marriage is all about. Rows,' I said, wagging my finger at her. 'Don't you dare think of ever getting married, right?'

I did another picture for Robin that night. This time I drew him in a warm red woolly jumper with a pair of massive feathery wings sticking out the back, brown to match his trousers, real robin colours, and he and Birdie were flying over the sea with a flock of seagulls, and they all had sticks of rock or candy-floss or portions of fish and chips in their beaks and way down below there was a beach and everyone was waving and pointing and smiling up at them.

Jo took it in to Robin at the hospital. This time I got my own picture back. It was a portrait of me. Well, it had my name on it in very wobbly letters. My hair was an orange scribble right down past my knees. My eyes were crossed. My arms stuck straight out of my neck. My legs were mostly hidden beneath a triangle of green frock, but my feet were vast and stuck out sideways.

'Hmmm,' I said. 'Is this supposed to be flattering?'

'He tried ever so hard,' said Jo. 'This was his third attempt.'

'What's this pointy thing sticking in me? A dagger? Did Mark add that?'

'It's an arrow, pointing to you, to show you're Charlie. And Mark doesn't want to stick any daggers in you, you daft girl. In fact he wants you to come to the hospital tomorrow to see Robin.'

'Oh, wow, His Lordship has given his orders, eh?' I said.

'Charlie?' said Jo. 'Oh, don't be like that.'

'Don't look so worried. I'll go. To see Robin.'

'Are you going to do him another picture?'

'How about one he can eat?'

I wanted to make him a proper robin cake in the shape of a bird, but I couldn't work out how to do it, and the wing tips and little claws would be far too

337

fiddly and break off. So in the end I made two ordinary round sponges and sandwiched them together with lots of butter cream and jam and then I made up this super brown butter icing with a bit of cocoa powder and smeared it over most of the cake, doing an extra feathery layer each side for wings, and then I stuck on two brown smarties for eyes and a yellow one for the beak, and I filled in the gap with new bright-red butter icing.

It all took much longer than I'd thought, and the robin cake still didn't look quite right.

'It's wonderful!' said Jo.

'No, it looks like the robin's been severely squashed,' I said, sighing.

I really wanted to stay up all night and try again, but I'd used up all the eggs and icing sugar and practically half our housekeeping money, so I couldn't.

I kept worrying about the stupid cake the next day at school. Or maybe I was worrying about going to the hospital. Or something.

I took my time going home from school.

'Come on, what kept you?' said Jo. 'We won't get there in time for Robin's tea at this rate.'

'I don't feel like trailing all the way over there,' I said. 'You go.'

'After you've made Robin the fantastic cake?'

'It's a stupid cake. But you can take it if you think he'd really like it.'

'You're the one that's being stupid. Dump your schoolbag, find your jacket, and let's get cracking,' said Jo. Firmly.

So I went to the hospital clutching my cake in a tin. Mark didn't smile at me, but he nodded. Robin put his head on one side shyly, but he had this great big grin on his face.

'It's *Charlie*!' he whispered – as if I were someone important.

I don't like little kids much. Especially little boys. But somehow I dumped my cake tin and put my arms round Robin and gave him a great big hug. He'd always been a skinny little thing but now he felt like one of those little glass animals that snap off an arm or a leg when you just look at them. I tried not to hug him too hard in case I hurt him. Then I had to hug Birdie too. His general appearance hadn't been improved by Robin's recent adventures. I didn't really enjoy having this filthy piece of cloth rubbed round my face, but I didn't complain.

My cake had got a bit bashed about inside the tin, but it was still just about recognizable as a robin. The real Robin didn't want to cut it at first, but I made Birdie pretend to be starving hungry and nibble a corner of the cake, so Robin gave in.

It wasn't a work of art *ornithologically* (ha!) but it certainly tasted good. Robin had a great big slice. So did Mark and Jo and two nurses and a couple of kids in the main ward that Robin had made friends with. I had a great big slice as well. Two, actually, just to check it tasted good all the way round.

'It's a lovely cake,' said Mark, giving me another

nod. Then he smiled at Jo. 'I expect you helped Charlie with it?'

I spluttered. 'Jo can't even make *toast*!'

I felt like clouting him with the cake tin. But I didn't. I sensed our relationship was still dead precarious. I still couldn't stick him. I didn't ever want to make friends with him. But I did want to be friends with Robin.

Mark took him to the seaside the next week. Bournemouth. I'd never been there.

'I have,' said Jo. 'Your grandma and grandpa used to take me there on holiday when I was little. In a big white hotel and they played tennis all day and whist in the evening and I just mooched about, too shy and stupid to make friends with any of the other kids.'

'Aaaaah!' I said, teasing her. 'Don't worry, *I'll* play with you next time we go to the seaside.'

'We could go to Bournemouth on Saturday,' said Jo, trying to sound casual. 'Meet up with Robin and Mark. Mark phoned and suggested it.'

Jo still had to do her supermarket shift early Saturday morning, but I met her at eight o'clock and we went straight to the station and set off for Bournemouth. Robin and Mark met us off the train. Robin looked a bit bigger and bouncier out of bed, though he was so well wrapped up against the sea breeze that he could barely move. Birdie's appearance had deteriorated even more because he'd dived into the sea by mistake when Robin was paddling in wellie boots – but at least he'd had a good wash.

It was a bit nippy for the beach but we walked right along the sands and I laboured long and hard making a sandcastle for Robin. He twittered beside me and Jo and Mark billed and cooed in the background. I was beginning to think I'd maybe done enough hard labour and that it was time I was let off for good behaviour – but I perked up a little when Mark bought us all ice creams.

It was far too cold to go swimming in the sea, of course, but we went to the Leisure Pool instead. Birdie took a nap in a locker while Robin splashed around happily with me. Robin still looked a bit too thin stripped to his bathing costume but he was very perky. Mark looked a right berk in his trunks. I practically fell about laughing.

We spent ages drying every tiny bit of Robin afterwards and wrapping him back in his one hundred and one layers and then we had hot chocolate to make sure he was well and truly warmed up before going out into the wind.

We went on the pier and Mark spent a small fortune on the cuddly-toy cranes. He's useless at them . . . but *eventually* he won a lop-sided parrot for

Robin and a simpering blue
bunny for Jo. And then he got this
hideous bug-eyed troll with long
orange hair – and gave it to me.

I wasn't particularly charmed with that little
seaside souvenir. But I tell you what I *did* get.
There's an amazing museum place in Bournemouth
called the Russell-Coates Gallery. It's this big
Victorian house and it's stuffed full of everything
Victorian and I went round and round peering at
everything, pretending I'd really stepped back
into the past. No nurseries, though – my
Lottie wouldn't have had a job.

Robin needed to have a wee so I
took him into this lavatory – and it was
a genuine Victorian one, with a special
picture down the pan and a great big
wooden seat. I tried it out too.

I hoped I'd be able to buy a postcard of it, but no
such luck. I bought lots of other postcards, though.
Not for Lottie's diary. It had become obvious to me
that Miss Beckworth was not going to approve of
my project. It was very much *my* way, not hers. And
yet there was no way I was going to change it now.
So I decided if I couldn't win a prize for best
Victorian project then I might as well make sure
that Jamie did. I bought all the postcards for him.

SEASIDE

Dear little Freddie pulled through! One night his fever rose alarmingly and he didn't know any of us and we all really felt this was the end — but towards dawn he quietened and grew calm and suddenly opened his eyes and said 'Mamma' as clear as anything. He took a long drink and then settled down into a peaceful sleep. He woke at lunchtime almost his old self, though his sweet curls were all in a tangle and his face pale and drawn. He lapped up all his broth and made it plain that he wanted more.

The Mistress cried, Mrs Angel cried, Eliza cried — and oh how I cried too! We were all so tired and strung out watching over little Freddie that the Master decided to take a week away from his business and hire rooms for us all at the seaside as soon as Freddie was fit to travel.

We went on the steam train, an amazing adventure! Victor was beside himself with glee, asking questions nineteen to the dozen — and Louisa insisted on sticking her head out of the

window and got
herself covered
in sooty smuts.

It was dark
when we arrived at long last and there was such
a to-do getting the children to bed and all our
belongings unpacked that I simply crawled into my
own bed and fell fast asleep while Eliza and Mrs
Angel were still joshing and giggling (we three
share a room in the seaside lodgings and it is very
companionable). But I awoke early. I looked in on
Freddie but he was still fast asleep, and there
wasn't a peep from Louisa or Victor either. So I
wrapped myself in my cloak and ran down to see
the sea.

I could not believe it. I knew it would be a very
large stretch of water, but I'd pictured it like the
river at home. I had no idea it would shimmer as
far as the eye could see. And it moved so, wave
after wave rolling over and over.

It was very cold in the early morning air but I
tore my boots and stockings off and paddled in
the shallows just to say I had done it! A fat

old woman told me I could use one of
her bathing machines if I cared to,
but I was happy enough just to let
the water whirl about my ankles.
My feet were blue with cold all
morning but I didn't care.

Then, when I took the three
children to the beach later that

morning there was an ice-cream man selling hokey-pokey for a penny a lump, even though it was the winter season. I had three pennies so I bought one for Louisa, one for Victor, and one for Freddie and me to share.

My first ice cream! This time my lips turned blue but I licked them warm again.

I still cannot say I enjoy being a servant — but it has its compensations!

CHRISTMAS

Jamie's Victorian project *did* win. Well, it was obvious it was going to. It was easy-peasy, simple-pimple to work it out. Though my postcards from Bournemouth certainly helped. They made Jamie's project much thicker and the pages clicked enticingly as you turned each page. These postcard pages were so bright and glossy that Miss Beckworth couldn't *help* being dazzled. All right, she puts lots of ticks and stars and *Well Dones!* on his sections on railway engines and factories and coal mines, and she liked his town and country pages and all his maps in the British Empire bit, and she went a bit overboard on his Crimean War with an *EXCELLENT!* underlined. My postcards just got a tick or two, but that was obviously because she didn't want to deface the beauty of the page.

Miss Beckworth held Jamie's project up and showed it to the class and all the goodie-goodies went Oooh and Aaah and all the baddie-baddies went Yuck and Boring and Swot and Teacher's Pet. I would normally count myself the baddest baddie-baddie – and yet I found myself thumping old Jamie on the back and saying, 'Well done, Clever Clogs.'

He went very red when I said that. Maybe I thumped a bit too hard. Then he had to go up to Miss Beckworth and shake her hand and *she* said 'Well done' too. She said she'd like to give him a little prize. She gave him a £5 book token and a little painted Victorian soldier. Jamie was dead chuffed.

I couldn't help feeling a bit wistful then. I waited for Miss Beckworth to hand out the rest of the projects. I was sure mine would have red lines all through it and *SEE ME, CHARLOTTE!* in cross capitals. But you'll never ever guess what! Miss Beckworth paused theatrically.

'Jamie's brilliant project tells us almost all there is to know about Victorian times. But there's one other project here that tells us what it *feels* like to be a Victorian.' And she held out MY project!!! 'I'm so impressed with your diary of Lottie the Nursery Maid that I'd like to award you a prize too, Charlotte.'

'Great! Good for you, Charlie,' said Jamie.

Yep! Good for me! Miss Beckworth beckoned me out to the front of the class and I had to go through the hand-shaking ceremony too, which was OK – but I kept thinking, am *I* getting a prize like Jamie? And I did! A £5 book token, and a tiny reproduction china doll the size of my little finger.

347

'Oh, she's sweet! Thank you very much, Miss Beckworth,' I said.

'Do you know what they used to call that sort of doll? They were called Frozen Charlottes,' said Miss Beckworth, and she actually grinned at me.

I appreciated her little joke. I actually sort of appreciated *her* for once. She asked me to read out some of my diary entries for Lottie. So I did. Everyone got a bit shuffly and sighing to start with – but by the time I'd got to the bottom of the first page *they were riveted*! I read on and on and not a single person said Yuck, so there!

Lisa and Angela got a teensy little bit snotty afterwards. Lisa especially, because her dad had done all her Victorian project on his posh computer with special loopy writing and graphics and it hadn't even had a special mention.

'You're really getting to be a teacher's pet now, Charlie,' said Lisa. 'I don't know who's the swottiest now, you or your precious Jamie.'

'He's not mine. And he's not precious either, come to that,' I said, snorting.

'*We* saw you putting your arm round him when his project won,' said Angela, giggling away.

'Purlease!' I said. 'Don't be so pathetic, Ange.'

'You're the one that's pathetic, Charlie, getting all matey with Jamie Edwards. He's the nerdiest boy in the whole class.'

'So?' I said fiercely.

'So what do you *see* in him?' said Lisa.

'He can be quite good fun sometimes. OK, he

348

does look a bit weird—'

'You're telling me!' said Lisa.

'And he wears the grottiest clothes,' said Angela.

'Yes, right, he's a total Arnie-Anorak, but I don't care.'

'She's gone off her rocker,' said Lisa to Angela.

'Completely nuts,' said Angela to Lisa.

'Yeah, you're mad, Charlie. You could probably get any boy in our class keen on you – well, apart from Dave Wood – yet you choose *Jamie* for a boyfriend.'

'He's NOT my boyfriend. You two aren't half slow at catching on. He's a friend who happens to be a boy – OK a nerdy, grotty, swotty boy – but so what?' I shouted. A little too loudly. Jamie himself came out the boys' cloakroom and stared. Lisa and Angela doubled up laughing. I felt myself going red. Totally screamingly scarlet.

BRIGHT RED

'Better leave the two lovebirds together,' said Lisa, and she tugged Angela away.

They went giggle giggle giggle down the corridor.

'Idiots,' I muttered. I blew hard up my nostrils, fluttering my fringe. 'Phew, isn't it hot in here?' I paused. 'What are you staring at?'

'Did you just say I was nerdy and grotty and swotty?' Jamie asked.

'Oh,' I groaned. 'No.'

'I heard you,' said Jamie, looking wounded.

'Well, all right, yes. But it wasn't my description,' I said.

'So everyone thinks I'm nerdy and grotty and swotty,' said Jamie.

'No. Yes. Well, a few of the girls maybe. And the boys. Don't look all upset, Jamie, I'm trying to make things better.'

'I'd hate it if you were trying to make things worse then,' said Jamie.

'Look, you're not daft, you must have twigged that's what they think,' I said.

'You *are* making it worse,' said Jamie.

'But you don't really care, do you, Jamie?'

'Don't I?' said Jamie.

'Well, *I* don't care what anyone thinks of me,' I said.

'Yes, but that's because everyone likes you,' said Jamie.

'No they don't. Not even Lisa and Angela much, and they're supposed to be my best friends.'

'And . . . did you say *I* was your friend too?' said Jamie, looking a bit perkier.

I shrugged. 'Mmm,' I said.

'You mean it? We're really friends? Even though I'm a boy? And a nerdy grotty swotty one at that?' Jamie didn't seem at all upset now. I wondered if he'd been pretending before. I wouldn't put it past him.

'I generally can't stick boys,' I said. 'But you're OK.'

'So are you,' said Jamie.

We stood there looking at each other. For two ultra-chatty people we suddenly seemed lost for words. And then there were these s-t-u-p-i-d slurpy kissy-kissy sounds. Angela and Lisa had crept back towards us.

'Look at them!'

'Gazing into each other's eyes, dumb-struck!'

'Go on then, Jamie, kiss her.'

'They'll be snogging at the school disco next week!'

They collapsed with laughter.

'Take no notice,' said Jamie calmly. 'Let the lower mortals prattle.'

'You what?' said Lisa.

'He's talking in some foreign lingo now,' said Angela.

'See if you two can understand plain English then,' I said – and I used some very short sharp shocking words to indicate that I wanted them to go away.

'Who is using that disgusting language?' said a familiar voice.

A teacher came stalking down the corridor. The one with the all-hearing ears. You've guessed right.

She gave me a detention too, even though it wasn't really my fault at all that I'd been reduced to blunt language. But I still felt *quite* fond of her, even though she was always so snappily strict. So when our top year had our special disco party and Miss Beckworth organized it and asked us to bring some refreshments from home I went overboard.

I went round to Jamie's house and hunted through the Victorian books – and found a great big fat one with lots of recipes called *Mrs Beeton's Book of Household Management*. I flipped through it until I found the *perfect* cake.

It needed quite a lot of ingredients but that was no problem. (For reasons I will divulge later!)

It took ages to make the special cake. I had to make this special lemon jelly and then pour a little bit into a big tin and then stud it with glacé cherries like jewels, and then I did another layer of jelly and stood sponge fingers all the way round the tin and *then* I made a special eggy custard and poured that on and let it all set and THEN the next day I dunked the tin very quickly in hot water and then, holding my breath and praying, I gently tipped it out onto a pretty plate like a little kid turning out a sandcastle. You know what often happens with sandcastles? They crumble and break, right? But my special Victorian cake came out whole and perfect, easy-peasy, simple-pimple.

It was a bit of a mega-problem getting it to school, though. I had to carry it on a tray and hope it wouldn't rain. My arms were aching terribly by the time I got to school. I was a bit late too, because I'd had to walk so carefully to keep my cake intact.

'Charlotte Enright, you're late for school,' said Miss Beckworth.

'Only half a second, Miss Beckworth. And it's in a very very good cause,' I said, propping my heavy tray on a desk and peeling back the protective tinfoil I'd arched over it.

'And what's this very good cause, might I ask?' said Miss Beckworth.

'You!' I said, pulling the last of the foil off with a flourish. 'I've made you a cake, Miss Beckworth. Well, it's for all of us at the disco, but it's in your honour and you've got to have the first slice. It's a Victorian cake. And you'll never ever guess what it's called!'

Miss Beckworth looked at my wondrous masterpiece. She blinked her all-seeing eyes. They twinkled as she met my gaze.

'I *can* guess,' said Miss Beckworth. 'In your own ultra-irritating phrase, it's easy-peasy, simple-pimple! It's an absolutely magnificent Charlotte Russe.'

She really *is* all-knowing! We shared the cake-cutting ceremony when it was nosh-time. I got a bit worried my Charlotte cake would collapse, but it stood its ground splendidly. And it tasted great too, mega-yummy. It was all gone in a matter of minutes – just a lick of lemon jelly and a few sponge crumbs left on the plate.

I made sure all my special friends got a slice. Then the disco started up. It wasn't a *real* evening disco with a proper DJ and strobe lighting. It was just an afternoon Christmas party in the school hall for

Year Six, with the headmaster playing these mostly ropy old discs. Hardly the most sophisticated exciting event of the century – though you'd maybe think it was, judging by the fuss Lisa and Angela and some of the other girls made.

We were allowed to change into our own home clothes, you see. The boys didn't think it much of a big deal. They looked *worse* out of school uniform.

I didn't try too hard either. I was too busy creating my cake to fuss about my outfit. And I can't actually win when it comes to cool clothes way in the front line of fashion. My kit comes from the label-free zones of Oxfam, Jumble and Car Boot Sales, especially nowadays. Though this might change soon. (Second hint of changes in the Enright family fortunes!)

Lisa and Angela and lots of the other girls tried very hard indeed. Lisa looked particularly lovely.

But Angela was the big surprise. She usually wore ordinary old jeans and jumpers when we were hanging round after school. But now her mum had bought her this new party-time outfit down the market. Angela's got too tall for kids' clothes so this was really grown-up gear. And Angela looked ultra-adult in it too.

'Look at *Angela*!'

You couldn't help looking at her. Everyone did. It was as if she'd become an entirely new girl to match her new outfit. When she danced the boys all circled round. Even Dave Wood.

354

Jamie's jaw dropped when he saw Angela too, but he didn't try to dance with her. He didn't dance with anyone at first. I danced with lots of people. Then I went and stood near Jamie. I waited. It started to get on my nerves.

'Come on, Jamie. Let's dance,' I said commandingly.

'I don't think I'm very good at dancing,' said Jamie.

He was right about that. He just stood and twitched a little at first.

'Let yourself *go* a bit,' I said, jumping about.

Jamie let himself go a bit too much. His arms and legs shot out all over the place. I had to stay well back to stop myself getting clouted. But I suppose he was trying.

Lisa was standing near us. I prepared myself for some ultra-sarcastic comments. But Lisa's eyes were a little too bright, her smile showing too much teeth. She wasn't watching Jamie and me. She was watching Angela and Dave.

'Hey, Jamie. I want to dance with Lisa for a bit,' I said.

'Good! I need a rest,' Jamie puffed.

So I danced with Lisa for a bit. And then I danced with some of the other girls. And some other boys. So did Lisa. And at long last Dave Wood came slithering up to her, because he'd been elbowed away from Angela by the rest of the boys. I expected Lisa to send Dave Wood off with a flea in his ear. I'd have added a swarm of stinging wasps and a buzz of killer bees. But would you believe it, Lisa just gave him this stupid smirk and danced with him devotedly. Lisa has got a very pretty head but it contains *no brain whatsoever*.

'Do you want to dance again, Charlie?' Jamie asked eagerly. 'I think I'm getting the hang of it now.'

He was a little optimistic. But we had fun all the same. The party ended at three and we were allowed to go home then.

Lisa and Dave Wood went off together, so she was happy.

Angela went off with half the boys in our class, so she

was happy.

I decided to go back to Jamie's

house because I was still a bit peckish in spite of my Charlotte Russe (the other refreshments weren't up to much) and I fancied one of his brother's toasted cheese sandwiches. We walked along Oxford Terrace together. I peered up at all the attic rooms right under the roofs and imagined Lottie looking out.

Jamie kept walking closer and closer to me, so that his schoolbag banged my shins several times. I turned to tell him off – and he kissed me on the cheek!

'What are you playing at?' I said furiously.

'I – I – well, you kept sticking your chin

356

up and looking up in the air so I thought you wanted me to kiss you,' Jamie stammered.

'Well, you got it seriously wrong, matie,' I said, giving him a shove. I scrubbed at the little wet patch on my cheek with the back of my hand. 'You do that again and I'll clock you one,' I said.

'Don't worry, I won't,' said Jamie. He sighed. 'I wish I could figure girls out. I especially wish I could figure *you* out, Charlie.'

'It's part of my deeply mysterious feminine charm,' I said, chuckling.

Jamie's brother came up trumps with another toasted sandwich and his mum asked if Jo and I could go round to their house on Boxing Day. They have a party every year. Jo got a bit worried when I told her and said she didn't think it sounded her cup of tea – well, glass of punch – but she's agreed to come with me because I've been astonishingly agreeable about *her* Christmas plans.

I shall give Jamie his Christmas present then. I've bought him a big fat paperback Victorian novel. *Jane Eyre* – by Charlotte Brontë, and inside the cover I've written: *This is a present by a Charlotte, from a Charlotte!*

I'm going to make Jamie's mum a special cake to eat at her party. I've got it all worked out. It's going to be a square cake, iced all over with a cake lid on top and marzipan ribbon, so it looks like a special gift box – for Boxing Day, get it?

I'm going to be so busy busy busy

making cakes in the Christmas holidays. I've got to make one for Grandma and Grandpa when Jo and I go over there on Christmas Eve – yuck! I had all sorts of good ideas but Jo talked it over with me and she thinks they'd like an ordinary conventional Christmas cake, white icing and HAPPY CHRISTMAS, boring boring boring – but I've said I'll do it.

I'm making one more cake – and this one's a special one.

Jo fixed a beautiful red breakfast in bed for us on Sunday (ruby grapefruit and raspberry Danish pastries and cranberry juice). When we'd eaten it all up we cuddled down in bed again and I started up one of our games and Jo tried to join in but I could tell she wasn't concentrating.

'Jo? What is it, eh?' I could feel her tense.

'Well . . . I want to talk to you about something,' she said.

I felt as if all the delicious red food inside me was being whisked in a blender. This was it. I knew what she was going to say. I wriggled away from her and lay stiffly in bed, waiting.

'It's about . . . Robin,' she said.

'And Mark,' I said, through clenched teeth.

'Well. Yes, I suppose so. Oh, Charlie. I don't know how to say this.'

'I'll say it for you,' I said. 'It's easy-peasy, simple-pimple. You

358

and Mark are going to get married and Robin's going to be my little brother and you'll be giving up all your jobs to look after him full-time and we'll have to sell our flat and go and live with them and I expect you want me to make you a flipping wedding cake as well, but if I have to come to your wedding I warn you, I won't throw confetti, I'll start throwing rocks at you,' and I turned over on my tummy and started to cry.

'What?' said Jo. '*What?*' And she started to laugh.

'It's not funny!' I sobbed. 'I want to stay here. With you. Just the two of us.'

'So do I,' said Jo. She shoved my tangled hair out of the way and said it straight into my ear. '*So do I!* That's what we're going to do. Now listen, Charlie! You've got it all wrong. Mark and I aren't getting married. He's still too fussed about his first marriage – and I don't think I ever *want* to get married. OK?'

'So you don't love him?'

'I don't know what I feel. I just want to let things develop. Slowly. In their own time. I hope I'll still see a lot of Mark and Robin – but I might not carry on working there. You know this Christmas job?'

You don't know about the Christmas job. Jo's stopped working at the Rosens'. The last big electrical goods shop in the town advertised for part-time staff to help them out over their busy Christmas trading time. Jo jumped in there and they took her on right away, working from nine to three. So we've got enough to keep up the mortgage payments – *and* a bit over. *That's* what I was hinting at earlier.

'You mean it's too tiring, working there and then going to look after Robin?' I said, leaning up on my elbows.

'The thing is, the shop manageress is going to have a baby. She wants to start her maternity leave in January – and even though I'm only temporary they're asking if I'm interested. It won't be for ever, of course, though she might decide she wants to stay at home with the baby – but it would still be great to get back to the work I like. But of course it would be full time, through till half past five.'

'I see. Well. You'll have to take it, Jo. I mean, it's great. But . . . what about Robin? He likes you a lot.'

'He likes you even more, Charlie. Mark hopes he'll be able to juggle his working hours and pick Robin up from school himself. Or maybe he'll have to find another child-minder. But in an absolute emergency I said you could always pick Robin up from school and look after him until Mark could come.'

'Mark wouldn't ever trust me with Robin!' I said.

'Yes he would. He knows that you're really very sensible and responsible,' said Jo.

'Me?' I said. 'OK. Tell Mark he can count on me. As long as he pays me!'

'Charlie!'

'So we can really stay here in our own flat, Jo?'

'You bet.'

'And we'll have our first Christmas here, just us two?'

'Ah. Well. That's the other thing I wanted to discuss.'

This time I did guess right.

'You want Robin and Mark to come round here for Christmas?'

'If that's all right with you, Charlie?'

I didn't want Mark to come at all. Still, it might be fun to have Robin bobbing about at Christmas.

So . . . I decided I'd better come up with something pretty special for our Christmas cake. I baked a square fruit cake and then carved out part of the front and made up a brown butter icing and did this posh basket weave all over to make it look like . . . a stable! With a big gold marzipan star and a fat pink marzipan angel perched on the roof.

(I'm going to get to eat the angel on Christmas Day – because I'm currently so angelic!) Then I made a marzipan Mary (Jo can eat her) and a marzipan Joseph (I suppose I *might* offer him to Mark) and a dear little marzipan baby Jesus clutching a white marzipan lamb (specially for Robin).

I piped a long message in front of all my Nativity figures.

PEACE ON EARTH.
GOOD WILL TO ALL MEN.

I never ever thought I'd be wishing Good Will to *any* man! I decided to add a bit.

AND GOOD WILL TO ALL WOMEN AND BOYS AND ESPECIALLY GIRLS!

THE END

ABOUT THE AUTHOR

JACQUELINE WILSON was born in Bath in 1945, but has spent most of her life in Kingston-on-Thames, Surrey. She always wanted to be a writer and wrote her first 'novel' when she was nine, filling countless Woolworth's exercise books as she grew up. She started work at a publishing company and then went on to work as a journalist on *Jackie* magazine (which was named after her) before turning to writing fiction full-time.

Since 1990 Jaqueline has written prolifically for children and has won many of the UK's top awards for children's books, including the Smarties Prize in 2000 and the Guardian Children's Fiction Award and the Children's Book of the Year in 1999. Jacqueline was awarded an OBE in the Queen's Birthday Honours list, in Golden Jubilee Year, 2002.

Over 10 million copies of Jacqueline's books have now been sold in the UK and approximately 50,000 copies of her books are sold each month. An avid reader herself, Jacqueline has a personal collection of more than 15,000 books.

She has one grown-up daughter.

'A brilliant young writer of wit and subtlety whose stories are never patronising and are often complex and many-layered'
THE TIMES

Jacqueline Wilson has a rare gift for writing lightly and amusingly about emotional issues'
BOOKSELLER

'Wilson writes like a child, and children instantly recognize themselves in her characters. The tone of voice is faultless, her stories are about the problems many children face, and her plots work with classic simplicity . . . a subtle art is concealed by artlessness, and some might call that genius'
DAILY TELEGRAPH

THE ILLUSTRATED MUM
Jacqueline Wilson

Star used to love Marigold, love me, love our life together. We three were the colourful ones, like the glowing pictures inked all over Marigold . . .

Covered from head to foot with glorious tattoos, Marigold is the brightest, most beautiful mother in the world. That's what Dolphin thinks (she just wishes her beautiful mum wouldn't stay out partying all night or go weird now and then). Her older sister, Star, isn't so sure any more. She loves Marigold too, but sometimes she just can't help wishing she were more *normal* . . .

A powerful and memorable tale for older readers from Jacqueline Wilson, the award-winning author of *The Suitcase Kid*, *Double Act*, *Bad Girls*, and many other titles.

'Disturbingly perceptive and provocative' *Guardian*

'A marvellous, poignant tale . . . Jacqueline Wilson's best yet' *Daily Telegraph*

WINNER OF THE CHILDREN'S BOOK OF THE YEAR AWARD AND THE GUARDIAN CHILDREN'S FICTION AWARD. SHORTLISTED FOR THE WHITBREAD AWARD.

0 440 863686

CORGI YEARLING BOOKS

THE JACQUELINE WILSON COLLECTION
Jacqueline Wilson

Two lively and hilarious tales from one of today's most popular authors for young readers.

THE STORY OF TRACY BEAKER
I'm Tracy Beaker. This is a book all about me. I'd read it if I were you. It's the most incredible dynamic heart-rending story. Honest . . .

'An appealing mix of events and reactions that are both entertaining and moving. A book that lingers in the mind long after it is put down' *Guardian*

THE BED AND BREAKFAST STAR
I'm Elsa, and I'm hoping to be a big star one day. I tell jokes all the time to try and cheer my family up. Trouble is, no-one seems to laugh much anymore. Not since we lost our lovely house and had to move into a bed and breakfast hotel.

'An unsentimental and truthful book that is even better for a strong sense of mischief' *Independent on Sunday*

0 440 863775

CORGI YEARLING BOOKS

THE DARE GAME
Jacqueline Wilson

I'm Tracy Beaker, the Great Inventor of Extremely Outrageous Dares – and I dare you not to say this is the most brilliant story ever!

I thought I was going to live happily ever after with Cam as my foster-mum. Well, ha ha! It hasn't turned out like that. Cam's so *mean*. She won't buy me designer clothes, so all the other kids at my new school laught at me. No wonder I bunk off and go to this special secret place. There are these two boys I meet there, Alexander and Football. We play this Dare Game – and I always win. I'm the greatest. I *am*!

The super-feisty star of the award-winning *The Story of Tracy Beaker* is back – in another brilliant story from Jacqueline Wilson, author of *The Illustrated Mum*, winner of the Children's Book of the Year and the Guardian Children's Fiction Prize.

'Wilson . . . is on top form yet again'
The Times Educational Supplement

0 440 86369 4

CORGI YEARLING BOOKS